W9-BOD-327

His hands were gentle...

...as they slowly slid from Vanessa's face to her neck and across the slope of her shoulders. He held her as though she were fragile glass. Cautious. Careful, lest she break.

When at last they drew apart, his eyes were narrowed on her with a look she couldn't fathom.

She struggled to cover the tremors that were still rocketing through her system. "Satisfied?" Her voice was husky with feeling.

His smile came then. A dark, dangerous smile that had her wondering at the way it made her heart contract.

"Not nearly. But I guess that will have to do. For now."

Why did his words sound like another challenge?

RAVES FOR R. C. RYAN'S NOVELS

THE LEGACY OF COPPER CREEK

"Solidly written romance. Rich, layered, vulnerable characters in Whit and Cara, coupled with strong chemistry and intense heat between them, proves Ryan does the contemporary Western love story well."
—RT Book Reviews

"What a perfect ending to a series... I love this story."
—SillyMelody.blogspot.com

"If you're looking to lose yourself in a fictional family that will steal your heart and pull you into the thick of things, this is the book for you. *Copper Creek* is where a wayward soul can find a home and have all their dreams come true."
—MommysaBookWhore.com

THE REBEL OF COPPER CREEK

"A winner. Ryan writes with a realism that brings readers deep into the world she's created. The characters all have an authenticity that touches the heart."
—RT Book Reviews

"An awesome story."
—NightOwlReviews.com

THE MAVERICK OF COPPER CREEK

"Ryan's storytelling is tinged with warmth and down-to-earth grit. Her authentic, distinctive characters will get to the heart of any reader. With a sweet plot infused with family love, a fiery romance, and a bit of mystery, Ryan does not disappoint."

—RT Book Reviews

"Full of sexy cowboys and a western feel that is undeniable...A well-written fun story that I really enjoyed."

—NightOwlReviews.com

JAKE

"A must-read...cozy enough to make you want to venture into the Wild West and find yourself a cowboy...And if you haven't read a Western romance before, R. C. Ryan is where you should start."

—ReviewsbyMolly.com

"Wonderful characters who quickly find a way into your heart...a glorious picture of the West from one of my favorite authors."

—FreshFiction.com

JOSH

"There's plenty of hot cowboys, action, and romance in this heady mix of a series that will leave you breathless."

—Parkersburg News and Sentinel (WV)

"A powerfully emotional tale that will connect with readers…Love a feel-good cowboy romance with a touch of suspense? Then pick up *Josh*."

—RomRevToday.com

QUINN

"Ryan takes readers to Big Sky country in a big way with her vivid visual dialogue as she gives us a touching love story with a mystery subplot. The characters, some good and one evil, will stay with you long after the book is closed."

—RT Book Reviews

"Engaging…Ryan paints a picturesque image of the rugged landscape and the boisterous, loving, close-knit Conway family."

—Publishers Weekly

MONTANA GLORY

"These not-to-be-missed books are guaranteed to warm your heart!"

—FreshFiction.com

"Wonderful romantic suspense tale starring a courageous heroine who is a lioness protecting her cub and a reluctant knight in shining armor…a terrific taut thriller."

—GenreGoRoundReviews.blogspot.com

MONTANA DESTINY

"5 stars!...R. C. Ryan delivers an ongoing, tantalizing mystery suspense with heartwarming romance. Sinfully yummy!"
—HuntressReviews.com

"Ryan's amazing genius at creating characters with heartfelt emotions, wit, and passion is awe-inspiring. I can't wait until *Montana Glory* comes out...so that I can revisit the McCord family!"
—TheRomanceReadersConnection.com

MONTANA LEGACY

A *Cosmopolitan* "Red Hot Read"

"A captivating start to a new series."
—BookPage

"Heart-melting sensuality...this engaging story skillfully refreshes a classic trilogy pattern and sets the stage for the stories to come."
—Library Journal

ALSO BY R. C. RYAN

Montana Legacy
Montana Destiny
Montana Glory

Quinn
Josh
Jake

The Maverick of Copper Creek
The Rebel of Copper Creek
The Legacy of Copper Creek

MATT

R. C. RYAN

FOREVER

NEW YORK   BOSTON

This book is a work of fiction. Names, characters, places, and incidents are the product of the author's imagination or are used fictitiously. Any resemblance to actual events, locales, or persons, living or dead, is coincidental.

Copyright © 2016 by Ruth Ryan Langan
Excerpt from *Luke* copyright © 2016 by Ruth Ryan Langan
All rights reserved. In accordance with the U.S. Copyright Act of 1976, the scanning, uploading, and electronic sharing of any part of this book without the permission of the publisher constitute unlawful piracy and theft of the author's intellectual property. If you would like to use material from the book (other than for review purposes), prior written permission must be obtained by contacting the publisher at permissions@hbgusa.com. Thank you for your support of the author's rights.

Forever
Hachette Book Group
1290 Avenue of the Americas
New York, NY 10104

www.HachetteBookGroup.com

Printed in the United States of America

First Edition: April 2016
10 9 8 7 6 5 4 3 2 1

OPM

Forever is an imprint of Grand Central Publishing.
The Forever name and logo are trademarks of Hachette Book Group, Inc.

The Hachette Speakers Bureau provides a wide range of authors for speaking events. To find out more, go to www.hachettespeakersbureau.com or call (866) 376-6591.

The publisher is not responsible for websites (or their content) that are not owned by the publisher.

ATTENTION CORPORATIONS AND ORGANIZATIONS:

Most Hachette Book Group books are available at quantity discounts with bulk purchase for educational, business, or sales promotional use. For information, please call or write:

Special Markets Department, Hachette Book Group
1290 Avenue of the Americas, New York, NY 10104
Telephone: 1-800-222-6747 Fax: 1-800-477-5925

For my son, Tom.
Firstborn.
Fiercely protective of his family.

And for my darling Tom.
First love. Though gone,
still watching over us all.

MATT

PROLOGUE

Glacier Ridge, Montana—1997

The town of Glacier Ridge dated to the 1860s. A time of Western migration, when millions of buffalo roamed the Montana plains. It had seen plenty of legends in its time. Miners discovering gold at Grasshopper Creek. Gen. George Armstrong Custer and his cavalry. Railroad tycoons and, later, oil barons. But the closest thing to legend now in the sleepy little town was the Malloy family. Rancher Francis Xavier Malloy was married to Grace Anne LaRou, the daughter of legendary Hollywood director Nelson LaRou, who had become famous in her own right by spending a lifetime photographing herds of wild mustangs that roamed the Montana wilderness. Collectors paid a fortune for her original photographs, and researchers and even government bureaucrats sought her advice on how to manage the wild horses. Add to that Frank and Grace's handsome, reckless sons, Patrick and Colin, and the fact that Patrick ran off and married a gorgeous girl named Bernadette when they were just seventeen, leaving the gossips with plenty of things to whisper about. Soon Patrick and Bernie gave birth to three good-looking sons who seemed to be as wild and reckless as their daddy and granddaddy, so folks around Glacier Ridge just naturally figured they'd have plenty to talk about for another generation or two.

It was a given that there was never a dull moment when the Malloys were around.

Twelve-year-old Matthew Malloy, already known as a wild child around the town of Glacier Ridge, was asleep in the top bunk, enjoying a dream. A dream that mirrored the day he'd spent up in the hills with his grandpop Frank, father Patrick, and uncle Colin, who, at twenty-two, was always laughing and teasing and seemed more like a big brother than an uncle. With the first snowstorm of the season rolling in, they'd driven the last of the herd to winter in the south pasture, and had spread a ton of hay from a flatbed truck before heading back to the ranch house for dinner.

Their sprawling Montana ranch was home to four generations of Malloys. Matt and his younger brothers, ten-year-old Luke and nine-year-old Reed, shared a section of the restored house with their parents, Patrick and Bernadette, who still behaved like teenagers, whispering behind their hands, stealing kisses when they thought no one was watching, and laughing over shared secrets. It was obvious to all who knew them that they were still crazy in love.

Frank Malloy, whose Irish ancestors had cleared this raw wilderness, loved sharing the ranch chores with his sons and grandsons, while his Gracie Girl, as he called his wife, often took to the hills for weeks at a time photographing the herds of mustangs that roamed the open range.

Gracie's father, crotchety old Nelson LaRou, was now slowed by age, forcing him to give up his opulent homes in Connecticut and Hollywood and move in with his daughter and her family on this ranch, which he called the middle of nowhere. Though he constantly complained about the rugged lifestyle, it was no secret that he reveled in the company of his only daughter and was adjusting to the slower pace of life on a working ranch. The family loved it when he regaled them with tales of all the famous movie stars of the past. If only he would use a hearing aid, all their lives might be a bit easier. Gracie liked to say her father heard only what he chose to.

In his sleep Matt was smiling at one of Uncle Colin's silly jokes, until the dream dissolved and he was jolted into wakefulness by the sound of a door slamming somewhere below, followed by a chorus of voices. Not that it was anything new. In a family the size of his, voices raised in anger and laughter, as well as the occasional thump of a fist, were as natural as the lowing of cattle.

But this was different somehow. He sat up in bed, completely awake, and heard a woman's voice that sounded too high, too shrill, to be his sweet grandmother Gracie's. And yet he knew it to be hers. And a low, deep growl that could only be that of his sweet-natured grandpop, Frank, sounding more like a wounded bear.

There were other voices. His uncle Colin cursing. The cultured tones of his great-grandfather Nelson, more a moan than a voice. And the low rumble of strangers, all trying to be heard above the din.

Matt ignored the ladder alongside his top bunk and jumped to the floor. He noted idly that his younger brothers were undisturbed by the commotion.

The words drifted up, clearer now as he opened the bedroom door and stepped into the hallway.

"Impossible. They can't be…"

"…I tell you…lost control in the snow."

"I saw more than one set of tire tracks when I went there to document it on film."

"They could have been made by Sheriff Graystoke's police car, Nelson." Deputy Archer Stone's mouth was a taut line of raw emotion. "Or by mine, or even one of the ranch trucks."

Matt was halfway down the stairs when the voices went abruptly silent. He glanced down to see half a dozen faces tilted upward, all eyes focused on him. His grandparents were in parkas tossed hastily over their robes, as were his great-grandfather, still holding a movie camera, and the ranch cook, Yancy Martin, hair in wild disarray. His uncle Colin was still in his torn denims and sheepskin parka, obviously caught finishing chores in the barn. Sheriff Eugene Graystoke and his deputy stood in snow-covered boots that were dripping water on the hardwood floor. And over by the door, still as a statue, was old Burke Cowley, his hair and clothes dusted with snow. He was a cowboy who had been with the family for as long as Matt could remember. He stood, eyes downcast, his agitation apparent only by the way he was twirling his Stetson around and around in his hands.

All of them looked grim.

It was Gracie, her face ghostly pale, her eyes red-rimmed from tears, who rushed toward her grandson.

"Oh, Matthew." She reached her arms as if to clutch him to her, but he shrank back, just out of reach.

He turned to the sheriff. "It's Mom and Dad, isn't it?"

No one spoke.

"Are they in the hospital?" At the sound of ten-year-old Luke's question, everyone looked beyond Matt to see the two younger boys, hair rumpled, eyes wide with a million questions, standing at the top of the stairs.

Matt turned pleading eyes to his grandfather. "What happened, Grandpop? Somebody tell us."

His family was rendered mute.

It was old Burke who lumbered across the room and put a big, wrinkly hand on the boy's shoulder, while he signaled for the two younger ones to come closer. "Your ma and pa were in an accident out on the highway. Their car slid off the road and hit a boulder. They're both gone."

"Gone where, Burke?" Nine-year-old Reed's voice raised to a youthful bellow. "You tell us right now. Where are they?"

Burke's jaw clenched, as if bracing for the blow he was about to deliver. Then the old man cleared his throat twice before he managed to say, "I'm sorry to tell you this, boys. They're dead. I hope you can take some comfort in the fact that your ma and pa died together, just the way they'd want it."

Colin crossed the distance between them, wrapping his three young nephews in a tight, hard embrace while his voice trembled. "I know this is a shock. I know what you're feeling, 'cause I'm feeling it, too. And I know I can't be your dad. Nobody else could ever be my brother

Patrick. But I swear I'll be here for the three of you." He turned to include the others, so locked in shock and grief they had no words. "All of us will be here for you. We're family. And we'll do everything in our power to keep you boys safe and happy."

"Happy?" The very word mocked Matt. He pushed free of his uncle's arms, staring defiantly at all of them.

Time stopped. He heard a buzz of voices, and felt hands reaching for him and his brothers as the family gathered around, determined to offer aid and comfort.

He was aware of only one thing. His sweet, pleasant dream had just become a nightmare. His mother and father, the people he loved more than anything in his young world, were dead. Gone too soon from his life.

And though he and his brothers had all these people willing to surround them with love, Matt knew that nothing, not now, not ever in this life, would be the same again.

CHAPTER ONE

Rome, Italy—Present Day

A limousine glided toward the sleek, private jet parked on the tarmac of Rome's Fiumicino Airport. The uniformed driver hurried around to open the door as two men exited.

Matt Malloy extended a handshake. "Thank you for your hospitality, Vittorio. And please thank your lovely wife for the tour of her family's vineyards. That was a bonus I hadn't expected. Tell Maria I hope I didn't overstay my welcome."

The handsome, white-haired man gave a vigorous shake of his head. "You know how much we enjoy your company, Matthew. The vineyard was all Maria's idea. She said to expect a case of her family's finest wine in time for your summer holidays. You do take a holiday from ranching, don't you?"

Matt chuckled. "Ranchers like to say our only day off is our funeral."

"Do not say that, even in jest." The older man shook his head before closing a big hand over Matt's shoulder. "It is always a pleasure doing business with you, my friend."

"The pleasure is mine." After a final handshake, Matt turned away and greeted the crew at the bottom of the steps before ascending to the plane's interior.

Within minutes the steps had been lifted and the hatch secured, then the pilot announced their departure.

As soon as they reached their required altitude, Matt unbuckled and retreated to the small bedroom in the rear of the aircraft. When he returned to the cabin, he had already shed his suit and tie and replaced them with denims, a comfortable flannel shirt with the sleeves rolled to the elbows, and a pair of well-worn Western boots. Just as easily he shed the attitude of a worldly, successful businessman and became once again a rancher, a man of the soil, eager to return to the life he loved.

Matt leaned over the shoulder of his pilot as the plane cast its shadow on the vast herds darkening the hills below. "Now there's a sight I never grow tired of."

"Can't say I blame you." Rick Fairfield, with his trim build and graying hair cut razor short, could never be mistaken for anything but a former military pilot. He adjusted his mirrored sunglasses. "After nearly three weeks out of the country, it's got to be a good feeling to be home again." He glanced at Stan Novak in the copilot's seat. "Let's bring this baby down."

Matt returned to the cabin and fastened his seat belt for landing. A short time later, after thanking the crew, he deposited his luggage in the bed of a truck that stood idling beside the small runway and climbed into the passenger seat.

Behind the wheel was Burke Cowley. Burke had spent his younger years tending herds on ranches from Montana to Calgary, until he'd settled on the Malloy Ranch, working his way from wrangler to ranch foreman. With his white hair, leathery skin from a lifetime in the weather, and courtly manners, he was a cowboy in the traditional mode. Strong, silent, watchful.

"Welcome home, Matt."

"Thanks, Burke. I see the weather's turning." Matt slipped into a battered parka.

"Springtime in Montana. Shirtsleeves one day, winter gear the next. Was it a good trip?"

Matt shrugged. "Satisfying. Is everyone home?"

"You bet." Burke nodded. "By now they've finished their chores and they're just waiting for you so they can enjoy the special dinner Yancy's been cooking all afternoon."

Matt was smiling as they drove along the wide gravel driveway that circled the barns before leading to the rear of the ranch house.

As Matt stepped down from the truck he turned. "You coming in?"

Burke grinned. "Wouldn't miss it. I'll just park this in the barn and be back in no time."

Matt hauled his luggage up the back-porch steps, experiencing the same little thrill of pleasure he always felt whenever he returned to his family home.

"Matthew." His grandmother was the first to greet him as he stepped inside and dropped his luggage in the mudroom.

Matt simply stared. "Gram Gracie, you never age."

"Go on. Look at all this gray hair."

Despite the strands of gray in her dark hair, she was as trim as a girl. She was wearing her trademark ankle-skimming denim skirt, Western boots, and a cotton shirt the color of a ripe plum, the sleeves rolled to the elbows.

She flew into his arms and hugged him before drawing a little away to look into his eyes. "I missed you."

"No more than I missed you."

Matt kept his arm around her as they made their way into the kitchen. "Hey, Yancy."

At his words the cook and housekeeper, who stood all of five feet two, his salt-and-pepper hair cut in a Dutch-boy bob, set aside a pair of oven mitts before hurrying over to extend his hand. "Welcome home, Matt."

"Thanks. I've missed this. And missed your cooking. Something smells wonderful."

The cook's face softened into a mile-wide smile. "I've fixed your favorite."

"Yancy's Fancy Chicken?" Matt used the term he'd used since childhood to describe the cook's special chicken dish that never failed to bring compliments. "If I'd known, I'd've had the pilot get me here even faster."

They were enjoying a shared laugh when a handsome man with a lion's mane of white hair entered from the dining room. Gracie's father paused for a moment. Standing ramrod straight, his starched white shirt and perfectly tailored gray pants brightened by a cherry-red silk scarf knotted at his throat, Nelson LaRou looked exactly like the director he'd once been, who had commanded an array of Hollywood's rich and famous.

He hurried toward them. "Welcome home, Matthew."

"Thanks, Great One." Matt ignored the outstretched hand and gathered his great-grandfather into his arms for a bear hug.

Though the old man remained straight backed, his stern countenance softened into a smile. It had taken him years here on the ranch to accept such casual signs of affection. In truth, he was still learning. And he liked it more than he would ever admit. Just as he loved the nickname the boys had given him all those years ago. *Great-grandfather* was just too long. They'd shortened it to Great One, but he sensed that it was more than a title. It spoke of the esteem in which they held him, which tickled him no end.

He cleared his throat. "How was Rome?"

"As amazing as ever. I wish you'd have come with me. Vittorio's wife took me on a tour of her family's vineyards. Every time I sampled another wine, I thought of you and all those fancy wines you brought from your places in Connecticut and California."

Nelson crossed to his favorite chair. "I hope you thought enough of me to bring some home with you."

"I'm having it shipped."

"It flipped?" He turned, cupping a hand to his ear. "Can you flip some my way?"

"*Shipped*, Great One. It's being shipped from Italy."

"Good. Good." Nelson settled into a comfortable easy chair in front of a huge stone fireplace just as the rest of the family began arriving.

The family's often-absent son Luke ambled in from the barn and rolled his sleeves, washing up at the big sink in the mudroom. Where Matt was tall and lean, his dark hair cut short for his trip to Rome, Luke was more muscular, honed by his never-ending treks to the mountains that called to him. Thick, long hair streamed over his collar.

He hurried over to welcome his brother back. "Another tough assignment, right Matt?"

"Right. But somebody has to do it. And I manfully accepted the challenge."

The two were still sharing grins when Reed strolled down the stairs and clapped Matt on the shoulder. Tall, wiry, with his long hair tied back in a ponytail and his rough beard in need of a trim, their youngest brother looked as though he'd just come in from months in the wilderness. "You're alone? I was hoping you'd bring a couple of Italian beauties with you."

"Wishful thinking, little brother. You'll have to go to Rome and do your own shopping."

"That works for me. Next time you're heading to Italy, you've got a traveling companion."

"You always say that, until it's time to actually go. Then you realize you'll need to wear a suit and tie and get a real haircut, and you find way too many things that need your attention here on the ranch."

Reed gave a mock sigh. "The trials of a cowboy. Never enough time for the ladies." He looked up. "Speaking of which, here's the ultimate cowboy now." He grinned at the handsome man in faded denims and plaid shirt strolling into the kitchen. "When's the last time you took a pretty lady out to dinner, Colin?"

His uncle was already shaking his head, sending curly dark hair spilling over his forehead. "So many females, so little time." He grabbed Matt in a bear hug. "'Bout time you got your hide back here. I was beginning to think you'd been seduced into moving to Rome permanently."

"I did give it some thought. But then I wondered who'd handle all the family business if I just up and relocated."

Matt's grandfather, Frank, chose that moment to walk in from the hallway. It was easy to see where his son and grandsons got their handsome Irish looks. From his twinkling blue eyes to his towering frame, he was every inch the successful rancher who'd tamed this rough land with sheer sweat and tears. Though his hair was streaked with gray and his stride was a bit slower, he was still able to work alongside his wranglers without missing a beat.

With a wink at his wife, he reached up and ruffled Matt's hair the way he had when his grandsons were little. "Any day you get ready to walk away, don't you worry, sonny boy. I can still negotiate contracts on behalf of the family business."

"Or hire a staff of lawyers to handle it for you."

At Matt's words, Frank pretended to groan. "You think it would take a staff to replace you, sonny boy?"

"At least a staff. Maybe an army." Matt grinned good-naturedly before accepting a longneck from Yancy's tray.

The others followed suit. Nelson accepted a martini, which Yancy had learned to make to the old man's specific directions.

When old Burke walked in, the family was complete. They touched drinks in a salute, and tipped them up to drink.

Matt looked around and felt his heart swell. He never grew tired of this scene. His brothers, his uncle, his grandparents, and his great-grandfather all here, as they'd been since he was a kid, surrounding him with love. Yancy cooking. Burke standing just slightly outside the circle, like a fierce, vigilant guardian angel.

Outside the floor-to-ceiling windows, the tops of the mountains in the distance were gilded with gold and pink and mauve shadows as the sun began to set.

Life, he thought, didn't get much better.

"Dinner's ready."

At Yancy's familiar words, they circled the big, wooden harvest table and took their places. Frank sat at the head, with his Gracie Girl at his right and their son, Colin, to his left. Matt sat beside Colin, with Burke beside him. Luke and Reed faced them on the other side, with Nelson holding court at the other end of the table.

After passing around platters of tender, marinated chicken, potatoes au gratin, and green beans fresh from the garden, Yancy took his place next to Reed.

Matt took a bite of chicken and gave a sigh of pleasure. "Yancy, after all that great Italian food, this is a real treat. I can't tell you how much I've missed this."

The cook's still-boyish face creased into a smile of pleasure at Matt's words.

"Okay." Luke pinned his older brother with a look. "Enough about the food. I want to know what happened with Mazzola International. Are they in?"

Matt put aside his fork before nodding. "They're in."

"They signed a contract?"

"Their lawyers still have some work to do. But Vittorio and I shook on it. And that's good enough for me."

Luke reached over to high-five his brother.

Matt laughed as he looked around the table at the others. "I figured that news would make Luke's day."

Colin shot a meaningful look at his nephew. "Does this mean you intend to give up all those reckless pursuits and settle down to raise cattle?"

"Reckless pursuits?" Luke arched a brow.

His uncle narrowed his gaze. "I caught a glimpse of you on your Harley, heading into the wilderness. You were doing one of your daredevil Evel Knievel imitations, as I recall."

Luke gave one of his famous rogue grins. "The way I see it, jumping a motorcycle off a cliff, or hiking through the mountains with nothing more than a camera, a rifle, and a bedroll—" he turned to his grandmother "—searching for that elusive white mustang stallion you've been tracking for years, is no distraction from work. They help prepare me to be a better cowboy."

"Or an aimless drifter," his great-grandfather muttered.

Luke's grin widened. "There's nothing aimless about it, Great One. It's preparing me for whatever life throws at me." He turned to Matt. "Enough about me. Tell us more about Rome."

Matt paused for dramatic effect before saying, "I brought back a little something for you, too, Reed."

Their younger brother looked up in surprise before narrowing his eyes in suspicion. "Okay. Give."

"I know how you've been hoping to make a mark in the green industry..."

Reed nodded. "Organic. Pure beef with no hormones, no antibiotics."

"Exactly. Leone Industries has agreed to a limited contract, to test the market. If they can see enough profit, they'll sign for the long term." He studied the excitement that had leapt into his brother's eyes. "Just remember. It's only a limited contract until they test the market."

"It's a foot in the door." Reed sat back, too excited to

finish his meal. "And there's an entire generation of buyers out there just waiting for this. If Leone Industries will give it a fair trial, this will become the gold standard for prime beef. And we'll be there first."

"Hah." Nelson sipped his martini and frowned. "Food fanatics. That's what they are. Now in my day——"

"Not now, Dad." Grace kept her tone light, but there was a hint of steel in her words. "Let Reed enjoy the moment. This is something he's been preparing for since he was barely out of his teens."

"You got that right, Gracie Girl." Frank Malloy patted his wife's hand before turning to his grandson. "You realize this means you'll have to work twice as hard to see that you have enough healthy cattle to fulfill this contract with Leone."

"I don't mind the work, Grandpop."

"I know you don't, sonny boy, and you never have. You've been tending your own herd since you were knee-high to a pup."

Reed flushed with pride. "I'll need to get busy segregating one herd and seeing that they meet all the requirements to be truly organic."

"And I'd like to get in one more trip to the mountains and see if I can spot a herd of mustangs for Gram Gracie before I settle down and do my lonesome cowboy routine."

At Luke's deadpan expression, they all burst into laughter.

"Yeah. That'll be the day, sonny boy." Frank squeezed his wife's hand.

All of a sudden, with so much good news springing from Matt's Italian trip, everyone seemed to be talking at once.

Matt sat back, looking around the table, listening to the chorus of voices, and smiling with satisfaction.

He'd missed this. All of it.

He'd grown impatient to get back to his roots.

But now, seeing the animation on their faces, hearing the excitement in their voices, he knew without a doubt it had all been worth waiting for.

CHAPTER TWO

Matt descended the stairs, feeling like a new man. There was nothing like a night spent in his own bed, after so many nights away.

Spying Yancy alone in the kitchen, he helped himself to coffee. "Am I the first one up?"

The cook set crisp bacon on a nest of paper napkins to drain. "The last."

"I am? Where is everyone?"

Yancy looked over. "Colin drove Great One to town. Luke, Reed, and Frank are up on Eagle's Ridge for the next week or so. Ms. Grace is out trailing one of her herds. No telling when she'll be back."

Matt walked to the floor-to-ceiling windows to stare at the mountain peaks in the distance just as Burke stepped into the kitchen from the mudroom.

"Then I guess I have some downtime coming. I think I'll head up to the hills for a week or so."

The ranch foreman's face creased into a smile. "I figured as much. Every time you come back from one of those fancy, high-powered trips, your first order of business is to get back to your roots. You going to drive one of the trucks, or ride old Beau?"

"I'm thinking Beau needs a workout as much as I do." Matt idly drained his coffee before setting the empty cup on the counter. "If anybody asks, I'll be up on North Ridge for a while."

"I'll let them know. You going to take time for breakfast?"

Matt shook his head and turned to Yancy. "Would you mind packing up some of that food?"

"I'll send as much as you can eat."

Matt shrugged. "I guess I'll take enough for a week or so."

"Done." The cook was already opening a pantry door and reaching for an array of zippered bags and pouches in various sizes.

Matt disappeared up the stairs and reappeared a short time later carrying a duffel filled with his gear, along with a rifle and ammunition.

Yancy handed him a parcel containing the food packets, all carefully labeled. "I sent a similar cache along with your grandmother. There's no telling how long Ms. Grace will be gone."

"As long as it takes to get the pictures she's aiming for." Matt tucked the parcel under his arm and started toward the mudroom, where he snatched up his hat before heading for the door.

"I'll see you in a week or so." He walked out the back door and headed toward the barn.

Not long after he was astride a big bay gelding, saddlebags overflowing, riding across a meadow that led to the hills, black with cattle.

Though it was early April, it still felt like winter in the hills surrounding the Malloy Ranch.

Matt stood in ankle-deep snow chopping wood. It was a chore he always found soul satisfying. Especially after weeks away from home.

It wasn't that he didn't enjoy wheeling and dealing with high-powered lawyers and corporate executives all over the world. And he certainly couldn't complain about the front-row seats at sporting events and the expensive dinners and shows. But even in the Eternal City, with its fine wines and fabulous food, after a week or more, it was like eating too much candy. He found himself craving the simple food, familiar chores, and nights with only the lowing of cattle to break the silence.

He slipped into his parka, which he'd tossed over a log, before filling his arms with fresh firewood. Nudging the door to the range shack open, he tracked snow across the floor to the fireplace, where he stacked the logs neatly before heading out for more.

When his cell phone rang, he plucked it from his pocket. "Hey, Gram Gracie. How's that herd of mustangs?"

"As wild as ever. They've added six pretty little fillies to the herd. There's a third mare big as a house and ready to deliver any day now."

"You hoping to capture the birth on film?"

"That I am. I've already been planning where to set up my cameras for the best angles. Now if only she'll cooperate and have that foal nearby. With these feisty mares,

I never know where I'll end up having to track her. I just hope she doesn't wander down one of those ravines. I really want these pictures for my collection."

"My money's on you, Gram Gracie." Matt paused. "Are you calling for my help?"

"In a way. But not with the herd. I just got a text reminding me about a meeting I'd agreed to. Some lawyer who represents a group of wild-animal federations had set it up, hoping for my take on the best way to preserve wild animals, especially those being removed from the government's endangered list. Since I'm away, I was hoping you could take my place at the meeting."

"Sorry. I'm not at the ranch. I'm up on North Ridge, spending some time at the range shack."

Everyone in the family knew about Matt's love of that particular section of land. From the time he'd been very young and missing his parents, he'd always found solace in this special place. He'd already staked it out as the spot he'd like to build his own house one day.

"Oh dear. How about Luke or Reed?"

"Up on Eagle's Ridge with Grandpop."

He heard his grandmother blow out a breath. "I guess this calls for desperate measures. Since the lawyer is traveling all this way, I'd say it isn't too much to ask him to travel just a bit more. Would you mind an intrusion on your privacy for an hour or two?"

Matt gave a dry laugh. "Never mind my privacy. What about the time he'll waste getting up here by horseback and down to the ranch again?"

"Since Burke is picking him up from his plane, maybe Burke could drive him up and wait until the two of you exchange views before he takes him back to town."

Matt shrugged. "I'll call and arrange it. Providing the phone service continues."

Gracie's tone softened. "I know. It's the same here. One minute a clear line, and the next my phone is dead for hours. Thank you, Matt darlin'. I owe you for this."

"I'm happy to help out."

"I know you are. I know, too, how much you value your alone time in the hills, especially after a long business trip. I'll find a way to make it up to you."

When she hung up, Matt dialed a number and spoke in staccato tones. "Burke. I promised my grandmother I'd meet with some animal activist lawyer. Instead of driving him to the ranch, would you mind driving him up here?"

The old man's tone was incredulous. "You're inviting someone to invade your privacy?"

"It's for Gracie. And it's only for an hour or so. I'd really like you to wait and take him back down as soon as we're through with our meeting."

"Sure thing. When should I expect him?"

"I don't have a clue. Gracie said it would be sometime today. I guess he'll call you when his plane gets in. And you may as well pack a bottle of Grandpop's good Irish whiskey while you're at it. A lot of these Eastern lawyers aren't happy with the local wine and longnecks we've got stashed up here. While I answer this guy's questions, maybe you could deliver supplies to the crew up in the pasture, and then drive him back to town when we're finished."

"Sure. I could do that." Burke cleared his throat. "Hell, son, I'll be happy to sit a spell with the wranglers. I haven't been up there for weeks. I'll head out as soon as the lawyer gets here."

Matt disconnected and stowed his phone in his pocket before bending to retrieve another armload of firewood. As he hauled it to the cabin, he thought about Burke. It didn't take much to make the old man happy these days. He'd been positively bubbling over with joy at joining the wranglers, if even for an hour or so.

He glanced out the window. He and Beau had time to ride across the north pasture and back before his precious solitude was interrupted by this unplanned bit of business.

Matt unsaddled his horse and filled the troughs with feed and water before stepping out of the lean-to behind the range shack that served as a storage shed and stall.

He'd had a great time riding across snow-covered pastures, drinking in the sights and sounds that nourished his soul. Using high-powered binoculars, he'd followed the path of a pair of eagles soaring on currents of air, and had paused to watch a pure white mustang stallion leading his herd toward a box canyon that offered shelter and food. He intended to relate the location to Gram Gracie, since she'd been hunting that stallion for a year or more. Every member of the family had spotted it at one time or another, but it always managed to disappear before she could capture it on film.

Hearing the sound of an engine, Matt ran a hand through his scruffy beard and rounded the cabin in time to see Burke just stepping down from the driver's side.

The old man was grinning like a fool as he circled the truck and opened the passenger door.

Matt stopped in midstride at the sight that greeted him.

The passenger was tall, blond, and gorgeous. She was wearing a charcoal suit jacket over a skinny little skirt that barely skimmed her thighs. When she stepped into the snow, her high-heeled shoes sank ankle-deep, causing her to hiss out a breath before she gamely forged ahead, extending her hand.

"Matthew Malloy? Vanessa Kettering." Her smile might have been forced, but the handshake was firm. It was obvious that she was a woman who didn't get easily flustered.

"Vanessa." Matt's hand closed around hers while he looked beyond her to old Burke, who was clearly enjoying this little turn of events as he retrieved a laptop case. "Do you prefer Vanessa or Miss Kettering?"

"My friends call me Nessa."

"Okay." He glanced down. "Sorry about the snow. This is springtime in Montana."

"It isn't something you can control." She managed a smile as she removed her sunglasses and looked around. "Though if I'd known our meeting would be in the hills, I'd have dressed more...appropriately."

"I'm sorry about that, as well. I agreed at the last minute to stand in for my grandmother." Matt led the way to the door and held it while she entered.

He shot the old cowboy a killing look before following her inside.

Burke set the leather bag on the table before walking to the door. "I'll just get those supplies you asked for, boss, and I'll be on my way up to the herd."

"Make yourself comfortable, Nessa." Matt turned. "I'll give you a hand with those supplies."

He trailed Burke out to the truck.

"Very funny. You could have called and told me to expect a woman."

"Yeah. I could have." Burke chuckled. "I even packed some of your grandpa's whiskey, just in case she drinks like all those other Eastern lawyers."

"You're enjoying this, aren't you, old man?"

Burke chuckled. "More than I should. I wish you could've seen your face. It was priceless."

Matt burst into laughter. "Okay. You got me. But you have to know I'll find a way to get even for this."

"Oh, don't I know it." Burke was whistling as he hauled a box of supplies to the cabin. He was still whistling as he walked back to the truck and drove away.

Matt glanced at the young woman, who bent to remove first one shoe, then the other, all the while wiping away the snow with a tissue. As she did, Matt found himself admiring her backside in the trim skirt that fit her like a second skin.

When she turned and caught him staring, he tried to cover himself by indicating a rocker in front of the fireplace. "Why don't you sit here and I'll crank up the heat?" Not that he wasn't already feeling more heat than he cared to admit.

While Vanessa settled into the rocker, he added a fresh log and kindling to the embers and soon had a fire blazing.

She gave a sigh of appreciation. "Oh, that feels good." She glanced around the tiny cabin. "Is there someplace I can freshen up?"

"Bathroom's over there." Matt pointed and she slipped into her shoes before crossing the room.

Matt remained where he was, clearly enjoying the view. She had a way of walking that he found fascinating. He figured she'd honed that power walk while competing with her male counterparts. Along with the trim skirt and softly flowing hair, it was a potent mix.

Minutes later she emerged and took her time looking around the room. "This is a lot more comfortable than it looks from the outside. When we first got here, I really thought Burke was having fun with me. Especially since he was grinning from ear to ear."

"Yeah. That's Burke." Matt clenched his jaw, wishing he could have a do-over for the day. If he'd known he would be stuck entertaining some female, he'd have sent her packing without the benefit of a meeting. After dealing with lawyers for the past three weeks, he was weary of the nitpicking that was a part of every negotiation. But having to deal with a female lawyer, and one with a killer body that already had him off stride, was more than he wanted to handle so soon after returning. "That old cowboy's always the joker."

Matt nodded toward the kitchen counter, where he'd unpacked the supplies he'd requested. "Would you like to warm up with coffee, beer, wine, or whiskey?"

She laughed. "I think I'd better keep a clear head while we have our discussion. I'll settle for coffee."

Matt filled a coffeemaker with water and freshly ground coffee. Soon the little cabin was perfumed with the fragrance.

He poured two cups and turned. Vanessa had already laid out several documents on either side of the wooden table in the center of the room, and her laptop was humming.

"Efficient. I like that." Determined to make the best of this, he set a cup in front of her and rounded to the other side. "The sooner we talk, the sooner you can get back to civilization." And the sooner he could get back to his privacy.

She nodded. "My thoughts exactly. Especially since the company jet will be returning from Helena to fly me back to Chicago as soon as I'm ready."

"Your wild-animal federations can afford a jet?"

"I'm afraid not. They're a loosely bound group of animal activists who pay me to represent them in Washington. But one of the board members, Clayton Anderson, made his company jet available, since he was heading on to Helena for business, and he'll be back to pick me up in a couple of hours."

"All right then." Eager to finish the meeting and get rid of this intrusion on his privacy, Matt took a seat and picked up the first page of the mound of documents. "Let's get to it. My grandmother said you want the Malloy take on wild-animal preservation, especially those being removed from the government's endangered species list."

"Exactly. The Malloy Ranch is successful enough to pack some clout with the officials who set the rules. We're hoping the Malloy name will make a difference."

Matt compressed his lips and decided to keep his thoughts to himself until he'd had more time to see just where this was leading.

CHAPTER THREE

I hate to nitpick, but I'd like to clarify this third paragraph." Matt indicated the words on the page, and Vanessa located them on hers before carefully reading.

Her head came up. "You agree with the government regarding the number of animals that have been removed from the endangered species list?"

"I haven't even heard of half these animals, Miss Kettering. I can only speak about those animals located in this part of the country."

She sat back, her arms crossed. "Now I'm 'Miss Kettering.' What happened to 'Nessa'?"

He grinned. "I guess I wanted to make my point."

"Point taken." Her own smile returned. "Please disregard the exotic animals on this list. We'll just concentrate on those located, as you said, in this part of the country. How do you feel about the government's annual roundup of mustangs?"

He sat a little straighter. "Now you've touched a nerve.
You have to know that my grandmother is devoted to her
mustangs."

"I know that. That's why I was so eager to meet with
her and hear her views on the subject."

"I assure you that my views will reflect hers. I've
grown up hearing her lament the mistreatment of those
wild horses. She's spent a lifetime trailing them, captur-
ing them on film, and seeing to it that our ranch hands
deliver precious feed whenever she locates a stranded,
starving herd."

Vanessa nodded. "But is she willing to lend her name
to a complaint we hope to present to Congress? We're asking that they rescind the law allowing the annual capture
and adoption of mustangs, along with the slaughter of those
considered too old or ill to be adopted by ranchers."

"I'm afraid, in that particular matter, I cannot speak for
my grandmother. In order to use her name, you'll need
her complete and unequivocal approval."

"Spoken like a lawyer." Vanessa set aside the documents and sat back, forcing a tired smile. "Is there any
coffee left?"

"Sure." Matt walked to the kitchen.

Vanessa took the moment to slowly exhale before glancing at the time on her cell phone. They'd been going over
the documents for more than an hour, and she was no
closer to having the Malloy stamp of approval on their
wish list. At this rate, she wouldn't be out of here until
after dark.

This day wasn't going at all as she'd planned. When
she'd been given the task of flying to Montana, she'd en-

visioned a quick meeting at a cozy ranch, and a long, leisurely dinner aboard the company jet while returning to Chicago. She'd actually set up a lunch meeting tomorrow with another client at one of her favorite restaurants on Lake Shore Drive.

She was most comfortable sticking to a busy schedule. As an only child, and the daughter of a high-profile workaholic, she was well suited to this lifestyle she'd carved out for herself. Whether enjoying a power lunch in the hallowed halls of Congress in Washington, DC, or grabbing a midnight drink with her coworkers in her cramped office in Chicago to discuss her next project, she was invigorated by the challenge of the next job, the next client. Now her entire agenda would have to be amended. Matt filled her cup, and then his own.

"Thanks." She looked over as he settled across from her and picked up the next page of the document.

Seeing him look so comfortable in faded denims had her resenting the fact that she'd felt compelled to dress like a proper lawyer for this meeting.

"If you'd like..." Her words trailed off at the sound of thunder rumbling across the hills. "Are you expecting a storm?"

He shrugged. "Sorry. I haven't been paying attention. But I wouldn't be surprised. This is Montana. We have a saying: If you don't like the weather today, stick around. It's bound to change by tomorrow."

She tried for a smile, but it was more like an anxious grimace.

"You afraid of storms?"

"No." She picked up a page of the document and tried to nonchalantly stare down, but the words were a blur.

Liar, she thought. She was absolutely terrified of thunderstorms, and had been since she was a girl. But it didn't seem prudent to admit that to a client. Especially one who looked as though nothing in the world would frighten him.

This bearded cowboy, with his shaggy hair in need of a trim, and those shrewd, laser-like eyes, wasn't like the men she knew. There was something unsettling about the way he seemed to anticipate what she would say even before she said it. He seemed much more knowledge-able about the law, and the world beyond these hills, than she'd expected. And yet he never tried to show off that knowledge the way most of the men around her would have. He seemed so comfortable with himself. With his life. With this isolation.

Isolation. Here she was, drinking way too much coffee and wishing she could be anywhere except here, in this cabin in the hills, with thunder rumbling across the sky like the devil himself was throwing a temper tantrum.

She drew in a deep breath, reminding herself that she'd come here hoping to snag a big name for their crusade. He hadn't exactly said no. He'd simply pointed out that he would not give his grandmother's name without her approval.

"All right. I'll hold off filling in your grandmother's name until I have a chance to speak with her." She drew a line through the words before glancing over. "But I'll continue to hope that once we meet, your grandmother will be as outraged as our conservancy is about the inhu-mane treatment of wild animals. Shall we move on to the next point?"

Matt nodded.

"How does your family feel about shooting wolves?"

He sat back, stretching out his long legs. "I'd say that depends on why the wolf is being shot. Was he attacking a herd? A wounded calf? For that matter, a wounded wrangler?"

"We'll take the wrangler off the table. Obviously, we all agree that a man has the right to defend himself. But to kill a wolf for going after a calf or a herd? Isn't that what wild creatures do instinctively?"

"True. But if, as you say, a man has the right to defend himself, what about his right to defend his property? Should he allow a wolf pack to decimate his herd?"

"I hardly think a few wolves could decimate an entire herd. Or is this really all about profit? And if so, just how many cattle can a pack of wolves eat?"

His lazy smile disappeared, though his tone remained without inflection. "Where is your home, Miss Kettering?"

"We're back to 'Miss Kettering.' I guess this is serious now. My home is Chicago, though I'm often in DC advocating for wild animals. But what's that got to do—?"

"I assume you've never spent any time on a working ranch."

"No, but—"

Matt stood and faced her, leaning both palms on the table so that they were eye to eye. "Ask any rancher what his day is like, and he'll tell you that no two are ever alike. Whether he's dealing with a blizzard rolling over his pasture in the middle of May, just as the cows are calving, or watching mudslides in September washing out an entire road, he has only himself and his wranglers to depend on. The government doesn't send out troops to lend a hand. Organizations dedicated to the preservation of wildlife don't offer to come in and help him relocate his herds to higher ground, or round up the predators that might use that opportunity to kill even more helpless cattle."

Though she flinched inwardly, Vanessa fought to keep her features neutral. It was a habit she'd mastered watching her father, a well-known prosecuting attorney in Chicago. "I'm sorry. I didn't realize you expected help from the government or from our conservancy to lend a hand"—she adopted her most authoritative lawyer's tone—"during your disasters."

"I don't. No sensible rancher would. I'm just pointing out the obvious. When the good people of Chicago experience a force of nature, they know the city, the state, and the federal government will all come to their aid. When ranchers here in Montana experience the wild forces of nature, we have only ourselves to count on. Do you understand what I mean by that?"

"Perfectly. But I don't see what that has to do with wild animals."

"They're cunning. They use such disasters to their advantage, running down exhausted cattle, dragging helpless newborns into the woods for a feast. A ravenous pack could kill dozens of cattle in a matter of days. I hope you understand that a responsible rancher will hunt them down and remove the danger from his herd."

"I...I'm sure I would do the same."

"Good." Matt visibly relaxed, just as another rumble of thunder shook the cabin. Seconds later, a streak of lightning turned the evening sky outside the window to neon before going dark.

Vanessa gripped the edge of the table and turned startled eyes to his. "Is it safe to be here?"

Matt shrugged. "I guess one place is as good as another in a storm." He crossed to the window to see the trees dipping and swaying in a wild dance. "Looks like the wind is picking up."

"Maybe I should go." Vanessa picked up her phone and realized that she had no service. "Oh dear. My phone is dead."

"That happens a lot up here in the hills." He noted that she'd gone pale. "Look, why don't we forget about our discussion for now and stop for dinner."

"Dinner?" She put a hand on her stomach. "I don't think I could eat a thing. Besides, we have to finish soon so I can return to town."

"We need a break. How about a drink?" He walked to the small kitchen counter. "Would you care for some wine?" Without waiting for her answer, he asked, "Do you prefer red or white?"

"Whatever you have."

"I have both."

"Red, then."

He picked up a bottle of cabernet and uncorked it before pouring it into two wineglasses.

When he handed her one, she managed a smile. "I wasn't expecting wine in a rustic cabin."

He returned her smile. "Don't let the looks of the place fool you. This may be my escape from the world, but when I'm up here, I prefer all the comforts of home." He sipped, nodded. "At least all the comforts that matter."

"And what matters to you?"

He led the way to the fireplace, where he stoked the fire.

Vanessa settled herself in one of the chairs, hoping the fire would take her mind off the storm raging outside.

"My family matters. This ranch matters. The herds up here in the hills matter. But what matters most is the Malloy name. We've built a reputation for integrity." He turned and smiled over the rim of his glass. "I'm sure you've noticed that I'm willing to fight tooth and nail to see that our good name doesn't get used indiscriminately by people with well-intentioned causes."

"So, it's not just about business with you?"

"It's good business to protect the family's reputation."

She lifted her glass in a salute. "Well said."

He gave a slight nod of his head. "Thanks." He chose the chair beside her and nudged an ottoman between them. "Put your feet up. And if you'd like to shed those shoes, be my guest." As he said it, he lifted his own feet to the ottoman, crossing one booted foot over the other.

Vanessa followed suit, and though she was tempted to remove her shoes and wiggle her toes, she decided to remain as professional as possible.

As the thunder and lightning increased in intensity, the skies opened up in a torrent of rain that pounded the roof.

When Vanessa tensed, Matt made his way to the kitchen, returning with the bottle of wine. He topped off her glass, and then his own, before settling back in the chair.

She glanced around nervously. "Do you think Burke will be back soon to pick me up?"

Matt shrugged. "He will if the roads are passable."

Her head came up sharply. "You think the storm will wash them away?"

"It happens."

"But how will we know?"

Again that careless shrug of his shoulder. "If Burke can make it here, he will. If he can't, we'll have our answer. Without phone service, there's no way for us to communicate."

"But we're...safe here." Though she said it as firmly as she could manage, the hesitation in her voice gave her away.

Matt reached over and patted her hand. "Yeah. We're safe here."

Vanessa sat very still, trying to show absolutely no emotion. She was sure this cowboy was just trying to be reassuring. But his touch had had the opposite effect. In fact, she was practically vibrating from it. Tiny darts of pleasure prickled along her spine.

Nerves, she told herself. A simple case of nerves. She'd always been this way in a storm. And this one was even more frightening, because she was feeling so far out of her element. Here she was in a remote cabin in the hills of Montana, spending way too much time on business that should have been cleared up during a simple meeting. And would have, if the woman she'd hoped to meet with hadn't been unavailable.

She shot a sideways glance at the man seated beside her. She'd expected to meet with some backwoods cowboy. Despite his wild, mountain-man look, Matthew Malloy just didn't fit the image at all. From the give-and-take so far, she saw he was smart, savvy, and tough enough to take care of himself and his family.

"You seem to have quite a bit of knowledge of law. Was that your college major?"

Her question brought a smile. "College, when I could manage the time, was spent on business as much as law.

Though I do admit to loving the challenge law school presented. I never finished, though."

"Why?"

He chuckled. "Life got in the way. And I told myself that if I could make the ranch successful enough, I could hire a big-city law firm."

"And did you?"

"Yeah. But I still like to read every line of a contract, especially since my signature seals the deal."

Vanessa grew thoughtful. No wonder his grandmother had recommended this particular grandson to handle the interview in her absence.

Matt got to his feet and walked to the small kitchen. "I think I'd better get some dinner started. If Burke comes, no harm done. But if he can't get through, you won't starve to death."

Vanessa looked up with a quick, nervous smile. "What can I do?"

He paused. "For now, why don't you just relax in front of the fire?"

As another rumble of thunder, closer now, shook the cabin, she nodded her agreement. Setting the glass of wine aside, she leaned her head back, fighting the tension that knotted her insides. Breathing deeply, she struggled to find a calm place in her mind. Not an easy thing to do, with so many appointments that would have to be juggled if she happened to be delayed here. She prided herself on always being on time. It was part and parcel of who she was. What she was. A disciplined, organized, efficient workaholic. And here she was, being asked to relax and roll with this fickle weather.

Within minutes, exhausted by the long flight, lulled

by the warmth of the fire and the wonderful aroma of onions in a skillet wafting on the air, she was able to blot out the thought of the storm raging outside, and the appointments she would miss, and was soon drifting on a cloud of contentment.

CHAPTER FOUR

Vanessa's head came up sharply as she jolted awake. She'd been asleep only a few minutes, but it was enough that she felt a quick rush of embarrassment at her lapse.

She turned her head to see Matt stirring something on the stove. She breathed deeply, feeling suddenly ravenous. She picked up her wineglass and strolled to the counter, where she perched on a wooden bar stool and watched Matt work.

He looked over. "Hungry?"

She nodded. "I didn't realize how much until now. Something smells wonderful."

"Yancy's chili. And I have some bread warming in the oven."

A giant rumble of thunder had him looking at her. "Sounds like the storm's directly overhead now. This should be the worst of it before it blows past."

She tried to take comfort in the thought that it would soon be over, but the sound of rain lashing the windows had her shivering.

Seeing it, Matt nodded toward a plaid afghan tossed over the end of a bunk. "Wrap that around you. It'll keep the cold at bay."

"Thanks. I think I will." She crossed the room and draped the warm plaid around her shoulders before returning to the counter.

Matt rummaged through some containers in the supplies he'd brought and gave a murmur of pleasure. "Here it is." He uncovered a plastic bowl filled with greens, before uncorking a bottle of liquid. "Yancy makes the best salad dressing in the world." He glanced at Vanessa. "I dare you to find one better in Chicago."

"That's a pretty bold bet." She shot him a knowing grin. "We have hundreds of fine restaurants in the Windy City."

"I've sampled a lot of them. But none could compare with Yancy's dressing."

She thought about arguing, but instead glanced around. "Will we eat at the table, or here at the counter?"

"Let's use the table." He nodded toward a cupboard beside him. "Dishes in there. You'll find silverware in that drawer."

While she set the table, he filled two salad bowls with greens and set the container of dressing beside them.

Vanessa carried them to the table.

Matt dropped the oven-warmed bread into a basket and snagged the bottle of wine before crossing to the table.

After tasting Yancy's dressing, Vanessa gave a sound of approval. "Oh, that's wonderful."

"I thought you'd like it." Matt broke off a piece of crusty bread. "This is home baked, too."

"Your cook could work in any fine restaurant in the country. What keeps him at your ranch?"

Matt grinned. "You'll have to ask him. He's got quite a tale to tell. But I suspect Yancy wouldn't be tempted to leave Montana for twice the salary."

He pushed away from the table and returned minutes later with two steaming bowls of chili. On a tray between them were dishes containing shredded cheese, red pepper flakes, snippets of green onion, and crispy crackers.

"Before you start eating, I'll bring you a glass of water."

When he set the glass in front of her, she shot him a look. "Do you think this is my first taste of chili?"

"It's your first taste of Yancy's chili." He dug in and was finishing his second spoonful when he heard the quick gasp of breath across the table.

He looked up in time to watch Vanessa down the water in one long swallow.

"That was—" she reached for a word to describe the eye-watering heat "—really spicy."

"The wranglers refer to it as Yancy Martin's gut-burning masterpiece."

"An apt description." She laughed as she attempted a second bite. This time, prepared for the quick burn, she merely smiled before adding a little cheese, onion, and cracker to the bowl. "But I have to say, this may be the best chili I've ever tasted."

Matt looked at her with new respect. "Any woman who can dig into Yancy's chili has to be a lot tougher than she looks."

"Thanks."

While Matt polished off a second bowl, Vanessa finished her first before sitting back and sipping her wine. "That was incredible. From the salad dressing to the chili. A really unexpected treat."

"I'm glad you liked it. I hope you won't take offense at the fact that the chili was a gift from the wild."

At her blank look, he smiled. "The meat was venison. A deer I tracked on the South Ridge a few months ago. Yancy managed to turn it into steaks, hamburger, and stew meat."

"Are you hoping to shock me?" She resisted touching a hand to her stomach, though the impulse was strong.

"Maybe. A little. But in truth, I think you ought to realize that there's another valid reason for killing animals in the wild. Though it may not be necessary in Chicago, here in Montana we not only care for the land, but we live off it. Deer are plentiful, and though some ranchers hunt them for sport, my family only kills enough to eat."

"Now that you've brought up the fact of sport hunting, I have to ask: Shouldn't it be regulated, for the sake of preserving wild species?"

He stared into his glass. "That sounds noble. But what about the rancher who can barely make ends meet by ranching? Is he to be denied the chance to open his land to hunters who pay very generously for the privilege of sleeping under the stars and stalking their prey on a range in Montana?"

"Again, you make it all about profit."

He glanced over. His eyes narrowed slightly. "And you make *profit* sound like a dirty word. For every successful rancher here in Montana, there are a dozen barely hanging on. There are ranches, many of them in the same family for generations, being auctioned off every month. Do you know what that does to a man whose only dream was to carry on the work of his father and grandfather? I've seen proud men reduced to tears because they've lost everything. So, if opening their land to hunters, or turning their places into dude ranches so city folk can experience life on a working ranch, helps pay the bills, I say more power to them."

Vanessa bit her lip. "You're very persuasive. You'd probably make a very good trial lawyer."

"Just hoping to give you another point of view."

"You have. And I intend to take it under advisement." She shoved away from the table. "Since you cooked, I insist on cleaning up."

As she filled the sink with hot water and began washing the dishes, Matt surprised her by walking up beside her and picking up a towel.

"I said I'd wash them."

"I appreciate that. And I'll dry." He reached over her head and returned a bowl to the cupboard.

Vanessa went very still, feeling a tingle along her spine.

When he returned a second bowl, the back of his hand brushed her hair and she experienced little pinpricks all along her skin.

It had to be fatigue. And the fact that she was jumpy because of the storm. Still, it had her holding herself stiffly until he'd put away all the dishes.

"How about a fresh pot of coffee?"

She merely nodded.

A short time later she carried two cups of coffee to the footstool positioned between the two rockers in front of the fire.

Matt followed with a plate of brownies.

As the storm blew itself out, they sat by the fire, nibbling Yancy's homemade brownies, sipping coffee, and taking opposing sides in the discussion about wild animals.

At least, Vanessa thought with a sigh of relief, they were no longer arguing. Rather, they both seemed to be enjoying the give-and-take, and the satisfaction each time one of them made a valid point in their favor.

As the fire burned low, Vanessa stifled a yawn.

Matt pointed to the bunk bed in the corner. "Let's face it. Burke isn't getting here tonight. If he could get through, he'd have been here hours ago. You can bunk there."

"Where will you sleep?"

He pointed to the pullout sofa bed.

She needed no coaxing. She barely had the energy to slip out of her shoes and suit jacket before draping the plaid afghan around herself and dropping onto the bunk.

She'd expected the bunk to be hard, and it was. But she was too tired to care. She was asleep almost as soon as her head touched the pillow.

Matt added another log to the fire and filled his cup with coffee before adding a splash of his grandfather's fine Irish whiskey. Easing off his boots, he settled himself into the rocker and nudged the footstool to a more comfortable position.

The rain gentled to a steady patter on the roof.

He leaned his head back, enjoying the sounds of the night and the hiss and snap of the logs on the grate.

He'd expected to resent this intrusion on his privacy.

Always before, he'd treated this alone time in the hills as his sacred right, especially after a long overseas trip. And this cabin was much more to him than a simple range shack. It was his very private domain. His haven. And had been, since the loss of his parents. But he had to admit that he'd enjoyed the spirited debate between himself and this woman. Vanessa Kettering. Nessa.

His lips curved into a smile. Nessa. The nickname suited her.

She was bright. Sharp. Quick with a response to every question he'd thrown at her.

And gorgeous.

He turned to glance at the woman asleep across the room. She'd drawn the plaid afghan up to her chin. Even with her eyes closed, he could see them. A rich maple-sugar brown that could sharpen with anger or go wide with fear. And when she smiled, they crinkled at the corners. That smile did something to his heart.

His first impression of her had been all wrong. With those long, long legs, the city suit, the designer shoes, and that mane of blond hair dancing in the breeze, she'd looked as out of place stepping out of Burke's truck in the wilderness as a prom queen at a mud-wrestling match. But once they got down to the business that had brought her here, she'd been an able opponent.

He had to admit that he'd actually enjoyed their little tug-of-war. And wouldn't mind going another round or two in the morning.

That admission had him smiling.

He drained his cup and got to his feet. Across the room he set the empty cup in the sink before turning to the pull-out sofa bed.

He preferred to sleep naked. But out of deference to his guest, he simply stripped off his shirt and peeled away his socks.

Climbing beneath the covers, he lay listening to the soft patter of raindrops on the roof.

It took him longer than usual to fall asleep. He tossed and turned, trying in vain to get comfortable. But an hour later he was still wide awake and crossing to the window to stare out into the darkness.

He absently reached for one of Nelson's fine cigars and held a flame to the tip. Smoke curled above his head as he studied his beloved hills, which were shrouded in darkness, looking like silent sentinels keeping watch over the herds they nurtured.

As a boy, he'd dreamed of traveling to exotic places to escape the tedious work that he and his brothers were expected to share. It had seemed, to a boy of twelve, that there were too many adults directing his life, taking away any chance of making his own choices. And yet the older he got, the more he learned, and the stronger his bond with this land and his family became. He'd traveled the world and hadn't once found a place that compared with this.

It was his roots. His anchor. His passion.

He stubbed out the last of his cigar and made his way back to bed, lying as still as possible, listening to the soft, steady sound of breathing from the figure across the room.

He was intrigued by her. Fascinated with her quick mind.

Who was he kidding? It wasn't her mind he'd coveted. Not only was she absolutely beautiful, but the entire time they'd been debating, he'd had to fight an overpowering desire to kiss her. That admission made him feel like a teenager with a crush on some hot movie star. And the fact that her mere presence in his space had him thinking things better left alone just added to his discomfort.

Sometime in the small hours of the night he finally fell into a deep, exhausted sleep. But only after assuring himself that he would find a way to send Vanessa Kettering back to Chicago first thing in the morning, even if it meant slogging through waist-high mud to do it.

And then he could return to the business of enjoying his wilderness.

He could savor the solitude that he'd always craved. The solitude that had always managed to soothe his lonely, restless soul. A soul that yearned for something...something indefinable triggered by the loss of his parents that no other relationship had since been able to fill.

CHAPTER FIVE

Vanessa awoke and lay very still, fighting through the last cobwebs of sleep. After a few moments of confusion, she remembered where she was. A cabin in the hills of Montana. And then a second thought. Matthew Malloy.

Keeping the blanket hugging her like a shield, she peered around in the dim light of the fire's embers. Spotting the figure on the sofa bed across the room, she tossed aside the blanket and made her way to the tiny bathroom.

She couldn't recall the last time she'd slept in her work clothes. She felt rumpled and thoroughly uncomfortable as she undressed and stepped under the shower's spray. Though the water was only lukewarm, it wasn't cold enough to have her shivering. Minutes later she dried herself and wrapped a towel around her hair before dressing in the same wrinkled clothes she'd slept in. Then she tossed her head and finger-combed her hair, letting it fall in soft waves about her shoulders.

She made her way to the kitchen and put on a pot of coffee. While it perked, she crossed to the fireplace and struggled to add a log to the embers. When she'd finished, she watched as a thin flame began to lick across the dry bark. Satisfied, she stepped back with a smile.

"Not bad for a city slicker."

Matt's voice had her swiveling her head to give him a startled look.

"Sorry," she said. "I didn't mean to wake you."

"Don't apologize. I'm usually awake at dawn. I'd have helped you with that log, but I didn't want to scare you and have you drop it on your foot."

"I probably would have. So thanks, I think. At least I managed by myself." She gave a self-conscious laugh, knowing he'd been watching her struggles. "Well, barely."

"You did just fine. You wrangled a log half your body weight into the fireplace. That takes some doing."

At his words of praise, she felt an unexpected glow.

When he stood up, she found herself gaping before she managed to look away. He was barefoot and naked to the waist, his denims unsnapped and low on his hips.

"I heard the shower. I hope you gave the water time to heat up."

"I didn't know it would get warmer."

A smile teased his lips. "You took a cold shower?"

"Not cold, exactly. But not really warm."

"I apologize. I should have warned you. The water tank is heated by the fireplace."

"Gee. Thanks for not telling me sooner."

"You're welcome." He crossed the room and paused outside the door to the bathroom. "But thanks to your efforts, I get to enjoy a really hot shower."

"Just remember. For that, you owe me big-time."

"I'll figure a way to pay you back." He shot her a wicked grin.

When he closed the door, Vanessa let out a long, slow breath. She could think of one way he could pay her back. What a gorgeous body. All sculpted muscle and sinew. A body so toned, he could be a poster boy for a major weight-training company. If this was any indication of what Montana cowboys were like, she wanted more.

How had she not noticed last night? She must have been a lot more travel weary than she'd realized.

A short time later she looked up from her coffee to see him wearing a flannel shirt with the sleeves rolled to the elbows and a pair of faded denims. As he bent to pull on his boots, his hair and heavily bearded chin sparkled in the light of the fire with little droplets of water from the shower.

He looked over with a grin. "I've got to say, the smell of that coffee has me starving."

"Me, too." She felt a quick rush of guilt, knowing it wasn't food she'd been thinking about.

"Since you made the coffee, I'll rustle up breakfast." He moved around the stove and grabbed a skillet, then went to work frying sausages and eggs with the ease of someone who knew his way around a kitchen.

"Something tells me this isn't your first time cooking for yourself."

He shrugged. "When you grow up on a ranch, you'd better know how to take care of yourself. There's nobody trailing behind to cater to your needs."

"How about your mother? Is she a good cook?"

He paused for just a fraction before flipping the eggs

onto two plates. "My parents died when I was twelve. An accident on a snow-covered road."

"I'm sorry." Vanessa accepted the plate from his hand and led the way to the table. As he sat across from her, she added, "I lost my mother when I was fifteen. Cancer."

He met her look across the table. "It never goes away, does it? There's always a shadow lingering somewhere in our mind."

She nodded.

For a few minutes they ate in silence, feeling an odd sense of shared pain.

Matt shoved back his chair and retrieved the coffeepot, topping off her cup and then his own.

When he sat down he leaned back. "Do you live at home, or do you have your own place?"

"I live with my father. I toy with the idea of getting my own place. But so far I've resisted, since I travel between Chicago and DC so often. We really enjoy each other's company. Often my dad works so late, I may as well live alone. But when he does manage to get home for supper, it's nice to have the time to visit and catch up on life."

Matt smiled. "What does your father do?"

"He's the district attorney for Cook County."

Matt's raised brow said more than words. "No wonder he often doesn't make it home for supper."

"Yeah." She shook her head. "And on top of that, he's a workaholic. He can't leave it at the office. Most nights he brings home stacks of documents to read late into the night."

"Those must be some pretty high-profile cases he's dealing with."

Vanessa nodded. "He often jokes that there must be

something in Chicago's air to bring so many criminals to his district."

Matt regarded her. "So that's why you went into law?"

She shrugged. "In the beginning. I've always wanted to be like my dad. Especially since losing my mother. He used to say the two of us were joined at the hip. If I get hurt, he bleeds. If I have a problem, he won't sleep until it's resolved. So it was a given that I'd study law. But midway through my courses, I realized that I didn't want to pursue criminal law. I found myself wanting to get involved in social justice."

"And that led to animal activism."

"Exactly. It's something I'm passionate about. And I think I can make a difference."

"Is your father disappointed that you didn't follow him into criminal law?"

She chuckled. "I'm sure he's had some twinges. He made it clear that there would always be a place for me on his staff. But I think he's proud of the fact that I want to make my own way."

Matt nodded. "He should be proud."

She eyed him over the rim of her cup. "Even though my choice has brought me to your doorstep to meddle with your privacy?"

He threw back his head and laughed. "Yeah. Lucky me. Now I get to spar with an animal activist who's passionate about saving every wolf, deer, and bear in these hills."

"Bear?" She raised a brow. "Have you seen bears in this area?"

He gave a negligent shrug. "Sure. And right about now they're waking from hibernation and feeling mean and hungry. Want to go on a mission to feed them?"

"That depends. Would I be the food?"

He wiggled his brows like a mock villain. "You'd be a tasty morsel, little lady."

That had her laughing aloud. "Gee, thanks."

He started to gather up the dishes, and once again, as she had the previous night, she stopped him. "You made breakfast. I can clean these."

"Okay." He got to his feet and removed his parka from a hook by the door. "I'll chop some logs. It'll give me a chance to see what damage that storm did."

When he was gone, Vanessa finished her coffee before picking up the dishes and heading toward the sink.

Yesterday she'd thought being stuck in this godforsaken wilderness was the worst possible situation. Today, after a good night's sleep and a satisfying breakfast, it was feeling more like an adventure.

Of course, having had a good look at the sexy cowboy sharing this adventure put a whole new spin on things.

As she washed the dishes and stowed them away, she found herself smiling. If she hurried, she might catch him chopping wood.

Visions of silly cowboy movies played through her mind. A gorgeous hunk, shirtless of course, working up a sweat while whittling away on a downed tree. A helpless maiden being scooped up in his arms, clinging breathlessly to her hero.

She shook her head to clear her thoughts. First of all, he may be gorgeous and hunky, but she was no helpless female in need of strong arms. And second, she was quite certain the cowboy who brought her here would be driving up very soon to return her to civilization.

And though she would miss the spirited give-and-take

of last night with Matthew Malloy, it was time she got
back to reality. If she spent too much time up here, she
might just lose touch altogether.

Matt gathered up an armload of logs and made his way to
the cabin just as Vanessa pulled open the door.

While she held it, he stepped inside and deposited the
wood alongside the fireplace.

"That was quick."

He wiped his hands on his pants before turning. "I
can't take credit for chopping all of this today. Some of it
was left over from yesterday."

"Is there much damage from the storm?"

He nodded toward the doorway. "See for yourself."

She stepped outside and he followed.

"There's no snow." She looked down. The ground,
which yesterday had been snow covered, was now a sea
of mud.

"Yeah. Better watch where you step. Some of that
could be ankle deep."

She paused to study a giant evergreen leaning at a pre-
carious angle. "Isn't that dangerous?"

Matt nodded. "I'll have the crew take it down as soon
as they can get up here with some chainsaws."

"What's holding it up?"

He shrugged. "Probably some roots buried deep
enough to keep it from falling all the way."

"Could it have crushed the cabin last night?"

He smiled. "From the angle it's leaning, I'd say it
was in a better position to take out a couple more trees."
He pointed. "It would have taken Noah's flood to carry
it this far."

She gave a sigh of relief.

Matt pointed to a rock ledge not far from the cabin. "If you stand up there, you can see for miles."

As she started forward he moved along beside her until they reached the ledge. He closed strong fingers around her wrist. "This is as far as you want to go." He pointed. "That ravine may not look too deep, because it's covered over with a wild tangle of brush. But it's actually a drop-off that falls hundreds of yards down. It would be like dropping from the top of one of your Chicago skyscrapers."

With a hand to her throat she stepped back from the edge, feeling a quick, jittery rush of panic.

"Are you afraid of heights?"

She shook her head. "I didn't think so. But that left me a little...shaky."

Or was it the nearness of this man as he surveyed his land? His kingdom? Or maybe it was the strength in those fingers as they'd closed around her wrist. The mere thought of him had her sweating. Whatever the reason, she was feeling breathless. And more than a little shaken.

At the sound of ringing, Matt retrieved his cell phone from his pocket. "Hey, Burke. I'm surprised we can get a signal up here." He listened, then added, "Okay. I'll tell her."

As he tucked his phone away he turned. "Burke thinks the trail is passable. He's leaving camp now. By the time he gets here, he'll have a pretty good idea of the damage done and whether or not he can make it back to the ranch."

Vanessa swallowed back a twinge of unexpected disappointment. Her little adventure had just come to an end.

"Well." She reached for the cell phone in the pocket of her skirt. "I guess I can phone home now."

She pressed the button for her father's number and was surprised when his message came on without a single ring.

"Hi, Dad. It's me. Sorry I couldn't get through to you until now. I'm hoping to be home before too late tonight."

Feeling oddly deflated at not being able to speak with her father, she turned toward the door. "I guess I'll just gather up my papers and be ready to leave. I wouldn't want to hold Burke up."

Before Matt could follow her inside, his phone rang again. He remained outside, listening in silence.

When he finally stepped into the cabin, he crossed to the kitchen and began filling a box with food containers.

She watched him. "Won't you need that?"

He shook his head. "Looks like I'm leaving, too. I'll have Burke haul this down the mountain while I ride behind on my horse."

"Is anything wrong?"

He looked over, his face devoid of emotion. "Just some storm damage at the ranch."

"I hope it's nothing serious."

He gave a shrug. "Nothing new in these parts." He set the box on the floor near the door. "I'm sure we'll handle it."

Hearing the sound of a truck's engine, she started past him. As her body brushed against his, she felt a sudden, shocking sexual jolt.

She paused for a mere moment, tipping her face up to his, her eyes wide, her breath catching in her throat.

Matt reached for the door, but instead of opening it, he

kept his voice low. "I'm sorry again you had to spend the night."

"I'm not." The words slipped out before she had time to think. Then, trying to cover her lapse, she bit her lower lip. "I'm not sorry, Matt. Whenever I look back on this, I'll think of it as my excellent Montana adventure."

He was staring at her mouth in a way that had her throat going dry. There was a hint of a smile on his lips. "I hope I won't be a villain in your memory."

"Far from it."

Something in the way she said it had him looking from her mouth to her eyes.

Alarmed that he could read her thoughts, she blindly reached a hand to the door, only to have her hand come in contact with his.

She pulled it away as though burned, but it was too late. The rush of heat had her cheeks going bright pink.

"Nessa…"

She looked up to see him watching her in that quiet, closed way.

Before she had a chance to think about what she was doing she stood on tiptoe and touched his mouth with a soft butterfly kiss as light as a snowflake.

His eyes narrowed. His hands gripped her shoulders and for a moment he hesitated, as though considering. Then he lowered his head, staring into her eyes before covering her lips with his.

He kissed her with a thoroughness that had all the breath backing up in her throat. His lips, warm and firm, moved over hers with an intensity that had her heart pounding in her temples. There was such controlled strength in him. In the way he held her. The way he touched her. The way he kissed her. It was the most purely sensual feeling she'd ever experienced. She had a sudden urgent desire to see all that cool composure slip away.

Caught by complete surprise, her papers slipped from her hands, spilling onto the floor as she leaned into him, craving more.

He lingered a moment longer, as though unable or unwilling to break contact.

Breathing hard, his fingers closed around her upper arms, and he held her a little away while his eyes narrowed on hers. "Sorry. My fault."

"No. Mine. I..." She stared at the documents on the floor, as though unaware of how they got there.

They both dropped to their knees, gathering the papers, studiously avoiding touching.

When they stood, they both heard the sound of a truck door being slammed.

As the cabin door opened, they stepped apart, neither of them willing to look at the other.

CHAPTER SIX

Burke stood in the open doorway. "I hope you're ready, Miss Kettering. We've got a long drive ahead of us through a sea of mud."

"I'm...ready." Completely flustered, she held her laptop and folders to her chest as she stepped outside.

Burke trailed her, carrying the box of supplies that had been sitting by the door.

Matt strode to the kitchen counter and filled the other boxes.

While Vanessa settled into the passenger side, Matt and Burke made several trips back and forth from the cabin to the truck, storing boxes in the rear of the vehicle.

Then, as the old cowboy climbed into the driver's side and started along a muddy trail, Vanessa turned in time to see Matt leading a horse from the lean-to behind the cabin.

She glanced at Burke, who merely grinned. "I warned Matt it would be a messy slog, but he wasn't about to leave old Beau behind."

"Do you think they'll make it?"

At the worried look in her eyes he merely chuckled. "No matter the condition of the trail, my money's always on Matt Malloy. That man could make it through a blizzard, a nor'easter, or the storm of the century."

"You make him sound like Superman."

"Better than that, Miss Kettering. Superman's fiction. Matt's a real flesh-and-blood cowboy. I don't think there's a crisis in these parts that Matt couldn't overcome."

Vanessa sat back, pondering the old man's words.

What was it about Matt Malloy that had her behaving like someone she didn't even know? Take that kiss. She'd actually initiated it. And why? At the moment she wasn't sure. But at the time, she'd been incapable of resisting the urge. And once started, she felt as though she'd unleashed a hurricane.

That mouth. Those clever lips. Those strong arms holding her as gently as if she were delicate crystal.

Instead of pushing away, she'd become completely caught up in the moment. She couldn't recall the last time a man's kiss had had such an effect on her. She'd been absolutely drowning in feelings, and all in the space of a couple of seconds.

Though she tried to keep from looking back, every once in a while she would swivel her head to see Matt on his horse, navigating the trail some distance behind their truck.

Before they were even halfway to the ranch, the truck was covered in mud, as were the horse and rider behind them. But despite the conditions of the trail, the horse never stumbled or slowed its pace. And the man astride his horse sat tall in the saddle, looking as regal as a king surveying his kingdom.

Old Burke glanced in the rearview mirror before turning his gaze on her. "How'd you like to be riding with him?"

She'd been thinking the same thing. Despite the terrible conditions of the trail, there was something so raw and primitive about Matt Malloy, she'd been daydreaming about riding behind him, her arms wrapped around his waist, her face pressed to his neck. The mere thought had her shivering.

"I guess I should be glad I wasn't dressed for riding."

He joined in her laughter. "My thoughts exactly. Though I do love my horse, I'll take the comfort of this truck anytime, especially after a storm like the one we had last night."

Her own laughter rang hollow in her ears. In truth, she would take the sea of mud anytime over the comfort of this truck, if only she could have her hands on Matt Malloy.

To keep from thinking about him, she plucked her cell phone from her pocket and dialed her father's cell. She left another message before calling his office, where she left a similar message.

Puzzled, she made a mental note to try him again on the plane ride home.

Matt had to keep forcing his attention back to the treacherous trail. The thought of Vanessa Kettering kept blurring his focus.

He prided himself on always being in control. Ever since the tragic death of his parents, he'd assumed the role of leader to his two younger brothers, though he was still as wild and free as he'd always been. He worked hard at leaving the spontaneous, juvenile behavior to Luke and Reed. He'd trained himself to be disciplined and deliberate, steering the family business in a safe direction, always weighing both sides of an issue before making a decision that he knew would affect his entire family.

And back there in the range shack he'd thrown caution to the wind to do something just for the hell of it.

He would like to blame it on the situation. A small, cramped cabin. A gorgeous, unexpected woman interrupting all his carefully laid plans of solitude. The fact that he'd been forced to watch her sleep just a few feet away. But the truth was that those were all flimsy excuses for his out-of-character behavior. He'd kissed her simply because he'd wanted to.

It was only a kiss, he told himself. But again, truth won out, and he was forced to admit that, despite the fact that he'd kept it as light as possible, that simple touch of her lips had been an assault on all his senses. An explosion of light in his brain, followed by a rush of heat before the floor beneath his feet began to go all crazy and actually tilt until he'd nearly lost his balance. And all the while, thoughts of taking her right there on the cold, hard floor of the cabin had played through his mind.

What in hell had happened to his logic? His common sense?

He didn't know what intrigued him more. The fact that he was actually sorry that Vanessa Kettering was leaving, or the fact that he'd behaved like some kind of lonely mountain man bidding a final farewell.

A mountain man. He ran a hand through his rough beard and swore. Wasn't that how she saw him? As some kind of Neanderthal?

Still, she hadn't slapped his face, though he'd deserved it. And he could tell himself that he read an invitation in her eyes, especially after that sweet little kiss she'd given him first, but that didn't give him the right to take advantage. She was a guest. Here to interview his grandmother. And the fact that she'd been forced to spend the night didn't give him any rights.

He swore. It had been just a quick kiss. And yet, even now, slogging through mud that required his full attention, he couldn't stop thinking about it. And about the woman who'd felt so damned good in his arms.

It was a lucky thing she was leaving. He wasn't going to see her again. Because if he did, he'd be tempted to share much more than a kiss.

Vanessa Kettering had been a lovely distraction, but now he needed to get his mind back on the family business.

Matt hosed down his mud-spattered horse and toweled him dry before turning him loose in a pasture. Though old Beau had stood perfectly still during the entire process, Matt could have sworn that sly animal was smiling and enjoying being pampered. And once in the pasture, the old horse kicked up its heels and broke into a gallop.

It was exactly how Matt felt. Some time in the hills, one unplanned kiss, and he felt like a stallion just turned loose in a field full of sleek mares.

He looked around at the portion of roof ripped from

one of the outbuildings. A section of fence was missing, obviously blown away in the wind. And a corral gate stood at an odd angle, having been nearly ripped off its hinges during the storm.

How much more, he wondered, had been damaged by last night's storm?

He trudged up to the house, where he kicked off his boots before bending to a sink in the mudroom to wash.

In the kitchen, a chorus of voices told him that most of the family had gathered around to meet their unexpected guest.

Yancy was pouring coffee while his grandfather and great-grandfather were chatting up Vanessa. Across the table, Luke and Reed, fresh off the range and looking like wild mountain men, were staring at the newcomer with obvious, wide-eyed approval, while Colin was leaning against the kitchen counter and, like the lone cowboy he was, watching from a discreet distance.

"…wind so strong last night it blew a section of fence onto the roof of the barn." Frank chuckled. "I'm just glad I wasn't out during the worst of it. I'd probably be up there, too."

He glanced over as Matt paused in the doorway. "Hey, sonny boy. You look like you've been out playing with the hogs."

"Yeah." Matt grinned. "Making mudpies. Since I assume you've all introduced yourselves to Miss Kettering, I'll leave you to visit. I'll be downstairs in a while."

When he was gone, the cook set out a plate of chocolate chip cookies still warm from the oven.

"My favorites." Nelson jokingly snatched up the entire plate and held it to one side. "Glad you made these for me, Yancy, but you should have made enough to go around."

"Talk about hogs…" Luke reached over his great-grandfather's shoulder and grabbed the plate from his hand. "You could at least give our houseguest the first choice."

With a laugh, Vanessa accepted one from the plate before Luke passed it around to the others.

"I'm getting mine while the getting's good." Burke helped himself to two, as did Colin.

Vanessa bit into one and gave a sigh of pleasure. "I can't remember the last time I tasted homemade cookies."

"Then you're traveling in the wrong circles, little lady." Yancy transferred another batch from the baking tin to a plate and handed it to Frank. "I bake something fresh every day."

She looked over. "You're kidding."

The cook shrugged. "On a ranch this size, with a family like the Malloys, it's as natural as breathing. I think every one of them has a sweet tooth."

She gave a shake of her head. "You bake every day? I feel like I fell into a parallel universe. What happened to my world of coffee shops on every corner, and baked goods that were fresh last week and filled with preservatives?"

Burke and Yancy shared a smile as Yancy poured himself a cup of coffee. "I recall feeling that way when I first arrived here. I looked around at this big house, and this loud, crazy family—"

"Hey. Who're you calling crazy?" Reed reached out and helped himself to a warm cookie.

Yancy continued as though he hadn't been interrupted.

"—and I realized that, no matter how isolated this place was from the rest of the world, I never wanted to leave."

"How long ago was that?" Vanessa asked.

"Thirty-five years ago."

"That long?" Vanessa helped herself to another cookie. "Have you ever regretted staying?"

"Just about every day," Luke answered for him.

That had the others laughing.

Yancy merely grinned. "Oh, I may have thought once or twice about exchanging kitchen duties for some time spent up in the hills with the herds, especially in the middle of summer." He looked down at himself—all five feet two inches—and rolled his eyes. "But then I see how hard those wranglers work, and I remind myself that I've got the best life of all."

"Just remember, Yancy." Nelson helped himself to another cookie. "This family's got dozens of guys who can babysit cattle. But there's only one guy on this ranch that could put Hollywood's gourmet cooks to shame. So don't even think about giving it up to ride herd on some ornery cows."

They were still laughing when Matt descended the stairs. He'd shaved off his rough beard and was dressed in a clean pair of denims, a crisp shirt, and shiny boots.

"I see we've got almost the entire family here. All that's missing—" He looked over as the back door burst open on a gust of wind and his grandmother kicked off mud-caked boots before hanging her parka on a hook. "I take that back. Now the entire gang is under one roof."

Gracie rolled her sleeves and washed before stepping into the kitchen.

As she did, Matt said, "Vanessa Kettering, this is the

woman you came here hoping to interview. Gracie, this is—"

"—the lawyer from the wildlife federation?" Gracie's face creased into a wide smile. "I'll be darned. Just when I was feeling bad about having a lawyer invade my grandson's privacy, it turns out to be a beautiful young woman."

"Yeah," Reed exchanged a knowing look with Luke and their uncle Colin. "What're the odds? If I'd been up in the hills, I'd probably have to share my range shack with a bobcat."

"Or a toothless old wrangler looking for work," Luke added.

While the others laughed, Gracie offered a handshake, giving Vanessa a long, considering appraisal. "Aren't you kind of young to be worrying about the fate of wild things?"

Vanessa clasped Gracie's hand. "I didn't realize there was an age requirement for this sort of work."

Gracie merely smiled. "You're right, of course. But most of the requests I get about the mustangs come from folks my age, who have the time to worry about such things. Most young people are too busy trying to jump-start a career to give a thought to the plight of wild animals."

"Here, Gracie Girl." Frank held a chair. As she sat, he put his arms around her and brushed the back of her neck with a kiss. "I was worried about you up in those hills in that storm."

She turned and touched a hand to his cheek. "I found shelter in a little cave beneath some rocky outcroppings. I'd have stayed in the truck, but the way it was rocking in that wind, I was afraid it might topple clean on its side. And by the time the storm blew over, the herd I'd been trailing was long gone. I was cold, wet, and I figured I'd better head home while the trails were still passable."

"I'm glad you did, my girl." Frank kissed her lips and kept his arms around her when she picked up the cup of coffee offered by Yancy.

His concern, and their obvious devotion to each other, wasn't lost on the others.

Matt turned to Burke. "I guess we'd better get Vanessa to town. She has a plane to catch."

Yancy offered his hand. "It was nice meeting you, Miss Kettering. If you're ever in Montana again, I hope you'll come back for a visit."

"I'd love to, Yancy. And call me Nessa. Thanks for the coffee and cookies. These were the best ever."

"My pleasure, Nessa." The cook was beaming.

Vanessa turned to the others, but before she could say her good-byes, there was a loud knock on the door.

Burke opened it to admit the sheriff and his deputy, who hung their hats on a hook and cleaned their boots on a rough boot-scrubbing mat before stepping into the kitchen.

Eugene Graystoke was a plainspoken, take-charge man who came from a long line of ranchers. Smart, dependable, and tough, he'd been sheriff for over twenty-five years. From the beginning, he'd quickly earned the trust of the folks in Glacier Ridge, who called on him for everything from a drunken ranch hand driving on the wrong side of the road to a family squabble that ended up in a brawl. He even aided in trailing an errant bull or two, when they managed to break through a section of fence.

His deputy, Archer Stone, had grown up in Glacier Ridge with Patrick and Bernadette. Ruggedly handsome, he walked with a swagger that was always more pronounced when he was in uniform.

After greeting the family, Eugene turned to Vanessa. "You'd be Miss Kettering?"

She seemed surprised. "I am. And you are . . . ?"

"Sheriff Eugene Graystoke, ma'am. My deputy, Archer Stone." The sheriff cleared his throat. "I was contacted by a Captain Dan McBride of the Cook County PD. You know him?"

She nodded. "I know of him."

The two men accepted coffee from Yancy before Eugene took a seat at the table and his deputy remained standing behind him.

The sheriff fixed Vanessa with a piercing look. "As I understand it, you accepted a flight on a corporate jet headed to Helena."

"That's right. But—"

He held up a hand. "I'll talk, ma'am. You'll just do me the courtesy of listening."

Seeing the grins on the faces of those around her, Vanessa felt heat stain her cheeks and fought to compose her features. It was obvious to her that this man was accustomed to taking charge.

"The jet made a quick stop at Glacier Ridge, then immediately after depositing a lone passenger—" he peered over the rims of his glasses "—it continued on to Helena. Anyone tracking that flight figured all its passengers were going directly to Helena."

"Tracking the flight...?" At his upturned palm she compressed her lips together and made a quick nod of her head.

"Good." He looked around at the others, aware that he had their complete attention. "Now, ma'am, this is where it gets tricky."

CHAPTER SEVEN

The family stared at Sheriff Graystoke with matching looks of puzzlement.

At their frowns, he held up a cell phone. "This was delivered to me by the Montana State Police. I'm told it's untraceable. Like they use on those spy thrillers on TV. When we're ready for a conference call, I'm to dial the number of Elliott Kettering."

"My father...?"

Without a word the sheriff entered the number in the speed dial, then turned on the speaker.

Seconds later an image came into focus on the phone's screen.

"Nessa?"

"Dad..." Vanessa reached for the phone, but the sheriff shook his head and continued holding it facing her as the others gathered around to watch and listen.

"Vanessa, this is Captain McBride."

Vanessa could make out the police officer's face next to her father's.

"Sorry, Elliott," he said to the man beside him. "I think it best if I set the scene, so to speak."

"I don't understa—"

McBride cut off Vanessa's protest. "As you know, your father's office has been involved in a very high-profile case."

Vanessa nodded. "DePietro."

"Exactly. In the past few days, the accused saw his air-tight alibi fall apart on the witness stand. If convicted, Diomedes DePietro will be going away for a very long time. At his age, he'll likely die in prison. A very well-connected man like that, about to see his empire crumble, will often resort to anything to remain free. In this case, immediately after the trial ended yesterday, your father received a threat stating that if his office continued its prosecution of this case, he would lose his most precious possession."

Vanessa looked at the image of her father in the phone.

"Nessa, he was telling me very plainly that his people would go after you."

"But I—"

"These people don't make idle threats. I have no doubt your life is in danger. The exact words were, 'Unless a mistrial is declared, Kettering will pay with the life of the one he holds most dear.' That can only be you, Nessa."

"And then," Captain McBride added, "when we got word that the plane parked in Helena, the same plane that would be bringing you home, had been damaged, we feared the worst."

"Damaged? It was a storm—"

"And how do you know that?" the police captain asked. "The fact that it happened during a storm just makes the local authorities reluctant to consider that it might have been a criminal act. But taken with this threat, it's far more likely that the damage to the landing gear was man-made and not the result of any storm. That's why we have federal agents going over every inch of that plane right now."

Her father ran a hand through his hair. "I've been trying to reach you ever since I got that threat. Then, when I heard about the damage to the plane, I was desperate to hear from you. But when you never answered—"

"What about Clayton Anderson and the crew? Were they injured? "

"No serious injuries," Captain McBride's voice rang out. "The hospital in Helena reported that all are doing fine. But they had no report of a female passenger."

"Oh, Dad. I didn't know. The storm made it impossible to communicate. And then when I tried to call you, I couldn't get through. Not even at your office." She studied his haggard appearance. "I can only imagine what you've been going through."

He gave a weary shake of his head.

Captain McBride cleared his throat. "The fact that you couldn't get through was no coincidence."

Vanessa's brow shot up.

"We insisted on taking all the phones that had any messages from DePietro to our lab to be tested for evidence. That included both your father's cell phone and his office phones."

Vanessa swallowed. "Then you think there's a very

real possibility that this man intends to make good on his threat."

The police captain's voice deepened with authority. "Until all the tests on the plane are completed, we will continue to believe that it was a first attempt. We aren't foolish enough to believe it will be the last. DePietro's network is vast. That's why we've suggested that you be taken to a safe house until this trial is over."

"A safe house?" Her voice rose with anger. "You must be kidding."

Her father's tone was abrupt. "This is serious, deadly business, Nessa. Until this trial ends, I need to know you're safe from DePietro's threats, if I'm to be free to do my job."

"What about *my* job, Dad? What am I supposed to do for the weeks, maybe months, that this trial goes on?"

Captain McBride interrupted. "Are you saying your job is as critical as your father's?"

Elliott Kettering held up a hand before Vanessa could say a word. "The captain doesn't mean to insinuate that my job is more important than yours, honey. Right now, we're all feeling a little shell-shocked, and we may be careless with our words." He took a breath. "Nessa, when I couldn't reach you, I went through hell and back."

His daughter fought back a sudden sting of tears. "I can't even imagine what you were thinking. I'm sorry, Dad. The Malloy Ranch is huge, and much of it is wilderness. Matthew Malloy explained that they often can't get phone service in such remote areas. So I didn't really think much about the fact that I couldn't reach you."

"Which was fortunate for all of us," the captain remarked. "If we couldn't track you, neither could

DePietro's people. That's why I've asked Sheriff Graystoke to take your cell phone and replace it with one from our lab that can't be tracked."

"But all my contacts—"

"—will be transferred to your new phone. But I'll ask you to keep your calls to a minimum while you are at a safe house."

Though Matt had remained silent during this exchange, he looked at his family.

As if reading his mind, his grandmother gave a quick nod of her head.

He broke his silence, in an aside to Vanessa. "If you don't like the idea of staying at a safe house, what would you think about spending time here?"

"And hide?" She looked horrified. "I have a job to do."

Matt nodded. "And you were doing it in Montana. You could continue doing it." Before she could protest, he added, "My family's ranch is the perfect place to be able to see and study wild animals in their natural habitat, and nobody around here will even question your presence."

"But you forget. Somebody knew I'd gone to Montana, if the captain's theory about the damage to the plane is correct."

The police captain shook his head. "Montana is a big place. The plane was damaged in Helena. That suggests that DePietro's people assume you're there. And now, since the place is crawling with feds, they've lost their only lead."

"But the pilot had to file a flight plan." Sheriff Graystoke spoke in staccato tones. "If these people look into it, they'll know the plane made a brief stop in Glacier Ridge."

Elliott Kettering's voice sounded as weary as he looked. "Nessa, taking you to a safe house will put my mind at ease. I'm not comfortable allowing a family I've never met to take my daughter into their home and see to her safety—"

"I can see to my own safety"—her voice lowered with repressed annoyance—"thank you."

At her outburst, Elliott gave his daughter a gentle smile. "Yes, you can. And always have. Don't you see? I need to be assured of your safety if I'm to do my job. There hasn't been time to investigate the Malloy family, as well as all its employees."

She took in a deep breath, wishing she'd been given time to consider.

Sheriff Graystoke used the silence to speak his mind. "I know you'll have to do a thorough investigation of anyone charged with the safety of your daughter. But until your authorities can do that, you have my word that the Malloy family gets high marks around here for honesty and integrity. I can't think of a safer place for your daughter to stay, as long as they're willing."

Elliott's weary voice held a note of optimism. "Nessa, maybe this Montana ranch could be a short-term solution. I'm told it's vast and sparsely populated. If you don't object, and the Malloys and Captain McBride agree, I suppose it could be your refuge, but only until the trial ends. And the way the trial is going, that could be within another week or so."

"Or months."

At his daughter's words he nodded. "Or months. But I believe it'll be more like weeks. Could you handle another week or two in the Montana wilderness?"

Hearing the plea in Elliott Kettering's tone, Matt lifted a hand to halt Vanessa's protest. "Since my grandmother was the one you've come to Montana to interview, it could be the perfect excuse to spend some time with her." He winked at Gracie, who was listening as intently as the rest of the family. "If you're lucky, you might even get invited along on one of her photo treks into the hills tracking her precious herds of mustangs."

At that, Vanessa's eyes widened.

They could all see the wheels turning in her mind.

Her father leaned closer to the camera. "What do you say, Nessa? Are you willing to stay in Montana until the trial is over?"

"I guess I have no choice. I can stay here and do what I love, or be stuck in a safe house somewhere, pacing the floor."

Elliott gave a long, deep sigh. "Thank you, my sweet Nessa."

"Will we be able to talk again?"

The police captain shook his head. "The less contact your father has with you, the safer you are."

His next words were directed at the Malloy family. "I hope you understand that it's my duty to have all of you thoroughly investigated. If there are any skeletons, this would be the time to reveal them before my investigators uncover them."

Matt spoke for all of them. "You're welcome to do your job, Captain."

Elliott Kettering continued drinking in the image of his daughter on the phone's FaceTime, as though memorizing every feature. "I can't tell you what this means to me, Mr. Malloy."

"It's Matt. And I'm happy to be of service, Mr. Kettering."

"It's Elliott. I know I'm asking a great deal. This will be an intrusion on your family's privacy. But all of you will have a worried father's eternal gratitude."

The police captain's face filled the screen. "Sheriff Graystoke, your number has been programmed into the cell phone for Miss Kettering. Vanessa, I can't stress enough just how serious this threat is. If you sense any danger, or even something that doesn't seem quite right, just turn on that phone and your location will be instantly relayed to your father and to our police headquarters. Even if you don't have time to call, we'll see this as a message from you. I'm going to disengage now. Say your good-byes quickly."

Elliott's voice was deep with passion. "I love you, Nessa."

Vanessa gave a long, deep sigh before saying the thing she'd said to her father since she was a teen. "I love you more, Dad."

As the two lawmen quietly took their leave of the family, the image disappeared, and the line went dead.

While Nessa sat with her chin in her hands, trying to digest all that she'd just heard, the Malloy family moved to the far side of the room, gathering around a fireplace surrounded by comfortable sofas and chairs, talking in low tones, giving her the privacy she deserved.

Grace sat by the fire, allowing the men to carry on a muted conversation while she studied the young woman alone at the table. Vanessa Kettering was obviously distraught by the news she'd just received, and struggling to make sense of it. But to her credit, she hadn't dissolved in tears or allowed herself to be overcome by fear. Instead she was sitting as still as a statue, her only movement a finger going around and around the rim of her empty cup. Probably mimicking a quick mind mulling every little nuance of the words so recently spoken.

Grace turned to her father. "Do you remember that movie you directed with that British actress? The one who showed up late every morning, keeping an entire cast and crew waiting?"

Nelson frowned. "Hillary Burnside. Nasty diva. Though nobody alive could equal her talent."

Grace smiled. "That's the one. Do you recall the plot?"

Nelson's eyes lit with the memory. "Of course. She had to seek shelter from a foreign agent bent on..." He stopped and shot her a look. "Her character felt completely out of place in that small New England town. But once she realized the danger was imminent, she became as clever and devious as the man who was tracking her."

Frank laced his fingers with hers. "This isn't a movie, Gracie Girl. This is real life."

"All too real," she whispered. "But all the same, we need to circle the wagons around this young woman. She may be caught by complete surprise, and very much aware of the danger she's been placed in, but I sense a smart woman who would rather die than show an ounce of fear."

She turned to Matt. "You spent some time with her in the cabin. What do you think?"

"That you have a pretty good sense of her. At least the woman I met. When she realized she was trapped in the hills, she adjusted. And though I sensed a deep-seated fear of storms, and the one that rolled over our heads was worse than most, she never gave in to the fear."

Grace glanced around at her family. "We'll need to remain alert."

Matt's eyes narrowed slightly, the only sign of his inner turmoil. "This is my responsibility. I was the one to suggest she stay here instead of go to a safe house."

"And I was the one she initially came here to interview. Her safety is on all of us." Grace sighed and stood. "And now, if you don't mind, I really need a shower and a change of clothes."

She crossed the room and touched a hand to Vanessa's shoulder. "Come with me and I'll show you to our guest suite."

Vanessa pushed back her chair.

Before they could walk away, Matt was beside them. "You go ahead, Gram Gracie. I'll show Vanessa to her room."

His grandmother shot him a grateful smile before heading up the stairs.

Matt retrieved Vanessa's briefcase and computer from the mudroom before leading the way up the stairs and along a hallway, where he opened a door and stood back, allowing her to precede him.

She looked around with interest.

The room was filled with light from a pair of floor-to-ceiling windows. Along with a king-sized bed, there was a wall of shelves holding an assortment of leather-bound books. A flat-screen TV was positioned atop a desk. A pair of chairs and a round table stood in a little alcove, inviting reading or just a comfortable place to enjoy the breathtaking scenery.

Matt opened a door leading to a spa-sized bathroom, with a glass-enclosed shower, jet tub, and marble counter with double sinks.

Vanessa managed a smile. "Am I sharing this with your entire family?"

"Afraid not. This is just for you."

She shook her head in wonder. "I wasn't expecting all this luxury."

"You mean way out here in the wilderness?" He affected a perfect drawl. "Well, you see, ma'am, the family's outhouse is out of commission this week, so you'll have to make do with this old thing."

She laughed and looked at him. "Thanks. I needed that."

His voice lowered. "I know you've just been handed a lot to deal with. But I hope you realize you're not alone. Just let us know what you need, and we'll see to it. My family and I are here for you."

She took in a breath. "I feel so guilty about bringing this to your doorstep."

"You didn't do anything to feel guilty about. This wasn't your choice. But now that we're aware of the threat, we can take precautions."

When she didn't say anything, he moved close enough to touch a hand to her cheek. Just a touch, but they both stepped back as though burned.

He was the first to look away.

As he headed toward the door he called over his shoulder, "Make yourself at home. And when you're ready, you'll find us either downstairs or out in one of the barns."

She looked down at her wrinkled suit. "I'm not dressed for a barn tour."

He turned back. "Yeah. What was I thinking? Meet me downstairs when you're ready to drive to town for some suitable clothes."

"Is it safe for me to show my face in town?"

He thought a moment. "I'll run it by the family. I'm sure we can come up with a plausible reason for you to be here."

CHAPTER EIGHT

Matt held the truck's door. "Climb in, Cousin Van."

"Cousin Van?" Vanessa couldn't help laughing. "Who came up with the name?"

"My great-grandfather." Matt rounded the cab and climbed into the driver's side, fastening his seatbelt before starting along the curving ribbon of driveway that led to the interstate. "He was always good at revising scripts. As of now, you're Burke's niece, Van Cowley, on your first-ever visit to our ranch. I think Burke is enjoying this as much as the rest of us, since he's never had a relative before. Real or fictional." He held up a hand. "No. Don't bother thanking me. You can thank the Great One for this."

"The Great One?"

"That's what we call our great-grandfather. He loves it, since he considers himself one of the greatest directors of all time. And, in fact, he was."

"Director of what?"

"Movies. He was a pretty famous Hollywood director back in the fifties. Nelson LaRou."

"Nelson LaRou." She looked over, eyes wide. "Oh my gosh. I've heard of him. But I never dreamed I was talking to a famous Hollywood director. Did he know all the movie stars?"

Matt nodded. "Not only knew them, but directed most of them in their biggest movies. He was a pretty big deal."

"So your grandmother grew up in Hollywood?"

"And in Connecticut, where they kept a second home. As you can imagine, old Nelson wasn't too happy about his daughter marrying a rancher and moving to Montana."

"But he's living here now. He must have had a change of heart."

"What he had was a change of health. And he realized that if he wanted to see his only child and his grandchildren, he'd have to swallow his pride and move to the middle of nowhere."

"Has he adjusted?"

"I'd say so. Or we've adjusted to him and his demands. Yancy has learned to make a mean martini, just the way old Nelson likes it. And every once in a while Yancy surprises us with some exotic dish that Nelson once had at the Hollywood Grill, one of his favorite places."

"You have such a fascinating family. A famous director. A revered grandmother who photographs herds of wild mustangs in the wilderness. And your grandfather, Frank, who's absolutely bedazzled by her every time he looks at her."

That had Matt smiling. "Yeah. You can see the love

and devotion whenever they're together. I can't picture one without the other."

"How about your hunky, rugged uncle Colin? Is he married?" When Matt shook his head, she asked, "Engaged?"

"Not a chance. There isn't even a serious romance going on. He's too busy riding herd on us, and on the ranch."

"One of these days the right woman will come along, and he'll find himself in over his head."

Matt shot her a sideways glance. "Are you speaking from experience?"

She flushed. "I only know what I've seen with my friends. Even the most dedicated singles among them cave when the love bug bites."

"Looks like they need better bug spray." They both laughed as they rolled along the highway.

Vanessa found herself fascinated by the view of rolling green hills in the distance, black with cattle. "When do we leave your land?"

"Not for another couple of miles."

"Miles?" She turned to Matt. "Do you sometimes have to pinch yourself when you see all this land and realize it belongs to your family?"

Matt smiled, trying to see it through a stranger's eyes. "I guess it looks impressive, but it's what I grew up with. Are you ever in awe when you look around your city?"

She laughed. "I don't own it. Besides, it's not exactly as awe inspiring as this."

"It would be to a kid who never saw a big city like Chicago before."

That had her nodding. "I guess you're right. Maybe we all take what we have for granted."

"Well, drink in your fill of Glacier Ridge, Montana, since it's the only view of a city you'll have for a few weeks."

Seeing the way she gripped her hands together in her lap, Matt felt a tug of annoyance at himself. She'd had barely a minute to herself to process all that had happened. "Sorry. Do you feel like talking?"

She fell silent and gathered her thoughts before saying, "I guess I'm still reeling. Part of me feels terrible that I can't be home to comfort my father. I can't even imagine what he's going through. I know he wants this conviction more than he's wanted anything in his career. But any threat against me has to be a huge distraction. I don't know how he'll be able to continue to focus through the rest of the trial."

"Exactly what the bad guys are hoping. If the DA drops the ball, they win." He cleared his throat. "Your dad's a pro. He'll figure out a way to use his anger and frustration against his opponent."

She turned her head to stare out the side window. Her voice sounded weary. "I hope you're right."

"What about you? How are you going to deal with the threat to your safety?"

"When I saw my mom growing sicker and weaker, I went into a real panic. What would we do? How could we live without her? And my dad told me something I'll never forget." She took a breath. "He said we all have times when we're so scared, we want to run and hide. And that's the time when we have to stand our ground and face down our fears." She took a deep breath. "I've already been through the worst. After losing my mother, I guess I can face anything life throws at me."

In a gesture of comfort he reached a hand to hers.

Her head came up sharply, and he abruptly returned his hand to the wheel.

For the next hour, as they drove toward town, Matt kept up a running commentary on the various points of interest.

Vanessa clutched her hands together and wondered about her reaction to this man. Her hands were still overly warm, and all he'd done was touch them.

A short time later, he tapped her shoulder and pointed to a lone cowboy on a hill. "There's my Montana."

She struggled to ignore a quick little thrill. She'd felt this same awareness when he'd been setting dishes in the cupboard over her head the previous night. She'd absorbed the same pinpricks of pleasure.

"And this is the famous town of Glacier Ridge."

She forced her attention to the place that she'd barely noticed on her arrival. It had been merely a tiny town on her way to an important interview.

"On this side of Main Street is D and B's Diner. It's owned and operated by Dot and Barb Parker, twin sisters who've been fixtures in this town for more than fifty years."

Vanessa studied the tidy little white building with a door and shutters painted with black-and-white polka dots. "Is that in honor of their namesake?"

Matt nodded. "You got it. Old Dot loves polka dots. That's all she wears, too. And since she claims to be older than Barb by four minutes, she insists on being in charge. But maybe that's a good thing, because she draws in families, and especially cowboys from all over the area with her dandy cowboy-sized burger, and chili almost as good as Yancy's."

He pointed. "And over there is Snips. It started out as a barbershop and beauty shop owned by Gert and Teddy Gleason. Now they've added a spa to the building next door. They haven't named it yet, but folks around here are calling it Dips."

At her puzzled look he explained, "They dip their hands and feet, and sometimes their entire body in all kinds of fancy mud and green tea baths and stuff. So… Dips."

"Snips and Dips. You've actually got a spa in Glacier Ridge." That had Vanessa shaking her head.

"So they tell me." Matt grinned. "Though I haven't been in there to see it for myself."

"Where do you get your hair cut?"

He shrugged. "Usually Yancy cuts our hair whenever we come in from the range looking too shaggy."

She gave him an admiring glance. "Give Yancy my compliments. He does a nice job."

Matt's smile turned into laughter. "I'll be sure to let him know you approve. He's been itching to get his hands on Reed's ponytail. But my brother's having none of it. So, if you'd like a trim while you're staying with us, just let Yancy know."

He pointed. "Over there is the police chief's office, and beside it, the jail."

"Does the town ever get any criminals?"

"A few, now and then. Mostly cowboys who come to town to spend their paychecks and drink too much at the Pig Sty."

Vanessa shot him a look. "You're kidding, aren't you? There's actually a bar called the Pig Sty?"

Matt pointed to the faded sign. "The real name is

Clay's Saloon. It's just across from the jail. Back in Grandpop Frankie's day, old Clay Olmsted used to own a pig farm until he decided there had to be an easier way to earn a living. So he sold his farm and moved to town. He bought an old, boarded-up store, called it Clay's Saloon, and never looked back. But folks around here mostly refer to it as Clay's Pig Sty."

Matt added with a laugh, "One of our early sheriffs, Vinny Thurgood, figured he ought to build his jail as close to the potential drunks as he could, so he built his office and jail right across the street from Clay's place. Of course, it was a dirt road when they both started out. But now it's a proper paved street, suitable for an important town like Glacier Ridge."

They laughed, then Matt pointed to the end of the street. "There's the courthouse, and up on the hill is the high school and church."

It was, Vanessa noted, the perfect picture of a small-town church, surrounded on three sides by a cemetery.

"And just beyond the city limits," Matt added, "is the fairgrounds. When the ranchers around here finish roundup, they always gather there for the annual rodeo. A mile or so beyond is the local airport, where you landed."

He turned the ranch truck, parking in front of a tidy little shop sporting a red-and-white-striped awning with the name Anything Goes.

Matt stepped out of the truck and circled around to the passenger side, holding the door for Vanessa. "Like the name says, you can find anything and everything right here."

He led her inside and winked at the pretty woman

heading toward them. "Hey, Trudy. I'd like you to meet Burke's cousin, Van Cowley."

"Nice to meet you, Van. What's that short for?"

"Van...Vanilla. My parents love the smell of it, the taste of it. So..." Vanessa shrugged, her cheeks turning a becoming shade of pink as she found herself getting caught up in the charade. "They named me Vanilla."

Matt covered his laughter with a cough, hoping nobody noticed.

"Well, Van, I'm Trudy Evans. This is my shop. What are you looking for?"

"She needs some ranch gear. Jeans. Boots. Shirts and...stuff." Matt was trying to choke back his laughter and not embarrass her further by mentioning underwear.

"Packed the wrong things for your visit, did you?"

At the woman's long, steady look, Vanessa found her cheeks growing warmer. "Yes, I...misjudged."

Matt backed away. "Yancy gave me a list of supplies to pick up. When I'm done with his shopping, I'll pick you up here and settle your account."

The woman nodded. "I'll take care of everything, Matthew."

Vanessa was already shaking her head. "I have my own credit card."

Matt smiled at her. "I'll settle with Burke when we get back to the ranch, since your card's no good here, Van."

At his emphasis of her phony name, Vanessa realized that she'd almost made a serious mistake. "Thanks."

She could see his shoulders shaking as he walked away, and knew he was getting a kick out of this. Not only that, but leaving her here alone to deal with this messy lie.

At that she gritted her teeth.

Vanilla Cowley.

She felt like a total idiot.

"Ready to shop, Van?"

"Sure thing, Trudy." She stood a little taller and decided she would let go of her embarrassment and try to enjoy the next hour or so by spending Matt Malloy's money. In fact, lots of his money.

It was the least she could do to even the score.

Trudy led Vanessa to the back room of the shop. It was equipped as a fitting room, with a three-way mirror and hooks along the walls for hanging clothes.

Vanessa set the underthings she'd chosen on a wooden bench in the corner.

"Now these are my best slimming jeans." Trudy held up a pair in Vanessa's size. "They've got a built-in tummy trimmer. Not that you need it," she added with an admiring glance. "But since you're just visiting, you probably don't want to bother with regular working jeans. Most of the ranchers around here just want something serviceable for mucking stalls and ranch chores."

"Why don't you leave both kinds?" Vanessa took them from Trudy's hands and set them aside. "I may as well give everything a try."

Trudy beamed. "You'll need some shirts and a sweater or sweatshirt. It can get pretty cold most mornings and evenings around here until later in the summer."

"And a pair of sturdy boots," Vanessa added.

"I'll be right back."

Vanessa could see Trudy rubbing her hands together. She was already counting her profits.

It took almost two hours trying on jeans, tops, boots,

and a parka, as well as a denim jacket. She even found a
baseball cap that she figured would come in handy.

Trudy paused in the doorway and took in the bench,
now holding an array of clothing.

Vanessa was dressed in slim denims, Western boots, and
a pretty pale blue turtleneck, topped off with the denim
jacket. "I think I'll wear these and you can bag the rest."

"You made good choices. Will there be anything else?"

Vanessa shook her head. But minutes later, as she was
looking around, she caught sight of a Western hat in the
softest brown suede. Pausing in front of a mirror she tried
it on, expecting to feel silly. Instead, she was pleasantly
surprised. Not only did it look right, with her hair falling
long and loose, but it felt perfect with her new outfit.

"You can add this to the bill."

Trudy walked over to cut off the tag. Glancing at the
clock on the wall she smiled. "You made good time. I see
Matthew has just finished with his order, too."

She motioned toward the street, where the ranch truck
was just pulling up, its back loaded with sacks of supplies.

Matt stepped out and paused in the doorway for a moment, staring intently at Vanessa, as though unwilling to
believe what he was seeing.

"Well." The smile came slowly, spreading across his
handsome features. "Now you look like Burke's niece.
That old cowboy's going to be mighty proud of you,
Van..."

He took some time reaching into his pocket and with-
drawing a credit card. When Trudy handed him a pen, he
seemed distracted as he signed it and returned the card
and receipt to his pocket.

He turned to Vanessa. "I think maybe we'll stop at Clay's Pig Sty for a beer and a sandwich before we head home."

"Okay." Vanessa offered a handshake to the shop's owner. "Thanks again for all your help, Trudy."

Before she could pick up the packages, Matt was there, grabbing a dozen handled bags.

Outside he stowed them in the truck before catching Vanessa's hand and leading her across the street. Once there he released her hand.

It took her a few moments before her breathing returned to normal. She didn't know if it was the way he was looking at her, or the fact that he'd held her hand as they crossed the street. It was such a sweet and unexpectedly courtly gesture. But for now, there was no time to figure it out as she stepped into the saloon.

Inside, they were assaulted by the smell of onions on a grill, and the sizzle of burgers.

Hank Williams was wailing about being so lonesome he could cry, and men's voices were punctuated by occasional curses and laughter.

A white-haired man in jeans and suspenders, his rolled sleeves revealing Popeye muscles, waved to them from behind the grill. "Matt Malloy. They let you off the ranch in the middle of the day? You got a broken arm or something?"

"Just had to pick up some supplies for Yancy." He cupped a hand to his mouth. "What's the special, Clay?"

"Pork sausage. Pulled pork sandwiches. And for the hungry—"

"And the brave," one of the cowboys at the bar shouted, to a chorus of raucous laughter.

"—there's stuffed pork chops."

"What's in the stuffing, Clay?" another customer shouted.

"I call it my mystery stuffing."

"That's why you've got to be brave to order it," the first cowboy added, to another round of laughter.

Matt joined in the laughter before turning to Vanessa. "Want to be brave, or do you want the pulled pork sandwich?"

"Pulled pork."

"And to drink?"

She shrugged. "Whatever you're having."

He had to shout their order to be heard above the noise. "Two longnecks, and two pulled pork sandwiches, Clay."

"Got it. Grab a table. I'll be right there." The old man bent to his grill.

Matt led the way through the haze of smoke to a table in the rear of the room where the music wasn't as loud.

A short time later the owner hurried over with their order.

"Clay Olmsted, I'd like you to meet Burke's niece, Van Cowley."

"Nice to meet you, Van." He set down two beers and two plates loaded with sandwiches and curly fries, as well as a big bowl of coleslaw. "Didn't know Burke had any kin. Never heard him talk about family in all the years I've known him."

"Well, I guess he never figured I'd come all this way to visit."

Clay straightened. "Where you from, Van?"

"Chica—"

Matt's voice drowned her out. "Saint Louis."

The old man looked from one to the other. "Never been there. To either place." As he ambled away, Vanessa lowered her head and stared hard at the table. "Sorry. This just isn't working."

Matt lay a hand over hers. "Hey. At least you know how to think on your feet. But—" he paused to bite back his grin "—Vanilla?"

She was shaking her head. "See? I'm no good at lying." She tried to pull her hand away.

He tightened his grasp. This time his laugh broke free. "Well, I have to say Vanilla Cowley is a stretch. But since you dug that hole, you're just going to have to stand in it."

She grinned. "Such a stupid name. But it was the first thing that came to mind."

"It works. You're doing just fine." His voice deepened even while his smile grew. "And you're looking just fine, too."

"You don't think it's too much. I mean the boots, the jacket, the...hat?"

"It's perfect. You're perfect."

"I wasn't sure about the hat. But once I put it on, it just felt right."

He picked up his beer and took a long pull, to keep himself from gushing. The truth was, that first glimpse of her back in the shop had all the breath backing up in his throat. In the course of a couple of hours she'd gone from cool, polished city lawyer to the most gorgeous country girl he'd ever seen. She wasn't just perfect. She was breathtaking.

She slanted him a catlike look. "I enjoyed spending your money."

He laughed out loud. "I just bet you did."

"I actually bought more than I needed. To get you back for laughing at me."

She bit into her sandwich, then shot him a look of amazement. "This is good."

"Why wouldn't it be?"

"I thought, the way those men were teasing, that the food would be horrible."

"Clay's a good cook. Maybe not as good as Yancy, but he knows his way around pork."

"Of course. The Pig Sty. I guess I forgot about that." She looked around at the gleaming floor and tables and chairs. "I guess with a name like that, I expected it to be filthy, and the food to be barely tolerable."

"Don't let a name fool you."

"This from the man who just gave me a new identity."

He looked around, relieved that nobody was near enough to overhear them. "You might want to keep that to yourself."

"Right." She sipped her beer and polished off the rest of her sandwich. "Vanilla Cowley knows how to keep secrets."

CHAPTER NINE

Matt walked to the counter to pay their bill.

Clay Olmsted rang it up and handed Matt his change before saying to the young woman beside him, "Bye, Van. Be sure and say hello to your uncle."

"My...?" She caught herself. "Yes. Uncle Burke. I'll do that. The pulled pork sandwich was the best."

The old man brightened. "Next time you're here, try the stuffed pork chops."

One of the regulars at the bar called out, "That's why we call him Colonel Clay. His secret ingredient is in the stuffing."

To a chorus of laughter, Matt and Vanessa walked outside.

Before crossing the street Matt caught her hand. At the truck he held the passenger door while she settled inside before circling around to climb up to the driver's side.

As they pulled away, a car fell into line some distance

behind them, leisurely trailing along Main Street until they left town and turned onto the interstate.

Vanessa swiveled her head, trying to take in all the things she'd missed on their way here.

"Oh, look at those hills in the distance."

Matt followed her direction, trying to see everything through her eyes.

"There's so much space here. I bet there are more cattle than people."

He nodded. "You'd be right about that."

"And it's all so clean and fresh and pretty. No streetlights. No throngs of pedestrians. No office buildings, or smoke from buses, or horns honking."

"Just remember you said all that when you complain about no fast food places, or easy transportation when you need a prescription for pain, or directions to the nearest hospital when a friend is about to deliver a baby."

She laughed. "Okay. Point taken. I'm sure there are plenty of drawbacks to living so far from civilization. But just allow me my fantasies for a little while longer, will you? It's called trying to make the best of a situation."

"And you are." He laid a hand over hers. "I know this isn't easy for you."

When she clasped her hands in her lap, he glanced in the rearview mirror. Though the car remained far behind them, he had an uneasy feeling. "How would you like to make a detour on the way back?"

She shrugged. "You're the driver."

"Okay." He slowed the truck before turning the wheel.

Though there were no exits, he merely left the highway and started across a bumpy stretch of field toward a distant hill.

The vehicle that had been trailing them stopped, but didn't follow.

"What's up here?" Vanessa was straining to see beyond the high ground.

Matt drove up and over the incline, cutting off their view of the highway. He continued on until they came to a swollen stream that was overflowing its banks.

He parked and stepped out before speaking to the sheriff on his cell phone. Scant minutes later he took Vanessa's hand and led her to a small promontory overlooking the water.

"This is Malloy Creek."

She turned to him. "You actually have a creek named for your family?"

He nodded. "My great-great-grandfather, the original Francis Xavier Malloy, came here from Ireland and cleared this land. When the state was charting its landmarks and asked the name of this creek, he decided to name it for himself."

Matt pointed to the hills beyond. "In the middle of summer, this will be nothing more than a small stream. But right now, with all the snow melting high in the hills, it's a gusher. Old Francis X. realized there was enough runoff to irrigate these fields. This was where his first herd of cattle grazed, and later, when he moved them to higher ground, this was where he planted enough crops to see him through the winter. According to legend, the minute he saw this place, he thought of the green fields of Ireland, and knew his future lay right here."

"That's nice." She shielded the sun from her eyes as she peered around. "I guess to someone far from home, it would be comforting to feel something familiar."

"Yeah." Matt held his silence and allowed her to drink in the view, knowing she was seeking her own comfort in a strange place.

Nearly an hour later they returned to the truck and headed for the ranch.

Matt noted that the car that had been trailing them was nowhere to be seen.

He'd reported its presence to Sheriff Graystoke, who had assured him it would be checked out immediately.

It could turn out to be a real threat, or it could mean that he was seeing danger where none existed. The sheriff had suggested another possible explanation for that car. It could be someone sent by the Chicago police to investigate the Malloy family.

Whatever the reason, he recognized a duty to report anything that seemed out of place. He had no intention of ignoring something that could prove to be a real danger.

He felt responsible for the woman entrusted to his family's care. Though neither of them had asked for this, he felt it was his job to keep Vanessa Kettering safe until she was able to return to the life she'd left.

After putting away all the things she'd bought in town, Vanessa stepped into the kitchen to find Yancy and Nelson sharing coffee at the big wooden table, their heads bent close in quiet conversation.

The both looked up as she entered.

"Sorry." She hesitated. "I didn't mean to interrupt anything."

"You didn't." Nelson waved her close. "We're talking about an unsolved Hollywood mystery from the fifties."

Yancy produced a thick hardcover book with a lurid

cover depicting a bloody female draped over the arm of a blood-soaked sofa. "Natasha Leonid. She was a legend in the thirties and forties." Yancy flushed. "I'm afraid Hollywood scandals are my passion. I love reading about them. I especially love the unsolved murders. And since Nelson lived through a lot of them, he knew the people involved."

Vanessa turned to Nelson. "Matt told me who you are. The minute I heard your name, I knew of you. What an exciting life you've led."

The old man puffed up his chest, obviously enjoying the moment.

Yancy motioned toward the coffeepot. "Would you like some?"

Vanessa shook her head. "Matt and I had lunch in town. I promised him I'd join him when I put my things away."

"He and the others are out in the barn." Yancy pointed toward the back door. "The first barn is for equipment. The second is where some of the horses or farm animals in need of attention are stabled." He glanced at her new clothes. "You look pretty, Nessa. You shouldn't go out there. You wouldn't want to get your new duds all dirty."

"These are work clothes, Yancy." She couldn't help grinning. "Though I can't imagine what kind of work I'll be doing."

Nelson set aside his cup. "You might want to stay here and join us for coffee. I'm not sure a big-city lawyer like yourself is ready to join the Malloy ranchers in their favorite pastime."

"I promised myself I'd earn my keep here."

"Then at least find a pair of rubber boots that fit you before you walk into the barn."

"If you say so." She turned toward the mudroom and exchanged her new leather boots for a pair of cracked rubber ones. As she opened the door she called over her shoulder, "What can be so hard about caring for a couple of farm animals? I think this could be fun."

The two men exchanged a look. And as the door closed behind her, they burst into peals of laughter.

Taking a last deep breath, Vanessa stepped from sunshine into the cavernous interior and paused to allow her eyes to adjust to the gloom. The first thing that assaulted her was the smell. It was an outhouse, only magnified a thousand times. And then there were the sounds of men's voices raised in laughter, bouncing off the walls.

Seeing her in the doorway, the voices stilled.

Luke called, "Hey. You're late."

"Late?"

"Yeah. Matt said you were putting away your gear. So we decided to work a little slower than usual so you wouldn't miss out on all the fun."

Getting into the spirit of teasing, Reed pointed to a wall of ranch implements hanging on hooks. "Grab some gloves and join us."

"Okay." Vanessa crossed to where Matt was standing. "Where do I find gloves?"

"Here." He reached into his back pocket and handed her a pair of well-worn leather gloves. "You'll need these."

She slipped them on and followed him to a stall, where Reed was knee-deep in wet, smelly straw.

"This is what the horses leave behind. It's part of a rancher's daily routine. We have to fork up the old straw and spread clean. Since you need to start slowly, we'll do the forking and leave the spreading to you."

"I thought…" She stopped to look around the empty stalls. "Where are the horses and sick animals?"

"No sick animals at the moment. But we turned the horses into the corral so we can get our work done in here." Matt led her toward a stall that had recently been cleaned and showed her how to spread fresh straw.

While she bent to her task, the three brothers cleaned the rest of the stalls, keeping up a steady stream of conversation and jokes, often at their own expense.

"So." Reed paused to rest his hands atop his pitchfork while he eyed Luke. "I heard your phone ringing around midnight. Who called?"

His brother shrugged. "Nobody."

"Is this the same nobody who said she never wanted to see you again?"

Instead of a reply, Luke gripped the handles of the wagon. "This is pretty full. I'll be right back."

Vanessa couldn't help staring at he shoved the overloaded wagon through the doors as if it weighed nothing. She'd expected his brothers to lend a hand.

He returned a short time later with the empty wagon, only to pick up his pitchfork and continue on as before without a word.

Matt joined in where his younger brother had left off. "You're not going to evade our questions, bro. So why did this nobody phone you if she never wanted to see you again?"

Luke never missed a beat as he lifted a heavy load and

deposited it in the wagon. "She didn't say anything about never 'speaking' to me again."

Matt and Reed exchanged a look before Matt deadpanned, "So when are you and nobody getting together again?"

"She wants me to join her and some friends at Clay's Pig Sty Friday night. And she said to bring Reed along."

Reed paused. "So she can look at me instead of you? Not that I don't understand," he added, "since I'm a whole lot better looking."

"She's invited some friends. One of them is Carrie."

Reed snorted. "If Carrie Riddle was standing in the doorway of our barn right this minute, wearing nothing but her birthday suit, I wouldn't bother to turn and give her a look."

Luke gave a laugh. "Oh, you'd look, bro. You may try to pass yourself off as a saint in front of our guest, but I know you better'n that. You'd look."

Matt and Vanessa stood back, enjoying the banter.

"Okay. So I'd look. Hell, I'm a guy. But that's as far as it goes. I'm not interested."

"You feeling sick?" Luke touched a hand to his brother's forehead. "Carrie Riddle's had the hots for you since she was fifteen. I'm not asking you to marry her. But you could at least go to town with me Friday night."

Matt shook his head. "I hate to be the bearer of bad news, but Burke is expecting both of you to spend this weekend up on the South Ridge helping him and Colin with the herd."

Luke turned to stare at his brother. "Then I guess you'll get your wish."

Reed looked puzzled.

"I think Carrie was planning on showing you her birthday suit. Now you won't have to worry about ignoring her."

Reed turned to Luke. "Well, that will solve your problem about your 'nobody.' She won't have to worry about seeing you again."

"There's always next week."

Matt glanced at Vanessa in time to see her convulsed in laughter. He was laughing as he ambled over. She kept her voice low. "Do they go on like this all the time?"

"Endlessly."

She shook her head. "And I thought nothing exciting ever happens in a small town."

Overhearing her, Reed called, "There should probably be a billboard just outside of town. Horny cowboys. Women in birthday suits. You just never know what you'll discover in Glacier Ridge, Montana."

Still laughing, Matt nodded toward the last cleaned stall. "Come on. I'll give you a hand and we can let these two get on with their fantasies."

"You mean Nobody and Birthday Suit don't really exist?"

"Oh, they're real." Luke hung his pitchfork on a hook before peeling off his work gloves. "But Friday night is big business in Clay's Pig Sty for every wrangler who gets a paycheck. And that means that every female old enough to drink, and some who ought to be home doing schoolwork, will be helping them spend it. Frankly, I'd rather muck stalls on a Friday night than have to head to town. So"—he turned to Matt—"herding cattle on the South Ridge sounds about perfect to me."

Matt watched Reed follow suit, hanging up his pitchfork before heading toward the open doorway of the barn. "You okay with the weekend plans?"

Reed shot him a quick grin. "Nobody's gonna miss me."

"I'll just bet she will."

They were still chuckling as they ambled out.

CHAPTER TEN

Matt led the way to the corral, where the horses were grazing. Leaning on the fence, he turned to Vanessa. "Do you ride?"

She nodded. "From the age of eight until I was twelve, I was horse crazy. I pestered my parents until they allowed me to take jumping lessons at a suburban hunt club. I know they were terrified that I'd be hurt, and they couldn't understand why I was so in love with horses, but they couldn't stand to see me pout, so they gave in."

"I bet you were great at pouting."

She chuckled. "It's an art form that most girls learn. Boys—" she shrugged "—not so much. It just isn't attractive on a boy. But I was a champion pouter. I wore down my poor parents until they would have rather taken a sharp stick to the eye than see me pout another day."

They laughed. Matt glanced skyward. "I think it's too

late to ride today, but if you want, we could take a couple of horses into the hills tomorrow."

She nodded. "I'd like that."

"It's a deal, as long as the weather cooperates." He turned toward the house. "We'd better clean up before supper."

Vanessa looked down at her dung-covered boots, grateful that Yancy and Nelson had urged her to leave her new ones behind. And then she realized that those two had known exactly what kind of work she'd be doing in the barn.

Those two sly old men. And they hadn't given her a word of warning. She laughed at herself as she walked beside Matt.

He glanced over. "What so funny?"

"Me. I really didn't have a clue what ranching was like. I guess I still don't."

"Don't beat yourself up over it. How could a Chicago lawyer know what the typical day is like on a ranch in Montana? Besides, there really is no typical day. Ranching is like bungee jumping. Every morning you take a leap of faith and expect that wherever you manage to land, at least you'll land on your feet."

"And if you land on your head? Then what?"

He held the back door and allowed her to precede him. "You get through your day while nursing a headache."

"Great. I'll try to land on my feet."

"I'd put money on that. You strike me as a woman who always lands on her feet." He eased off his boots and headed toward the oversized sink.

Vanessa did the same and watched as he lathered up to his elbows, then placed his hands under the faucet. The water poured out in a steady stream.

"A hands-free sink. I'm impressed."

He winked. "Maybe we knew a city lawyer was coming, and we didn't want to look like yokels."

She washed and reached for a thick white towel from a stack on the shelf above them. "Or maybe the city lawyer needs to alter her mental image of Montana ranchers."

He smiled. "Actually you can thank Reed for this, and for dozens of other New Age gadgets. He's our tech nerd. Reed's favorite hobby is browsing through catalogs of all the latest equipment. He just informed us that he's thinking of ordering a drone."

She turned to him. "A drone? What for?"

He shrugged. "To keep track of things. With a spread this size, we usually do flyovers with one of our planes to check on the herds every week or so."

Vanessa shook her head. "A drone. Who'd have thought?"

As they stepped into the kitchen, Yancy looked up from the oven. "Well, did you get a chance to do a little work, Nessa?"

She nodded. "I'm grateful that you suggested those rubber boots."

"Got a taste of mucking stalls, did you?"

"I did. And I got to step in a lot of yucky straw and other things too disgusting to mention."

The old cook grinned. "Consider that your ranch baptism."

"Are you saying it will get easier after that?"

"Not at all. But next time you volunteer, you'll be prepared for the worst." He stirred something on the stove. "Dinner in an hour."

"Just enough time for a long, hot shower," Matt muttered.

"That sounds heavenly." She trailed Matt to the stairway.

Once in her room she stripped off her filthy clothes, which had been brand-new just hours earlier, and stood beneath a hot spray, sighing with pure pleasure.

An hour later, dressed in clean denims and a simple cotton shirt the color of raspberries, her hair flowing long and loose below her shoulders, she made her way downstairs and followed the sound of voices and laughter to the kitchen.

While Yancy put the finishing touches on the meal, the rest of the family was gathered around a big, open fireplace on the far side of the kitchen. Their comfortable chairs had been arranged in a semicircle to take advantage of both the fire and the amazing view of the sun setting on the peaks of the hills in the distance.

"...comes with an instruction book as thick as a Bible." Reed was gesturing with his longneck. "I can't wait to get my hands on it."

"The instruction book or the drone?" Luke shot a grin at the others, who were enjoying Reed's obvious excitement.

"Both."

Matt beckoned Vanessa over. He pointed to a tray on the counter, holding an array of bottles and glasses. "What would you like to drink before we eat?"

She noted the opened bottle of pinot grigio, and the glass in Gracie's hand. "I think I'll try that."

Matt handed her a stem glass of pale, chilled wine.

"So when do we get to see this glorious new toy?" Frank asked.

"It might take a while. First I have to look into any rules and regulations that might bar its use in Montana."

Nelson frowned. "Rules and regulations. In my day . . ."

Grace shot him a look that had him pausing.

"The company guaranteed delivery by the end of the month." Reed turned to his brothers. "But don't even think about using it until I get a chance to read through the manual. I don't want anyone messing with it and screwing up the controls."

Matt winked at Vanessa and said in an aside, "Our technonerd is at it again."

Overhearing, Luke added, "I know a couple of women at Clay's Pig Sty who wish Reed could get as excited about seeing them on Friday night as he does about his gadgets."

"It doesn't matter what they think." Colin looked at his nephews. "You're both spending the weekend up in the hills with the herd."

Reed finished his beer. "Actually, I prefer the company of cattle to anything I'd find at Clay's."

"There's something twisted in that mind of yours, bro." Luke tipped up his longneck just as Yancy set a salad bowl and a cruet of his homemade dressing in the center of the table.

"Dinner's ready." Yancy sliced roast beef on a platter before setting it aside.

Nelson finished his martini and nibbled the olive before pushing out of the big, overstuffed chair he'd claimed by the fire. He strolled to his usual spot at one end of the table. "I hope you made your au gratin potatoes to go with that fine beef, Yancy."

"I did, Great One." Yancy set a casserole dish on the table.

Vanessa found herself smiling at his use of the old gentleman's nickname. As Matt had said, "Great One" suited Nelson LaRou perfectly. From his tailored pants and shirt, to the apricot silk ascot that would look over the top on any other man, he could only be called great. The Great One.

Her smile grew when Frank and Grace held hands as they crossed the room. Frank held her chair as she took her seat. Then he settled himself at the head of the table.

Matt put a hand beneath Vanessa's elbow, leading her toward the table as the rest of them took their places.

Burke sat beside Colin, while Yancy moved back and forth from the stove to the table, handing out platters of roast beef, a dish of steamed vegetables, and a basket of crusty bread still warm from the oven.

As they helped themselves before passing the dishes around, Vanessa couldn't believe the amount of food. But then, they had all engaged in hard, physical labor the entire day.

"Your roast beef is done to perfection, Yancy." Nelson reached for the casserole. "And your au gratin potatoes—" he touched thumb and finger to his lips "—sublime."

"And this bread." Grace looked over at the cook. "You've added something."

"Asiago. And just a bit of herbs."

"It's wonderful."

Yancy beamed. He turned to Colin. "That rainstorm may have done us a favor. Most of the snow disappeared just in time for calving."

Colin nodded. "But now we have the mud to contend with. I just hope we get a few mild weeks and lots of sunshine to dry up the ground before they drop their calves."

Vanessa was listening with interest. "The cows don't give birth in the barns?"

Matt shook his head. "That might work on a small spread. Our herds number in the thousands. We've got teams of wranglers with each herd, assisting with difficult births. And for a first-time mother, there are plenty of those. But for those days immediately following the birth, the cow and her calf are vulnerable to everything nature can throw at them. Snowstorms. Predators."

"Are they in enclosures?"

"They're on open range."

"How can you possibly keep them all safe?"

"We can't. But we do our best. We post wranglers to ride the perimeter of the herds through the night. That helps to discourage predators. But a few always manage to slip past and snatch a newborn. Don't forget. Hunger makes them bold."

She tried not to shiver at the image that came to mind. A hungry wolf dragging a bleeding newborn into the brush, where others waited for a feast. And then a cow, heavy with milk, waiting for a calf that would never return.

This wasn't what she wanted to think about over such a wonderful meal.

Later, as the conversation swirled around her, Vanessa looked at her empty plate. Even though her appetite had been curbed by her thoughts, she'd managed to eat more in one sitting than she would usually consume in two or three days.

Grace smiled at her family around the table. "How about dessert in the family room?"

"Sounds perfect." Frank pushed back his chair and offered his arm to his wife.

The others followed them past a formal dining room and into a large room dominated on one wall by a huge stone fireplace. Across the room were floor-to-ceiling windows looking out at rolling hills that only days ago were covered in snow. Now, after that storm, they were already showing hints of spring green.

As they settled into comfortable chairs and sofas, Yancy passed around cups of steaming coffee before cutting into a chocolate cake layered with cherry filling and topped with cherry-vanilla ice cream.

When Vanessa bit into it, she couldn't help sighing. "Oh, Yancy, I don't think I've ever tasted anything better."

"Thank you, Nessa." He was beaming as he took a seat by the fire and helped himself to dessert.

"I can't remember the last time I ate this much at one time," she said with a laugh.

"Nothing like a good meal after a day of ranch chores." Luke helped himself to a second slice topped with more ice cream.

"Well, Vanessa." Grace sipped her coffee. "Now that you've seen our town, what do you think?"

"It's a pretty little town. I enjoyed myself. Just as Matt promised, I found everything I needed at Anything Goes. And we had a great lunch at Clay's . . . saloon."

"Go ahead," Reed teased. "You can say Pig Sty."

Everyone laughed.

"All right. Lunch at Clay's Pig Sty was surprisingly good."

"But not as good as dinner, right?" Yancy winked at Reed.

"Of course not. After a meal like this, Clay would have to become a gourmet chef to top it."

Again, the cook beamed at her praise.

Luke shot a knowing smile at Reed. "And now that you've become...intimately involved with our barns, how would you rate them?"

Amid much laughter she kept a perfectly straight face. "Really big. Really stinky. And the hardest work I've done in years. But I will admit that when I was young, I took jumping lessons, and after every class I was required to groom my horse and hose down her stall, as well. I would rate hosing as a much easier manner of hygiene than shoveling."

"So hosing has your vote?" Reed looked around at the others.

"Definitely."

Luke slapped a hand to his forehead. "Why didn't you think about putting drains in every stall when you built that barn, Grandpop? Think of all the work you could have saved us."

Frank nodded. "In fact, I'm thinking that very thing. Technonerd, is there a solution to our problem of no drains?"

Reed pretended to think before saying solemnly, "Just think of all the manure we'd waste, putting it down the drain. I vote that we get more willing workers."

"And where do we get these workers?"

Reed looked pointedly at Colin. "I do believe it's your duty to find a wife and begin producing your share of workers, Uncle."

Colin nearly choked on his coffee while the others laughed.

Luke joined in the fun. "I think you should skip the hills this weekend and spend your time at the Pig Sty. I've heard any number of women say they'd like to have Colin Malloy's baby."

Colin said with a straight face, "I just may take you up on this and go wife hunting at the Pig Sty. I'm sure that would make my family proud."

The teasing continued until the fire had burned to embers.

With a yawn, Grace set aside her empty cup. "I don't know about the rest of you, but I need my sleep. And tonight, it's in a real bed. I love trailing my mustangs in the wilderness, but after a while, I start missing my bed."

"And the husband who keeps your feet warm," Frank added.

One by one the others got to their feet and called good night before taking to the stairs.

Grace paused. "Vanessa, if there's anything at all that you want or need, please let us know. I hope you'll be comfortable while you're here."

"Thank you, Mrs...."

"Gracie," the older woman prompted.

"Thank you, Gracie. I really appreciate all that you're doing for me."

Vanessa stood and thanked Yancy again for the lovely dinner before calling good night to the others.

Matt put a hand under her elbow as they walked up the stairs. At her door he paused, and she saw the same look in his eyes that she'd seen in the cabin, just before he'd so shockingly kissed her.

She couldn't control the sudden pounding of her heart.

"Good night..." His hand was on her shoulder. Just the lightest touch, but she could feel it clear to her toes.

His head was lowering, and she knew with absolute certainty that he was going to kiss her.

She stood perfectly still, waiting. Wanting. Yearning.

Matt's phone rang.

With a muttered oath he retrieved his cell phone from his pocket and looked at the ID before saying, "Sorry. Bad timing. But I have to take this."

"Of course." Stung by the way the mood had been shattered, her tone was sharper than she'd intended. "I wouldn't want to intrude on your personal life."

Vanessa turned away and opened her bedroom door.

Just then she heard Matt say, "Yes, Sheriff."

She paused and saw the frown that furrowed his brow.

Putting a hand on his arm she whispered, "If that's about me, I'd like to hear."

He touched the Speaker button, and together they both heard the sheriff say, "Our state boys are trying to get a verification from the Chicago PD on that vehicle you saw tailing you today."

Vanessa's head came up sharply and she stared pointedly at Matt.

"Captain McBride suggested that it was probably sent by the Chicago PD to keep an eye on your family until they've had a chance to check you out."

Matt's tone was low with anger. "First of all, if this is a sample of Chicago's finest, they get a failing grade. If I could spot their car following my truck, they're amateurs. And second, the Chicago PD has had hours to get back to you on this, Eugene. I don't like this one bit."

The sheriff's tone was rough. "I'm with you on this, Matt. I'm really sorry. You did everything right, but they're letting it slide on their end."

"Or they think we're a bunch of hicks and they don't need to be invisible."

"That could be." A hint of weariness crept into the sheriff's voice. "As soon as we get a response from Chicago, I'll pass it along to you. In the meantime, stay alert to anything."

"Yeah. 'Night."

As Matt slid his cell phone into his pocket, he heard a hiss of anger from the woman beside him.

Looking into Vanessa's eyes, which were dark with fury, he braced himself for the storm he could see coming.

CHAPTER ELEVEN

So that was the reason for the sudden romantic side trip this afternoon?"

"Romantic side trip?" Matt was thrown off stride.

"When you showed me that amazing creek named after your ancestor. At the time, I couldn't decide if you wanted to get me alone, or if you were trying to impress me. And now I realize you just wanted to play hide-and-seek with the car behind us. And you never bothered to mention it to me?"

"I didn't want you to be alarmed until I knew whether or not it was a threat."

"So you just decided to pat me on the head. 'Don't you worry your itty-bitty mind, little lady. I'm here to protect you.'"

"It wasn't like that—"

"It *was* like that. This is my life. My safety we're talking about. I don't want to be kept in the dark while my big, fierce protector takes charge."

"Look, I was wrong. I made a mistake in judgment—"

"You bet you did." She jammed a finger in his chest. "I won't be treated like some helpless female who's going to fall apart at the first hint of danger. We're talking about someone who's made serious threats against me. I have the right to know everything that's going on, if I'm going to make the choices that help me stay alive."

"You're right—"

"And furthermore, if you ever dare to keep such a thing from me again—"

He caught her finger and deliberately lowered it from his chest. "I get it."

"I hope you mean that."

The slight tremble in her voice sounded a warning. Realizing that she was close to tears, Matt went from angry to frustrated and then to sudden alarm that she would cry in front of him. "Look. I told you I get it."

"You'd better, because..." She blinked, then blinked again, furiously. "I can take care of mys—"

Matt froze. No. Not tears. He'd rather face an angry drunk in the saloon, or a blizzard up in the hills, without any shelter or gear, than face a single tear from a woman's eyes. Especially this woman, who was fighting so desperately to be strong.

But it was too late. Moisture slid from beneath her tightly closed lids and rolled down her cheeks.

She lifted a fist to her face and angrily swiped at them, but they just fell harder, faster.

She started to turn away. "I'm so furious right now..."

Oh hell. Though the last thing he wanted to do was

touch her, he had no choice. "Wait. Listen." He turned her into his arms and could feel the front of his shirt growing damp. "It's all right to cry…"

She tried to push away. "I am not crying—"

"Of course not. I get it." He pressed his lips to the hair at her temple. "But sometimes it's okay to just let it all out."

"I'm just so angry. You had no right—"

"I didn't. And you have every right to be mad."

He waited until the waterworks stopped before reaching into his pocket and handing her his handkerchief.

She wouldn't look at him as she blew her nose and wiped the last of the tears from her cheeks. When she finally stepped back he closed his hands over her upper arms, holding her when she tried to turn away. "Nessa, I'm really sorry. I overstepped my bounds. Blame it on my genes. All the Malloys inherited them. We're really vain enough or stupid enough to believe we have the power and the muscle and the will to rule the world. I guess we're legends in our own minds."

She was silent for so long, he worried that he'd only made things worse by trying to make a joke.

She lifted her head. Though her eyes were still red and puffy, there was a glint of something in them. Amusement? Understanding?

"Okay. I guess I overreacted. And that's something in my genes."

He tried for a smile. "Am I forgiven?"

She took in a deep breath. "As long as you promise you'll never do it again."

"Cross my heart."

She started to turn away, then turned back, a hint of

a smile touching her lips. "Sorry about the tears. I really hate crying."

"I get it. I'm not too fond of seeing them."

She stepped into her room. "Good night, Matt."

"Good night, Nessa."

He waited until she closed her door before moving on to his own room. Once there he crossed to the wall of windows to stare at the darkened hills in the distance.

Damned independent female.

And wasn't she damned gorgeous, even when she was mad?

Especially when she was mad.

If ever he'd wanted to kiss her, it was then. But with that temper, she'd have cut out his heart and fed it to the wolves.

He was grinning as he undressed. Not a bad way to die.

Vanessa showered and dressed in her new denims and a lemon-yellow T-shirt. Tucking her pant legs into leather boots, she grabbed up her denim jacket and headed down the stairs.

In the kitchen, Frank and Gracie were sipping coffee in front of the fireplace, while Yancy was busy at the stove.

She glanced around. "Are we the first ones up?"

Yancy shook his head. "The last. Luke, Reed, and Colin left at dawn to head to the South Ridge."

"The Great One?" Just saying that name had her smiling.

"Heading to town with Burke. His annual physical at the clinic. He'll be there most of the day."

"And Matt?" It galled her to have to ask, but she felt connected somehow to him, and found herself hoping he hadn't gone along with the others.

"In the barn. Tackling morning chores. He'll be in soon."

She turned away. "Maybe I'll give him a hand."

Yancy indicated a tray of mugs and glasses, along with a carafe and a tall pitcher on the counter. "Suit yourself. But you might want to help yourself to coffee and juice first."

"Thank you." She poured herself a glass of orange juice and tasted before looking over at him. "Did you make this fresh?"

He shrugged. "Is there any other way?"

"I buy mine by the half gallon at the store."

He gave a mock shudder.

Gracie beckoned her over. "How did you sleep, Nessa?"

"Very well, thanks." A lie. She'd tossed and turned for hours after that little scene with Matt. It still irritated her that he'd kept secret the fact that he'd thought they were being followed. And then, after wrestling with the lingering anger, she'd had to deal with the sinking feeling that DePietro's people could already know where she was staying. Not a good night. But she would never admit it to these good people.

"I want to thank you again for making me feel so welcome. It can't be easy to have a stranger in your house."

Frank linked his fingers with Gracie's and shot her a blazing smile. "We love having you, Nessa. Don't we, Gracie Girl?"

"Indeed. I told Frankie last night that it's rather nice for me to have another woman around. I've been living with all these men for so long now, it's really pleasant to hear a woman's voice in the mix."

They looked over as the back door opened and Matt trudged into the mudroom, kicking off his boots, tossing his gloves on a shelf, and hanging his hat on a hook on the wall.

They could hear the water flowing before he finally stepped into the kitchen. He greeted his grandparents, while his gaze remained steady on Vanessa.

"'Morning." He stayed where he was.

"Good morning. I'm sorry I'm too late to lend a hand with the mucking."

He smiled then, as he realized this was her way of saying that all was forgiven. "You were going to help?"

"That was the plan. But then I got sidetracked with Frank and Gracie."

"There'll be other mornings." He turned toward the stairs. "I'll be down in half an hour."

"Make it fifteen minutes," Yancy called. "Breakfast is almost ready."

Vanessa watched until Matt disappeared up the stairs. When she turned, both Frank and Gracie were staring at her.

She busied herself at the counter, pouring a cup of coffee. Then she turned to them. "Would you like more?"

Frank held out his cup and she crossed to him, topping off his cup and then Gracie's. And still the two were looking at her so steadily, she was grateful to turn away and replace the carafe on the counter. She was even more grateful that the two of them began carrying on a conversation, allowing her to relax.

Matt was as good as his word, strolling into the kitchen just as Yancy was setting a stack of pancakes in the center of the table.

He took a seat beside Vanessa and held a platter of ham and eggs toward her while she filled her plate. "I heard the caravan leaving around five. They'll be up on Eagle's Ridge by now."

Frank nodded. "A good day for it, too. I was afraid we might get another storm, but it blew over around midnight, and that sunshine is just what we need."

He held the plate of pancakes while Gracie helped herself.

She ladled warm maple syrup with walnuts and blueberries over the stack. After her first bite she smiled at the cook. "Yancy, you always know just what I'm craving after a trip to the hills."

"You're just like your daddy. The Great One loves his cookies. You love your walnut-and-blueberry pancakes."

Frank closed a hand over hers. "If you'd like the moon to go with it, just say the word, Gracie Girl."

Her smile bloomed. "And you'd fetch it, wouldn't you?"

"You know I would."

Vanessa felt a trickle of warmth around her heart. These two sweet people were so in love it felt like an invasion of privacy to be allowed to watch and listen.

When they'd finished breakfast, Frank held Gracie's chair. "Ready to head into town, Gracie Girl?"

"I am." Hand-in-hand they turned to Matt and Vanessa. "We're off to Glacier Ridge," Gracie announced.

Matt set down his cup. "Any reason in particular?"

"Just a date with my girl." Frank winked at his wife before turning to Yancy. "We'll probably be home by supper time, but if we're late, don't wait for us."

They left, still holding hands.

Matt glanced at Vanessa. "Ready to take the horses for a run?"

"Maybe not a run. But I wouldn't mind a nice, slow canter across the field."

"Let's do it." He stood. "Great breakfast, Yancy. If anyone asks, we'll be up in the pasture."

"You've got a good day for it." Yancy was already clearing the table as Matt and Vanessa made their way toward the corral.

Matt left Vanessa standing in the sunlight, watching the horses play in a fenced pasture. Minutes later he led two saddled horses from the barn.

"This is Ginger." He held the reins while Vanessa pulled herself into the saddle of a palomino mare with a flaxen mane and tail.

She accepted the reins while he mounted old Beau. Then she leaned over her horse's head to run a hand along her silken mane. "Ginger is beautiful."

Matt nodded. "She's one of Gracie's favorites. You'll need to keep control. She likes to have her head."

"A female with an attitude." Vanessa laughed. "No wonder I already like her."

As they started across the back field, Matt pointed toward a windswept parcel of land surrounded by a wrought-iron fence. "That's our family plot."

Nessa's eyes widened. "Your own private cemetery?"

He laughed at her tone. "Yeah. It's not so unusual. This is where they lived. This is where they should be allowed to spend eternity."

They dismounted, and Matt opened a pretty gate before leading her inside the enclosure. The grave markers were simple stones bearing the names of family members, their birth and death dates clearly etched.

Matt paused beside a double marker. "These are my parents."

Reading their names, and the same date of death, sent a tiny shiver along her spine. "They were so young."

Matt nodded. "The Great One will never be persuaded it was an accident. He's convinced there was a second set of tracks in the snow when he first went to record the scene on film. It's the director in him," Matt explained as she arched her brow. "But with so many other vehicles arriving so quickly, it couldn't be proven. And we were all so stunned, we couldn't focus on anything except the fact that they were gone."

She touched his shoulder. "I'm sorry."

"Thanks." He took a moment to run his hand along the top of the stone before turning away.

Still feeling the warmth of her touch, he helped her into the saddle before pulling himself up on Beau. As they started out, Matt trailed behind for a moment, watching the way Vanessa handled her horse, until he was satisfied that they were a good fit.

What a pretty picture they made. Two blondes out for a morning ride. Nessa's hair streamed out behind her, and Ginger's mane and tail drifted on the breeze.

There were a million chores he ought to be seeing to. But he was happily ignoring all of them to show Vanessa Kettering around the ranch.

A female with an attitude. No wonder I already like her.

Her words played through his mind.

It occurred to him that he was enjoying the time spent with this woman way more than he'd expected to.

He would sort out the why of it another time. For now, he intended to simply enjoy the day, and the pleasant company.

He urged old Beau into a trot until they caught up with Ginger. Slowing his horse, they moved along at an easy gait until they reached the top of the hill.

They paused to look out over the undulating hills and valleys spread out around and below.

"Oh, Matt." Vanessa sighed. "This is like something in a movie. It's so vast and so breathtaking. How can your family ever possibly see to all of it?"

"It takes a lot of work."

"And to think that your ancestors did this on their own."

"Yeah." He took a moment to drink it in, and realized that it was only through the eyes of others that he truly understood just what his family had accomplished. "With so much acreage, it's a good thing we have planes."

"You mentioned them before. How many?"

"Just two small prop planes."

"Who pilots them?"

"We take turns."

She shook her head. "I guess I shouldn't be surprised. After all, this is Montana, and you're living and working on land the size of a city. But do all of you fly?"

He nodded. "All but Great One. Even Gram Gracie has her pilot's license, though she rarely needs it, since she usually flies with Grandpop."

She chuckled. "Is there anything you don't do?"

"I haven't parachuted out of a plane yet, but there's always tomorrow to try a new challenge. And don't mention it to Luke or Reed. Those two are always up for a dare."

"Are they as reckless as they appear?"

"Even more. I can't think of a single thing they haven't tried. If it's dangerous, they're first in line to go for it."

"And you?"

He shrugged and decided to change the subject. "See that creek down there?"

She nodded.

"I'll race you."

He saw the light that came into her eyes.

"You're on." She nudged Ginger into a run and set off at a furious pace.

Matt watched for a moment, enjoying the sight of her, leaning low over her mount, pale hair streaming behind her back.

He'd known instinctively she couldn't resist a challenge, which was why he'd issued this one.

He gave Beau his head, knowing the big horse was itching to run.

It was thrilling to feel all that unleashed power as the gelding stretched out its long legs and ate up the distance, easily passing the smaller, lighter mare.

As they raced past, he heard her rich, ripe oath.

"Same to you, ma'am," he drawled. "I'll see you at the finish line." He lifted his hat in a salute as he flashed by.

CHAPTER TWELVE

Ready for a break?"

Without waiting for her reply, Matt slid from his horse. Vanessa did the same. They'd been in the saddle for more than an hour.

She pressed a hand to the small of her back. "How far have we gone?"

Matt shrugged. "A couple of miles. Sorry, I forgot that it's been years since you rode a horse."

"I'm a bit rusty, but I'll be fine."

They walked along the ridge of a hill, and paused to drink in the view of hills carpeted with pale spring grass that had cropped up overnight, thanks to the rain. For as far as they could see, the higher elevations were darkened with cattle.

She stared out at the panoramic view. "Are your grandparents really on a date?"

"You bet." He chuckled at the look on her face. "Poor

Grandpop dies a little every time his Gracie goes off on one of her camera safaris."

"Then why does he let her go?"

"Let her go?" He turned to her with a look of surprise. "Did you just hear yourself? Those two have been a team for almost fifty years. But I've never known either of them to monitor the activities of the other. They're completely free, which is why their bond is so tight."

Her smile was slow in coming as his words sank in. "Oh, Matt. That's just beautiful. They seem so old-fashioned. But their attitude is really fresh and modern."

"Yeah. They're quite a pair." His smile said much more than his simple words.

"Where will they go on their date?"

He shrugged. "I know they'll make a stop at Anything Goes and stock up on whatever they need. Then probably some old-time movie at Flicks. That's the only theater in town. Half the movies they show were directed by the Great One. He's become Glacier Ridge's famous adopted son. And then Grandpop will want to stop for some apple pie along with all the gossip fit to repeat at D and B's Diner. Dot and Barb know everything that's happening almost before it happens. And they're only too happy to share everything they know with all their customers."

That had Vanessa laughing. "It must be such fun to be part of a small town where everybody knows everybody else."

"Not to mention everybody else's business."

"I guess that's the downside of a small town."

Matt held Ginger's reins. "Ready to get back in the saddle?"

"I am if you are." Vanessa pulled herself up before taking the reins.

When Matt was astride Beau, they moved out at a relaxed pace, while Matt took the time to point out places of interest.

"That creek is where I learned to swim."

"Did your father teach you?"

He shook his head. "It was an unintended consequence. I got tossed by a mustang and landed in the water. I probably swallowed half the creek, bobbing up and down like a cork, hollering for help, until I realized I was all alone, and if I wanted to live, I'd better swim to shore."

"Just like that?" She looked horrified. "You could have drowned and nobody would have ever known."

He laughed. "Yeah. That thought crossed my mind. And that's a really strong motivation to learn to swim. There's no better teacher than necessity."

She could only shake her head as she considered what a tragedy it could have been for his family. Still, this family seemed to thrive on adventure and danger.

What had Burke said? He'd put his money on Matt. Better than a fictional Superman. He was a real-life cowboy. One who'd apparently learned his lessons the hard way.

They meandered along the banks of the stream and paused to allow the horses to drink.

Vanessa slid from the saddle and perched on a fallen log. Matt did the same.

She looked over at him. "I love your private family cemetery. It must be nice to have all your ancestors so close, including your parents."

"Yeah. It feels right knowing they're here on the land

they all loved." He looked over. "How about you? Visit your mother's grave?"

She shook her head. "In the first year or two my dad and I went nearly every week. We'd sit there and cry and hold each other. I know it forged a bond between us that we hadn't had before."

"And now? Still visit her grave?"

"Not often. We both came to the realization that it was painful. Like pulling a scab off a wound that had just begun to heal. So we found new ways to honor Mom. My dad hosts an annual golf outing in her memory, and I serve as hostess at the awards dinner. All the profits go to finding a cure for breast cancer."

"That's nice. It had to be hard, though, losing your mother just when you were about to have so many firsts."

"Firsts?"

He shrugged. "I'm assuming first date, first high school dance. First kiss?"

She arched a brow. "Are you asking, or merely speculating?"

He laughed. "Sorry. I thought I was being subtle about getting into your personal life."

She joined in the laughter. "Actually it was all of the above. Not to mention first love. His name was Todd Brody, he played football, and all the girls had a crush on him. He asked me to senior prom, and I forced my poor dad to go shopping with me for a pink, sparkly gown, and Cinderella shoes that looked like they were made of glass. I even talked Dad into letting me wear my mother's necklace. Then, halfway through the dance, I found Todd in the girls' bathroom in a really hot liplock with Heidi, head cheerleader and prom queen."

"Wow. How'd you react to that?"

"It was pretty predictable. First I started to back out. All I wanted to do was hide somewhere. Then my temper took over and I confronted them, telling them both exactly how I really felt. And then I called my dad, crying hysterically, and begged him to come and get me." She shook her head, remembering. "Poor Dad thought I'd been attacked or something. He arrived with fire in his eyes, ready to defend his baby's honor. But by then I'd taken another look around and decided I wasn't going to run away. Instead, I'd make everyone know that I didn't care that much—" she snapped her fingers "—about Todd Brody and Heidi-boyfriend-stealer. So while my dad was watching, I found Heidi's date standing around looking lost, and I asked him to dance. About that same time Heidi had discovered that Todd had two left feet, but when she came looking for her date, he was too busy dancing with me to bother. And we were both having the time of our lives."

Vanessa started laughing as she remembered. "At the end of the dance, my dad drove me home and I told him what had happened. He said he was proud of me for not hiding or running away from the pain of embarrassment." She shook her head. "That's when he gave me what I will always think of as 'the lecture.' He reminded me that life is never fair. But no matter what it throws at us, or how often we get knocked to the ground, we have to be strong enough to get up and try again. And then he said, 'Remember that Garth Brooks song you love? Honey, you could have missed the pain, but then you'd have also had to miss the dance.'"

Matt studied her with interest. "A really cool lesson."

She nodded. "And a really cool song with a message. I'm sure you've been told pretty much the same."

He grew thoughtful. "After the accident that took our parents, Grandpop used to remind me that every hurdle we're forced to jump makes us stronger. I figured he was the strongest one of all. But one day I caught him in the barn, mucking stalls, and when I walked over to help, I realized he was silently weeping."

"Oh." Vanessa touched a hand to Matt's arm.

Matt went very still. "That was the first time I saw my grandfather cry. I vowed, if I had anything to say about things, it would be the last. I decided that I'd never do anything to break his heart."

"So you've become the fierce protector. Big brother to your reckless younger siblings, Luke and Reed. Caretaker of your uncle, your grandparents, even Burke and Yancy…"

He was shaking his head. "It's not like that."

"Then you're not hearing what I'm hearing."

He fell silent.

She touched a hand to his. "I remember one of my college courses. We had to map out every classmate's birth order, to see if they fit the prevailing statistics. Those who didn't were then asked to provide additional information. Some were changed by the death of a sibling. Others by a traumatic incident in the family. I'd call yours a double whammy."

He looked at her.

"Firstborn and also loss of parents. Both guaranteed to make you want to take charge."

"Bingo." He smiled. "What about you?"

"Same thing. An only child is most often anxious to

please the parents. The loss of my mother made me even more determined to please the survivor. So I'll never know if I'm a lawyer because it was my heart's desire, or because I know how much it means to my dad."

He turned his hand palm up and linked his fingers with hers. "Do we have no choice in these matters?"

She looked down at their joined hands and fought to dismiss the sudden rush of warmth. "I think there's no point in fighting it. We're doomed."

"Maybe that's a good thing." His smile added to her warmth. "So you're saying we may as well just go with our feelings?"

"Why not?"

"I was hoping you'd say that. I hope you won't mind if I start now." He leaned close and nibbled the corner of her mouth.

"Wait." She put a hand to his chest, pushing away. "I wasn't suggesting..." She stood, breaking contact.

"I was." In one quick motion he stood up beside her, gathering her close. "That kiss back at the cabin left me curious."

"It was just a quick good-bye when I thought I was leaving."

"A very nice good-bye. And now...hello again."

He covered her mouth in a kiss that wiped her mind blank of every thought but one. The man had moves. Really good moves. This felt so good, so right, she never wanted it to end.

She wrapped her arms around his waist and held on as the world seemed to ever so slowly spin and dip, leaving her lightheaded, while a burst of heat poured through her, leaving her limbs weak.

For the space of a heartbeat he held her a little away, as though trying to assess what had just happened. And then, with great care, he framed her face with his hands and kissed her with a thoroughness that had them both sighing.

His hands were gentle as they slowly slid from her face to her neck and across the slope of her shoulders. He held her as though she were fragile glass. Cautious. Careful, lest she break.

When at last they drew apart, his eyes were narrowed on her with a look she couldn't fathom.

She struggled to cover the tremors that were still rocketing through her system. "Satisfied?" Her voice was husky with feeling.

His smile came then. A dark, dangerous smile that had her wondering at the way her heart contracted.

"Not nearly. But I guess that will have to do. For now."

Why did his words sound like another challenge?

He caught the reins of her mare and handed them to her.

She could feel the shocking tremors along her arm at the mere touch of his hand on hers.

She pulled herself into the saddle and waited for him to mount Beau.

As they rode across a meadow, she struggled to focus on the amazing scenery. It was impossible. All she could think of was that kiss and the way it messed with her mind.

This man was unlike any she'd ever known. There was danger here, she thought. But not the kind she wanted to run from. What was so mind-blowing was the fact that she knew she was walking into the eye of the storm, and she wanted to run headlong into it.

As the two horses and riders came up over a rise, they slowed to a walk.

Vanessa was laughing as she turned to Matt. "Now that Ginger and I are comfortable with each other, I challenge you to another race. I think we're ready to give you and Beau a run for your money."

"Just can't get enough of losing, can y—?" His words cut off as he caught sight of a black SUV barely visible in a stand of evergreens about a hundred yards away.

"Stay here." His staccato words stung the air as he turned Beau in the direction of the vehicle.

It took Vanessa several seconds before she made out the car and realized what had him so upset.

Ignoring his order, she turned Ginger and followed.

Before Matt was halfway there the car's engine revved and it took off, spitting dirt from its wheels as it gained speed and disappeared into a stretch of woods.

Matt memorized as much of the license plate as he could before it was gone. Knowing he couldn't catch up with the retreating vehicle, he dropped to his knees in the dirt, searching for anything that might have been left behind. Finding the remains of a half-smoked cigar, he wrapped it in his handkerchief and tucked it into his pocket.

"Who were they?" Vanessa remained in the saddle.

"I couldn't see. The windows were darkened. It was a Montana license plate, but it could have been a rental."

He pulled out his cell phone and pressed the sheriff's number.

Vanessa dismounted and walked close enough to hear the bark of the familiar voice.

"Sheriff Eugene Graystoke here. What's up, Matt?"

After describing what he'd seen, and as much of the license plate number as he could recall, the sheriff's voice grew louder with excitement. "Would anyone at the house have spotted them?"

"Not likely. My grandparents are in town. The rest are up in the hills with the herds. Yancy is the only one at home, and if he's busy in the kitchen, he may not have seen or heard a thing. But we'll head home now and ask."

"I'll have the state boys check the car rental places. There aren't that many in this area, but they could have driven from Helena or even any small airport in Montana."

"One of them smokes a cigar. I have what's left of it."

"Good. I'll want that and anything else you find. And Matt, it goes without saying that you're not to let Miss Kettering out of your sight."

Matt saw the way her eyes narrowed slightly. "I understand."

When he disconnected, he took his time returning his phone to his shirt pocket.

When he turned, he decided to keep things light. He touched a finger to her mouth. "Is that a pout?"

She slapped his hand away. "First you once again rush off without letting me in on what you spotted. And now your sheriff tells you not to let me out of your sight? Does your sheriff really believe you can just snap your fingers and I'll be safe?"

Matt sobered instantly, all hint of humor wiped from his eyes. "That's what he'd like. But he's been in this business long enough to know that he can't always get what he wants. That's why we all have to work together until your father's trial is over." He lowered his voice. "I know you resent feeling helpless. You're used to seeing to your own safety, and this has you rattled. But look at it from the sheriff's point of view. He's been given the job of keeping a big-city district attorney's daughter safe on his watch. Knowing Eugene the way I do, he'd much rather have you locked in a cell than roaming free on our ranch. But as long as he's stuck with this deal, he'll do everything in his power to deliver you safely. Even at the cost of his own life."

Those words took all the wind out of her sails.

She lowered her head for a moment, to hide the emotions that flitted through her mind.

When she lifted her head in that proud, almost haughty manner he'd come to recognize, Matt knew that she'd come to terms with the reality of her situation.

"I'm sorry. I must sound like a spoiled, entitled brat. And I want you to know that I appreciate all that you and your family, as well as Sheriff Graystoke and the Montana State Police, are doing on my behalf. I really resent having so many people working so hard just to keep me safe from some monster."

"I know. But as soon as the trial ends, so will the threat to you."

"Well, that's our hope." She met his look with a clear eye. "Unless, of course, DePietro has ordered revenge regardless of the outcome."

Matt clasped her hand. "In that case, we'll keep on working until all of his men are caught and rendered useless."

She glanced at their hands. "Thanks, Matt. You're a good influence on me. I'm almost ready to believe you."

"Believe me." He held her hand a moment longer, closing it between both of his and giving her a long, lingering look before catching the reins and holding them while she mounted.

When he was in the saddle, he kept Beau alongside Ginger as they crossed the meadow in silence and made their way to the barn.

Once inside, as Matt turned their horses into stalls and added feed and water to their troughs, Vanessa sank down on a bale of hay and thought about what had just happened.

She thought she would be safe here because of the isolation of this vast ranch. But even here, someone had managed to find her, and had been watching for a chance to do her harm. Unless, of course, the sheriff could find another plausible explanation.

And if she wasn't safe here, then where?

She shivered.

She wanted to believe that Matt and his family could offer her a refuge. But somewhere in the dark recesses of her mind was the thread of fear that an evil man, on trial in Chicago, had already found a way to carry out his threat.

CHAPTER THIRTEEN

As they stepped from the barn, Matt could see the sheriff's car parked near the back door. A ranch truck came into view. Behind the wheel was Frank, with Gracie beside him in the passenger seat.

Matt took Vanessa's hand and strolled leisurely toward the house, hoping to give the sheriff time to speak privately to his grandparents, without fear of Vanessa overhearing.

The three were standing on the back porch, heads bent in quiet conversation.

As he drew near, Matt called out, "Sheriff? Any news?"

The lawman shook his head.

Matt's eyes narrowed slightly on his grandfather. "You cut your date short?"

Frank shrugged. "When Eugene called us with the news, we decided we'd rather enjoy Yancy's dinner than whatever Dot and Barb were offering at the diner."

Matt held the door while the others trooped inside, where Yancy was frosting a four-layer torte.

The cook looked up in surprise. "You're back early." He looked beyond Frank and Gracie to add, "Hello, Sheriff."

"Yancy." Eugene Graystoke removed his Stetson. "You see any vehicles around here today?"

Yancy glanced from the sheriff to Matt, who stood slightly behind his grandparents. "Has something happened?"

"Nessa and I spotted a car up in the hills. It had darkened windows, so we couldn't see inside."

Vanessa was worrying the cuff of her shirt. The only sign of agitation.

Yancy shook his head. "I didn't see a thing. Didn't hear anything, either. Could they have driven in from the Interstate?"

"Not likely." Matt frowned. "But they could have taken a back road, if they knew the area well enough."

Eugene sighed. "I knew it was a long shot. If they're checking out the ranch, they wouldn't be careless enough to be seen from the house. But the fact that you spotted them, Matt, tells me they may not know a whole lot about just how sprawling your ranch is. They may have thought they could conceal themselves in the woods and watch all the comings and goings from a safe distance. I'd bet money they weren't expecting you to come riding in practically on top of them."

He turned to Frank. "If you don't mind, I'd like to talk to Burke and the boys up in the hills. They may have seen something unusual."

Frank nodded. "You want to call them or head on up there?"

Eugene thought a minute. "No sense riding all that way when a call can let them know what I'm after, as long as they happen to be in an area that has phone service. I'd like everyone here, including your wranglers guarding the herds in hill country, to report anything out of the ordinary."

Frank clapped a hand on the sheriff's shoulder. "Consider it done."

Eugene headed for the door. "I'll make that call outside." He paused and looked at Vanessa. "I'm sorry this adds to your distress, Miss Kettering. I hope you know I'm doing everything in my power to keep you safe."

"I know that, Sheriff." She managed a smile. "And I appreciate all your help."

When the sheriff stepped outside, she turned to Matt's grandparents. "I'm so sorry this caused you to cut your date short."

Gracie squeezed her hand. "Frankie and I have had more dates than we can count." She shot a quick glance at her husband before adding, "On the way home, we talked about my next trek to the hills."

Matt raised an eyebrow. "You just got back."

"But I came back early because of the weather. Just look at all that sunshine. With new foals arriving, the mustangs will be forced to stay in one place for a while, until the mares and their newborns are able to travel. This is the perfect time for me to set up my gear and chronicle the new life cycle."

His grandmother exchanged a glance with her husband before turning to Vanessa. "I'd say it's the perfect opportunity for you, too. Now that you're not on any sort of timetable, how would you like to accompany me into the hills and immerse yourself in the life of wild horses?"

Vanessa's eyes widened with excitement. "You wouldn't mind having me along?"

"I'd welcome the company. But I need to warn you about a few things. I travel light, and it's pretty primitive up there. I can't count on the herd stopping near one of our cabins or shelters at night. I cook over a campfire and sleep under the stars, unless the weather turns. Then I sleep in my truck."

"But I'd get to see the mustangs up close?"

"As close as they'll allow. You may get to witness a birth or two. And sometimes a death. Just remember, this is nature, raw and natural. It won't be pretty and airbrushed. It can be wonderful, but it can also be heart-breakingly brutal."

"I understand. When do we leave?"

Gracie gave a laugh of delight. "Oh, what fun to have a traveling companion who's young and eager. Let's shoot for tomorrow morning. Unless Mother Nature decides otherwise."

"I'll go up and pack now."

"Remember. We travel light. I prefer to dress in layers. You'll need a parka and boots for chilly or rainy mornings and nights, and something for warm afternoons. We sleep in our clothes, and we have to be prepared to head out whenever the herd starts moving."

As Vanessa started up the stairs, Matt remained in the kitchen. His voice was low. "You think it's wise to do this now?"

"I can't think of a better time." Gracie linked hands with her husband. "Frankie and I discussed it on the way home. If someone is targeting our houseguest, it's too late to keep her presence here a secret. But it would be almost impossible for them to find her in those hills."

"They found her today, while riding across the meadow."

"That could have been an accident. As Eugene pointed out, they may have thought they could hide out in the woods and watch the ranch. They may have been caught completely by surprise when you and Vanessa spotted them."

"Maybe." His eyes narrowed. "But I don't like the idea of you and Nessa alone in the hills."

She touched a hand to his arm. "I feel quite certain that you and Frankie will see to it that we're never completely alone."

He smiled then and felt his tense shoulders relax. "You're a sly one, Gracie Malloy."

"I just happen to know my men." She turned away. "Yancy, I'm really looking forward to tasting that torte after dinner."

The old man smiled. "I'll see there's enough left over to send along with you on your trek tomorrow."

"That would be grand."

As she and Frank walked away, Matt let himself out of the house and made his way to the barn.

There he did what he always did when his mind was troubled. He chose a pitchfork from a hook along the wall and began mucking stalls.

There was nothing like hard, physical work to free him to turn a problem over and over until he'd looked at it from every possible angle.

He and his family, along with all the wranglers, would

have to form a protective ring around the two women while keeping just out of sight. Not an easy thing anywhere, but especially in the wilderness. With mustangs, there was no set pattern. No trail or path. They moved at the whim of nature and their stallion leader.

Still, it had to be done. If a vehicle could breach the safety of their isolated ranch, it made sense to take Vanessa high in the hills, and hope it was enough to discourage anyone bent on evil from following.

He paused to clench a fist. He would move heaven and earth to keep Gracie and Vanessa safe, while still leaving them free to savor their journey into the wild.

Vanessa studied the meager clothes in her closet. It wouldn't be difficult making a decision about what to take along on her trek to the wilderness.

The wilderness.

Grinning wildly, she did a quick little turn. Oh, how she wanted to share this news with her father. She'd actually fished out her cell phone before it dawned on her that she could no longer indulge in that lovely ritual. Always, she'd enjoyed sharing every bit of good news with him, before calling her friends, especially her best friend, Lauren. Lauren McCotter, who'd been her BFF since kindergarten.

Though she and Lauren had followed very different career paths, they managed to meet at least once a week or so, either for morning coffee or a drink after work, to catch up on each other's life. They had a shared history that was a tighter bond than that of sisters. Lauren was the sister she'd never had.

She sat down on the edge of the bed, fighting a sudden

ache around her heart. The reality of her situation hit her
with all the force of a physical blow. She'd been cut off
from everything that was familiar and comfortable. Her father. Her friends. The people she worked with. And all
because some madman, who thought himself above the
law, was willing to do whatever it took to stay out of prison.

She felt a rush of love for her father, knowing how he
must be torn between his duty to the people who trusted
him to prosecute such men, and his fierce need to protect his only child. How he must be suffering as he went
about his daily routine, keeping his feelings carefully hidden beneath a façade of cool reserve.

Through the years she'd watched him handle the me-
dia after a sensational criminal case. He'd earned a reputation for being low-key and thoroughly professional.
One investigative reporter, eager to earn his stripes by
breaking through that wall of reserve, had, after a par-
ticularly grueling interview, given Elliott Kettering the
nickname Iceman.

It pained Nessa to see the man she adored misunder-
stood and ridiculed. But, as he'd reminded her often, it
came with the territory. The district attorney of any large
city was fair game for criticism. As her father said, he
was damned if he won a high-profile trial and damned if
he lost. And always, he was suspected of hoping to use
his position to move on to higher office, even when that
wasn't the case at all.

And now this threat to her safety was just another price
to be paid.

As Elliott Kettering's daughter, she needed to be as
strong as he'd always been.

She stood and paced to the window. She would put

aside her fears and get through this. And what better way to spend her time than with Grace Malloy, one of the most respected researchers in the field of wild horses?

Spotting movement outside the barn, she watched as Matt led a horse toward a corral. She couldn't take her eyes off him. Everything about the man exuded strength and confidence and purpose. The way he walked, those long strides matching that of the horse. The slow, easy lift of his hand as he removed the lead rope and ran an open palm over the horse's muzzle.

She gave an involuntary shiver, and thought about his hands holding her, touching her.

He was the epitome of a Western hero. All muscle and strength and easy charm. And ever since their uncomfortable introduction, she couldn't stop thinking about him.

She'd thought, earlier today, that he had chosen that isolated area near the stream for his own advantage. And when he'd kissed her, she'd been certain of it. But then he'd been the one to step back from that ever-so-tempting edge and suggest they return to the ranch. She'd actually had a moment of keen disappointment before coming to her senses.

He'd been right, of course. They needed to keep this on a purely professional level.

Maybe she was just a little annoyed that he'd been the first to do the sensible thing, when in the past she'd always assumed that role. Or maybe she was suffering some regret that they couldn't have let the passion they were feeling play out to its logical conclusion. If so, she didn't want to probe this too deeply.

She huffed out a breath. And hadn't she once again spent way too much time thinking about Matt Malloy?

She crossed her arms over her chest, turned away, and walked to the closet.

Time to make a decision about what to pack for tomorrow's grand adventure. She was traveling to the wilderness to see, up close and personal, a herd of wild horses. While she and Gracie were alone together, she would have plenty of time to interview the foremost authority on how mustangs lived and how they survived.

And when she returned to Chicago, and later to DC, she could report back to the wildlife organizations she represented how to make the lives of these beautiful creatures safer and better.

This was a rare opportunity, one she'd never dreamed possible, and she planned on making the most of it.

CHAPTER FOURTEEN

By the time Vanessa descended the stairs for dinner, she could hear muted voices in the kitchen. She walked in to find everybody gathered around the fireplace, enjoying drinks and appetizers. Even Colin, Luke, and Reed, as well as Burke, were there, fresh from their duties with the herds. It was obvious from the look of them that they'd barely had time to shower and change. Their faces were heavily bearded, their hair in need of a trim.

Yancy held a tray of drinks for her inspection.

"Thank you." She accepted a glass of wine and turned to the others.

Reed, heavily bearded, shaggy hair tied back in a ponytail, his well-worn denims faded and torn, had the look of an Old West gunslinger as he turned to her. "I hear you're about to go on one of Gram Gracie's famous wilderness treks."

Vanessa's smile widened. "I can't wait."

"It shows. You look like a kid at Christmas."

"Is it that obvious?"

Nelson, enjoying his martini, eyed her over the rim of his glass. "I can't imagine a fashionable, big-city lawyer like you climbing over mountains and slopping through muddy fields just to get close to a bunch of smelly creatures."

"Where's your romance, Dad?" Grace touched a hand to his arm. "If you were directing Vanessa in a film, you'd have soft music playing in the background while she danced through a field of wildflowers."

Something about her words had Matt lifting his head to stare at Vanessa through narrowed eyes.

Nelson nodded. "I would indeed. Beautiful women in fields of wildflowers sell movies. But I was never fooled by what I was doing. Movies are pretend. You're taking her into the harshness of the real world, Gracie Anne." He turned to Frank. "Of course, there was a time when I couldn't imagine a daughter of mine living on a ranch, let alone climbing all over Hell's Half Acre chasing wild animals."

"And now, you're living on a ranch yourself, Great One." Luke tipped up his longneck and drank, while the others shared smiles.

"True enough." Nelson set aside his empty glass. "It took some getting used to. But I have to say, Yancy's fine food and excellent martini skills have made the transition smooth enough." He looked around at his daughter and son-in-law, his grandson Colin, and then at his three great-grandsons, all of them rugged and handsome enough to have been leading men in his films. He gave one of those lazy, satisfied smiles. "Not that being with all of you hasn't been enough reward. But there's something to be said for fine food and liquor."

"Spoken like a true Hollywood icon," Luke drawled.

Burke accepted a longneck and, as was his custom, stood just outside the circle of family, like a guardian angel watching and listening in silence.

When Yancy announced that dinner was ready, they moved across the room, settling comfortably at the big harvest table.

Luke held a huge platter while his great-grandfather helped himself to a chicken breast. The others at the table easily passed around a Caesar salad, tiny new garden peas, and a basket of sourdough rolls fresh from the oven.

Nelson took a first bite and turned to the cook with a look of absolute delight. "Chicken cordon bleu?"

Yancy grinned. "You've been talking about it for weeks now. I figured it was time I took the hint."

"But this is—" the old man took a second bite and closed his eyes for a moment "—exactly the way they served it at the Brasseri."

Yancy couldn't hide his pleasure. "Glad to hear I nailed it."

"More than. Oh, this takes me back…"

Around the table the family shared knowing looks. They had no doubt they were about to be entertained by the Great One's memories of a bygone Hollywood.

"Anthony would pick me up in the limousine at exactly six o'clock. We would drive to the Brasseri, and Marcel, my favorite waiter, would set a martini in front of me the moment I was seated in a booth."

"Always a booth, and never a table," Luke explained to Vanessa.

"Exactly right. Tables were for the tourists who came in to stare at celebrities. Or for the gossip columnists," he added with a trace of contempt, "who spent a fortune tipping the waiters for any hint of scandal they could reveal in their rags."

"Even Marcel?" Frank nudged Gracie, knowing that would raise his father-in-law's hackles.

"Marcel was above such things. Totally incorruptible. He knew more secrets than anyone in Hollywood, but took them all to his grave. That's why, while the others came and went, he remained as head waiter at the Brasseri for over twenty years."

Vanessa turned to Grace. "Did you ever go along with your father?"

Grace shook her head. "Rarely. Over Dad's objections, Mother insisted that I attend a private girls' school in Connecticut, as she had."

"Which meant that I was forced to fly across the country regularly, just to spend time with my wife and daughter." Nelson chuckled. "It was the price I paid to love the most beautiful woman in Connecticut. That is until Grace Anne chose to attend college at UCLA over the elite Eastern university that had been her mother's alma mater. Madeline was horrified, of course, because it meant that she would have to return to the glitter of Hollywood if she wanted to see her own daughter."

"And then," Frank interjected, "just when Nelson thought he'd won the upper hand in their marital tug-of-war, my Gracie Girl made a fateful trip to Montana to photograph some scenery for her final year in filmmaking at UCLA, and ended up leaving both Connecticut and California behind."

Vanessa, caught up in the story, looked over with surprise. "You never went home?"

Grace linked her fingers with Frank's. "I never even went back to graduate. Nothing was going to make me leave this handsome cowboy for even a week."

Colin leaned back in his chair and regarded his parents. "And I've been thankful ever since."

Luke slapped his uncle on the back. "Not as thankful as all the pretty ladies in Glacier Ridge. Who would they drool over if you weren't around to make their hearts flutter?"

Colin gave a dry laugh. "In case you haven't noticed, you and your brothers have replaced me as hunk of the day."

"You might want to look around the next time you're in town." Reed exchanged a grin with his brothers. "Word is, every rancher in Glacier Ridge keeps his wife and daughters locked indoors until Colin Malloy leaves town."

"Trust me." Colin huffed a breath. "They're all safe. I'm not even looking."

"But they are. And drooling," Luke added as the others laughed.

"Speaking of drooling…" Grace turned to Yancy. "I think we'll take our dessert in the great room. And as soon as possible. I've been thinking about that torte for hours."

"Yes, ma'am." Yancy began setting plates and cups on a trolley, along with a carafe of coffee and a bottle of fine whiskey.

As they made their way to the great room, Frank huddled with Burke, who reported on the herds, the wranglers, and the weather in the hills, before being apprised of Gracie's latest plans to journey there.

"So, Nessa." Reed waited until his great-grandfather was comfortably settled into a big, overstuffed chair by the fire before sitting nearby and stretching out his long legs to the warmth. "Have you decided what you'll take along on your first visit to the wilderness?"

"I thought some jeans, a hoodie, maybe a parka, and boots."

"Well, that takes care of tomorrow morning." Reed grinned at his brothers across the room. "What about the days after?"

She shot a puzzled look at Grace. "Didn't you say we'd be traveling light?"

"I did. Just ignore the teasing. But Reed's right. You may want to add a few things. You'll need a couple of tees or a tank. Shorts. Sunblock. And I'd advise you to bring along some sturdy work gloves."

"And if you don't have room for the work gloves, at least make room for the shorts." Reed's smile went up a notch.

Yancy moved among them, serving his torte with dollops of chocolate chip ice cream, along with cups of coffee.

Nelson looked up after his first taste. "Is that hazelnut I detect, Yancy?"

"You've got a refined palate, Great One. It is hazelnut."

The old man brought his fingers to his lips in an exaggerated display of delight. "You've outdone yourself again, my man. I do believe this torte is better than any I ever tasted at the Brasseri."

Yancy made a formal bow. "The highest compliment ever."

"And well deserved."

Around the room the others were too busy enjoying their dessert to bother with words.

Yancy set a trolley along one wall, in case anyone wanted seconds. Then he settled into his favorite, well-worn chair by the fire and sipped his coffee.

Seeing him, Vanessa looked surprised. "You're not having any of this fabulous torte, Yancy?"

He gave her a pleased smile. "I'm glad you think it's fabulous. My real dessert is watching everyone enjoying the things I made. Truth is, I never had a sweet tooth. Now, if this were chili, I'd have seconds and thirds."

"Then I'll just have yours, too." Luke ambled across the room and cut another huge slice before mounding it with ice cream.

"Careful," Colin called. "All those pretty young things in town like their cowboys lean."

"You sure about that?" Luke winked at his brother Reed. "Now that our old uncle is past looking at women..."

"Who're you calling old?" Colin sipped his coffee.

Reed couldn't resist jumping in. "Luke's right. You said you're not even looking at women anymore. I'd say that makes you old."

"I'm only ten years older than Matt." Colin turned to his nephew. "Why aren't you defending me?"

Matt grinned. "You're on your own, old man."

Colin nodded toward his father. "You going to let these upstarts talk to your son this way?"

Frank dropped an arm around Gracie's shoulders. "Son, I've learned that there's only one thing that ever stops a man from looking at beautiful women. That's when he's snagged the most beautiful woman of all. And since I've already got her, and I'm too content after such a fine meal to do more than listen, I'll just let the four of you carry on." He turned to Vanessa. "See what we have to put up with? They're constantly ragging on one another, and we'd probably send them all packing and tell them to find their own ranches if they weren't so helpful around this big ol' ranch."

"Helpful?" Reed shot a knowing look at his brothers. "Grandpop, if you sent the four of us packing, you'd have to hire an entire army of wranglers to replace all these muscles and brains."

"You forgot to mention egos." The older man's eyes danced with laughter as he turned to Burke. "And I mean giant egos."

That had Burke roaring with laughter.

Reed crossed the room and held out a bottle of whiskey. "I think your brain just short-circuited, Grandpop. How about a splash to give it a jump-start?"

Still laughing, Frank held out his cup.

Reed turned to the others. "Any takers?"

Nelson lifted his cup. "I wouldn't mind a bit."

"I'll have some, too, son," Burke's eyes were crinkled in glee.

The rest declined, and Reed replaced the bottle on the trolley.

Vanessa had a sudden thought. "My cell phone didn't work up in the hills." She turned to Grace.

Frank answered for Gracie. "That's true, darlin'. They're pretty unreliable. Way up there, you're pretty much on your own."

"So, if there's…trouble…" She flushed. "Not that I'm expecting any but…"

Frank gave her a reassuring smile. "My Gracie Girl knows how to get the word out if she has any trouble."

Beside him, his wife nodded. "I have my rifle, Nessa. If I fire it, they'll hear it clear across the hills and come running from all directions."

"Have you ever had to fire it?"

The older woman gave her a gentle smile. "A time or two. Just to see if my men were paying attention."

They all laughed as Burke explained. "When Miss Gracie calls, this entire ranch drops everything to get to her."

Frank kissed his wife's cheek. "That's because she's the heart and soul of this place."

"And don't you ever forget that." She tried to sound stern, but everyone in the room could hear the warmth in her voice.

A short time later, as the fire burned low, Grace was the first to get to her feet. "Time I turned in. You might want to think about it, too, Nessa. We have a long day ahead of us tomorrow."

As she and Frank made their way upstairs, the others began drifting off to their rooms, calling good night as they did.

When Vanessa set aside her cup and got to her feet, Matt stood. "I'll see you to your room."

"That's not necessary. If you'd like to stay and chat with Burke…"

The old cowboy shook his head. "I'm heading to the bunkhouse. We'll be leaving for the herd before dawn." He crossed to her and took her hand in a courtly gesture.

"You'll have a grand time with Miss Grace. I hope you soak it all up."

"Thank you, Burke. I can't wait. Good night."

As she climbed the stairs, Matt followed. When they came to her room, he reached around her and opened the door. Once she was inside, he surprised her by stepping in behind her before leaning against the closed door.

She turned. "Is there something you want to say?"

"Something I need to do." His voice was low. Quiet.

His eyes were so clearly focused on her, she felt the magnetic pull of them. "If you're here to warn me…"

Without a word he dragged her against him. Her hands automatically lifted to his chest, as though to brace herself, but there was no time.

And when his mouth covered hers, there were no thoughts but one. Oh how she'd wanted this. Only this.

When he wrapped her in those strong arms, she felt the quiet strength of him and thrilled to it.

The more he drew out the kiss, the more her body softened, melted into him, until she could feel him in every part of her.

He lifted his head just enough to nuzzle her cheek, her eye, her forehead.

She gave a long, deep sigh. "You were so quiet tonight, I was afraid you were angry that I was going with Gracie." She lifted a hand to his jaw. "I know I shouldn't be taking any chances, but…"

"You've got a right to be concerned." His words, spoken against her temple, sent shivers along her spine. "But try to put everything aside and just enjoy this time with my grandmother. It's a once-in-a-lifetime experience."

"It is." She looked into his eyes. "But if you're not angry, why were you so quiet?"

"I'm not a patient man. And all evening, while my family was having such a good time teasing you, I just wanted you alone. For this." He lowered his head and took her mouth again.

Curls of pleasure had her insides quivering.

He changed the angle of the kiss and gathered her against him.

She returned his kisses with a hunger that caught them both by surprise.

When at last he lifted his head, he framed her face with his big hands and stared at her with a look that burned clear through to her soul. "I'm leaving now."

"You could . . . stay."

"Not tonight. You need your sleep." He studied her a minute longer before turning toward the door.

As he opened it he muttered huskily, "When you come back, I'll want a whole lot more than a few stolen kisses."

He stepped away and pulled the door shut behind him.

She studied the closed door before crossing the room to stand at the window and stare at the night sky.

Matt's words had her touching a hand to her heart, which was pounding inside her chest.

When you come back, I'll want a whole lot more than a few stolen kisses.

Not just words.

It had been a promise. A promise that left her absolutely breathless.

CHAPTER FIFTEEN

It wasn't yet light outside when Vanessa descended the stairs and dropped her backpack in a corner of the kitchen.

Gracie and Frank were huddled in front of the fireplace, heads bent in quiet conversation.

Yancy was draining bacon on a bed of paper towels.

Matt and Burke stomped in from the barn, pausing to remove their boots and hang their hats on pegs along the wall before washing at the big sink in the mudroom.

Spotting Vanessa, Grace hurried over. "I figured you'd be up early. How'd you sleep?"

"Badly. Too excited, I guess."

"You'll sleep tonight."

Frank chuckled. "That's a fact. After climbing around these mountains, trying to keep up with my Gracie Girl, I guarantee you'll sleep like a baby."

Vanessa was working overtime to keep from staring at

Matt, but when she turned his way, he winked, and she could feel her face getting all warm.

"'Morning, Nessa."

"Good morning." She ducked her head, wishing she could control the blush spreading up her throat and across her cheeks. She hadn't reacted to a guy this way since she was sixteen. But it was impossible to act all cool and composed after last night, and the promise he'd made. Just the thought of it made her body tingle.

He nodded toward the backpack. "That's it?"

"Yeah." She turned to Grace. "I added a tee and tank and some shorts, but I don't have any work gloves."

"We've got a shelf full of them in the barn. Remember to pick up a pair before we head out."

"Okay." Vanessa chose a glass of orange juice from a tray on the counter.

Matt snagged a mug of coffee and handed it to Burke before taking a second one for himself.

"Breakfast is ready," Yancy called. "Actually, this is a second breakfast. I served Luke and Reed and Colin theirs more than an hour ago. They're halfway to Eagle's Ridge by now."

Matt held a chair for Vanessa before sitting beside her. He held a platter of scrambled eggs while she served herself. "You'd better take more than that," he said, grinning at the small portion on her plate.

"I don't think I can eat a thing. Nerves, I guess."

"That's all right." Frank dug into his bacon and eggs. "I saw all the food Yancy packed up for you and Gracie. You could survive up in the hills for a month or more and still not run out of things to eat."

"Yancy understands the way an appetite sharpens when

you're living in the hills." Grace slathered wild strawberry preserves on her toast. "You did send along some of that torte, I hope?"

Yancy nodded. "I made sure that was the first thing I packed, Miss Grace."

"Good. The rest is lovely, of course. But that torte..." She let her smile speak for itself as she finished eating.

Half an hour later she and Frank shoved away from the table and led the way toward the mudroom, with Vanessa trailing behind.

She turned. "Thank you for that great breakfast, Yancy. And for all the food you're sending along with us."

"You're welcome, Nessa. Now relax and enjoy your trek into the wilderness. With Miss Grace along as tour guide, I'm sure you'll have a grand adventure."

Before she could pick up her backpack, Matt snatched it up and moved along beside her as they made their way to the barn.

He handed her a pair of work gloves. "See if these fit."

After trying them, she nodded and he tucked them in with her things before stowing the backpack in the truck and holding open the passenger door.

Before she could climb up, Matt laid a hand on her arm. Just a touch, but she felt the quick curl of heat as she turned to him.

"Yancy's right. With Gram Gracie along, you'll have the time of your life."

"I hope so. I'm so eager to see a herd of wild horses, I'm twitching."

"Yeah. I can feel it." He leaned in and touched his mouth to hers.

It was the merest touch of his lips to hers, but it affected her so deeply she couldn't feel her hands or feet as she turned and climbed into the truck and fumbled with the seat belt.

Matt closed the door and reached in the open window, tugging on a lock of her hair. "Go make some memories."

Grace set a rifle on a rack behind the driver's seat. Vanessa lifted a brow in question, but she merely grinned. "I don't suppose you shoot?"

At Vanessa's quick shake of her head, Grace touched her hand. "Not a problem, Nessa. I shoot well enough for both of us. And I'd never go into the wilderness without my rifle."

She turned the key in the ignition, and the truck rolled out of the barn. Instead of heading along the gravel driveway, she drove the truck across a flat stretch of ground.

As the older woman waved and called something to Frank, Vanessa stared at the reflection in the side-view mirror of Matt standing straight and tall, his eyes now hidden behind sunglasses.

As eager as she was for this adventure, she had the sudden, almost overpowering desire to run back and fall into his arms and beg him to kiss her one more time.

Go make some memories.

With a sweet smile she sat back and looked around as they drove across a pasture before veering up and up to a high, grassy meadow. Fields so green they seemed like a Hollywood set. The green gradually gave way to a background of colorful bitterroot. And still the truck continued, following no particular trail as it climbed and climbed until they came to the edge of the wooded area. Once there, all Vanessa's senses sharpened. The bright sun became dappled, and the air was heavy with the fragrance of evergreen and wildflowers. Colorful birds darted from tree to tree. And as her eyes adjusted to the dim light, she could make out movement. A herd of deer. An eagle lifting from the forest ground with something dangling from its beak.

As the eagle soared, so did her heart. She felt wild joy and a sense of quiet peace. The teeming streets of her city faded away, as did the danger that hovered like a dark shadow. She was actually in the wilderness of Montana, with Grace Anne LaRou as her tour guide. And waiting for her back at the ranch was a handsome cowboy whose kisses promised paradise.

Hours later the truck came up over a rise, and Vanessa gave an audible gasp at the panorama spread out before them. To one side were bleak, barren mountains rising up like a vertical wall from a half-moon-shaped lake, glistening in the sun. On the other side was a series of grassy ranges, each one folding into the next, for as far as the eye could see. And all of them ringed by towering mountain peaks in the distance.

"Oh, this looks like some sort of lost world."

At Vanessa's words, Grace nodded. "That's exactly how I think of it. My very own uncharted, untouched piece of heaven."

She put the truck in gear, and they drove slowly along a high ridge until Grace parked the vehicle under a rock ledge.

"I've used this spot before. It's a good place to make

base camp. There's a stream over there"—she pointed to a rock-strewn bank and sunlit water meandering just beyond a stand of trees—"and a cave here, once we make certain there aren't any bears calling it their home."

"Bears?"

"Just a precaution," Grace said with a reassuring smile. "Afterward, we'll walk a bit, see if we can find any trace of the herd. But we'll return and sleep here tonight. If the weather holds, we can sleep under the stars." Her tone lowered. "There's nothing quite like sleeping under the stars. Ever tried it?"

Vanessa shook her head. "Not even when I was a kid at camp. We always slept in cabins."

"Then you're in for a treat. But if it rains, we'll have shelter under that shelf of rock." She turned to Vanessa. "First we'll check out this cave."

The two women exited the truck and Grace led the way, carrying a battery-operated lantern. She switched it on before stepping into the cave. Vanessa, trailing behind, looked around nervously, praying she didn't see feral eyes looking back at her.

When they'd checked out the cave and found it empty and, though small, high enough for them to stand in, they walked back out into the brilliant sunlight.

Grace turned off the lantern and set it in the back of the truck, which was littered with her photographic equipment. She looked at Vanessa. "You ready to hike these hills?"

"I can't wait."

Grace smiled. "Let's do it."

* * *

They hiked for nearly an hour, with Grace pausing every so often to kneel in the grass and examine the ground for signs of horses.

Each time she stopped, Vanessa used the time to stare around with a feeling of awe. This amazing place was even more than she'd hoped for. Sweeping vistas of lush rangeland and breathtaking views of mountains towering in the distance, looking exactly like the pictures she'd carried in her mind.

Here there were no highways. Not even rough roads or the tracks from farm implements. No man-made buildings. No people. The Old West. Raw and untamed. Looking as it had for centuries. A land untouched by human hands.

"Ah." Hearing the exclamation from Grace, Vanessa hurried over.

"Look." Grace pointed to something in the grass. "Fresh droppings. A lot of them."

"But how do you know it's from horses and not some other animals?"

Grace stood. "Each animal has its own distinct markings. In this area there are pronghorns, elk, even higher up there—" she pointed to the mountain peaks "—Rocky Mountain goats. But this tells me the horses are near. And since it's fresh, they'll be close by, giving the mares time to deliver their foals and grow sleek and fat on all this grass."

Vanessa's heart was beating overtime. "Will we keep on climbing?"

Grace shook her head. "This sunlight will fade quickly once the sun drifts behind that ridge. We'll head back to camp now and settle in for the night. It's time to figure out what we'll have for dinner."

Vanessa touched a hand to her stomach. "I'd forgotten about food. But now that you mention it, I know I'll be ready to eat after we get back."

"Nerves beginning to fade?" Grace asked with a grin.

"Yeah." Vanessa took a moment to look around before turning to follow Grace's lead. "Now that I'm here, and it's even better than I'd hoped, I'm feeling... relieved."

"You're going to feel even better when we see what special things Yancy sent along."

"Oh, I hope he sent along some of that chicken."

"You can have my share. I'm just hoping he packed a big slice of that chocolate-hazelnut torte," Grace said, laughing.

"How did you find this place?"

Vanessa sat with her back against a boulder, which was still warm from the fading sun, enjoying Yancy's chicken cordon bleu and a roll heated over a firepit Grace had fashioned of some rocks and tree branches.

"I was twenty years old, a college senior, using my spring break to do a film study of the Montana wilderness." Grace paused to eat the last bite of Yancy's torte before setting aside the plastic plate and filling a cup with coffee. "While up here, I saw my first herd of wild horses. There was this wonderful black stallion standing perfectly still on a rock ledge, keeping watch over his herd grazing in a meadow below. I turned my long-range lens on him and began filming. He was magnificent. I lost my heart in an instant." Her voice lowered. "Sadly, he spotted me, leapt down from the ledge, and began herding his mares and their young in the opposite direction. I wasn't just disappointed. I was determined to see him again, and to film him with his herd. It became my obsession."

"Did you ever find him?"

Grace smiled. "Not that year. Before I could pack up and try to track the herd, the most handsome man I'd ever seen rode up out of the wilderness, and I lost my heart for the second time in a single day. Francis Xavier Malloy was simply magnificent. So much better than any of the Hollywood actors I knew who pretended to be cowboys. This man was the real thing. And when I learned that I was on his land, and that he didn't have a wife and children, and he looked at me in the same wild, almost primitive way that stallion had looked, I knew that I never wanted to leave."

"It must have been a terrible shock to your parents."

"*Shock* is much too mild a word." Grace chuckled. "You heard what Dad said last night. It was bad enough that I'd gone off to Montana without a chaperone. But to learn that I intended to stay and marry a rancher I barely knew—he was ready to have me committed."

"How did your mother react?"

Grace smiled. "Mother was the one who really surprised me. I'd expected her to be too embarrassed to even admit to her society friends what I'd done. Instead, she called me to say that she wasn't at all surprised that I was marrying my first love. She said she would expect no less of her daughter, and that she wished me and my rancher all happiness. She offered to come to the wedding without Dad, since he was sulking, but I told her we intended to marry quickly and without any fuss, and that she could come to Montana and meet him whenever she could persuade Dad to join her."

"Wow." Vanessa poured herself a cup of coffee and wrapped her hands around it in the chill of evening. "What did she think of your Frank?"

Grace's voice softened. "Mother died that year, before she had the chance to meet him. But it was enough to know I'd had her blessing." She brightened. "I've always felt that even after her passing, she was pressing Dad to soften his heart and get to know his only child's husband. And, of course, you can see how successful she was."

She and Vanessa shared a smile.

"That's really sweet."

"Yes, it is. I'm a lucky woman." Grace stifled a yawn. "And now, we'd better get our bedrolls ready. I have a feeling I'll be asleep in no time."

After banking the fire, she and Vanessa set their bedrolls close enough to enjoy the warmth of the hot embers through the night.

As Vanessa snuggled in, she stared at the canopy of stars overhead. Grace was right. This wasn't like anything she'd ever experienced. She'd never before seen stars so big and bright, it felt as though she could reach up and touch them. And the night air, though chilly, whispered over her face, leaving her feeling fresh and clean.

Make some memories, Matt had whispered. And oh, wasn't she just?

Oh Dad, she thought. *If only you could be here, safe and sound, away from danger, away from the all-consuming work that takes up so much of your time, to share this with me.*

And then she thought about Matt Malloy. How would

she describe him to her father? A cowboy. A rancher. A businessman. A man she would trust with her life, though she'd known him a scant few days.

With a feeling of deep contentment, she drifted into sleep.

CHAPTER SIXTEEN

Vanessa turned toward the warmth at her back before opening her eyes to see that Grace had added a fresh log to their fire.

She yawned, stretched, then sat up with a start. "Did I oversleep? How long have you been up?"

"Relax, Nessa. I just woke a few minutes ago, and thought I'd stoke the fire before breakfast."

Vanessa slipped out of her bedroll and pulled on her hiking boots before stowing her bedding in the back of the truck. "Tell me what I can do."

Grace was busy uncovering a metal storage bin and removing several packets. She handed over a blackened coffeepot that looked as though it had seen years of wilderness treks. "If you'll take this to that creek over there and fill it, we'll have coffee."

Vanessa returned and spooned ground coffee into the basket before placing the pot on a grate over the fire. Soon the air was perfumed with the wonderful fragrance of coffee, along with the mouthwatering aroma of onion-laced skillet potatoes, as well as ham and eggs.

"All the comforts of home," Grace proclaimed as she filled two plates.

As the two women dug into their breakfast, Grace couldn't help grinning at her young friend. "No loss of appetite this morning, I gather?"

Vanessa laughed. "I'm starving."

"That's what hiking these hills does to a body. I'm always hungry up here."

"I can understand why. We must have walked miles yesterday."

"We'll walk even more today. But I promise you, we won't even notice."

"I'd walk through fire just to see a herd of mustangs."

"I remember those same feelings of utter excitement. It's always been the same for me. The magnetic pull of wild horses. Just knowing they're close by has my heart beating faster. Now, tell me how you felt sleeping under the stars."

"It was just as you said. But I really never expected it to be so grand."

"You don't mind the lack of modern facilities?"

"What lack?" Vanessa lifted her hands to encompass the green hills, the blue sky with its puffy clouds, the stream gurgling behind them. "It seems to me we have all the comforts of home, and none of the annoyances. No phones ringing. No schedules or deadlines." She sighed, searching for words. "Honestly? Though I would have never believed I could be saying this, I think I could learn to love this way of life."

"Now you're in trouble," Grace said with a laugh. At Vanessa's expression she added, "That's exactly how I got hooked. A night under the stars. A herd of mustangs. A handsome cowboy..."

Vanessa felt her face grow warm.

"Speaking of which... What do you think of my grandson?"

Trying to be coy, Vanessa shrugged. "Which one?"

Grace threw back her head and laughed. "Try that on someone else. I've seen the way you and Matthew look at each other. You're not even aware he has two brothers."

Vanessa couldn't help joining in the laughter. "Am I so transparent?"

"To anyone who bothers to look at you, Nessa." Grace turned. "Let's get this campsite put to rights so we can get on the trail."

The two women worked together, banking the fire, cleaning their dishes in the stream, and stowing them inside the metal container stored in the back of the truck.

After checking their supplies in their backpacks, and adding Grace's rifle and the photographic supplies, which they divided between them, they set off across the high meadow in search of the herd, with Grace leading the way.

As they crested a hill, they paused to enjoy the view. The hills around them, each one folding into the next, were green and gold, with a sky so blue it hurt to look at it. The sun shot the distant peaks with shimmering gold and mauve while a mist drifted over the lake far below.

"I think you're my good luck charm, Nessa." Grace slipped on a pair of sunglasses. "I don't think I've ever seen a prettier day."

As they walked, they chatted amiably.

"Matt said he was twelve when his parents died."

"Yes." Grace paused to lower her backpack to the grass before sitting on a smooth, sun-warmed rock. "Sudden death changes the lives of everyone involved. Until then, Frankie and I had more happiness than anyone deserves in this life. Two sons who loved this ranch as much as we did. A beautiful daughter-in-law who loved us as much as we loved her. And three grandsons who delighted all of us, just by being."

She looked toward the brooding mountains. "We were all so carefree. Our biggest concern was doubling our herds and topping the previous year's profits. And then, suddenly, none of that mattered. All of us were changed forever."

She met Vanessa's look. "Matthew and his brothers were as carefree as boys can be, especially boys growing up on a vast ranch, being best friends, doing all the rough-and-tumble things boys do. But from the moment they were given the news of their loss, Matthew was no longer just a twelve-year-old boy. He became, in an instant, guardian and protector to two younger ones. My wild, fearless, dangerous grandson became—" she shrugged "—responsible."

She lifted her head, as though speaking to the air around her. "That singular event changed our entire family. Our son Colin had been the kid brother who had adored his older brother. All he'd ever wanted was to be like Patrick. And now he had to step up and become not only father to three lost boys, but also the only son to Frankie and me. And we were in such grief, we were nearly blinded by it. So was my father, who'd come to live with us so he could watch his family grow, and suddenly he had to bury a grandson and watch his great-grandsons struggle with their loss. And then there were Burke and Yancy, whose losses were as great as ours. They may not be blood, but they're family just the same."

Vanessa caught Grace's hand. Squeezed. "I'm sure you all struggled."

Grace nodded. "Of course you understand. Matthew told me you lost your mother as a teen. Once death touches you, you feel vulnerable. You—"

Vanessa finished for her. "—You realize it can happen to you and to all those you love. You can never again take anything for granted. In the blink of an eye, it can all be taken away."

Grace stood and wrapped her arms around Vanessa, and the two women embraced, letting the tears flow as they shared a strange and painful bond.

For Vanessa, it was an epiphany. She had never before shared her grief with a woman who had likewise suffered such loss.

They'd hiked for several hours before Grace suddenly held up a hand and pointed.

Vanessa was stopped in her tracks by the sight of a herd of horses just ahead. Their leader, a ghostly gray stallion, stood a little apart from the others, head lifted in the air, alert to any danger.

Grace pointed again, and Vanessa smiled at the black-and-white spotted mare calmly grazing while her foal nursed.

Vanessa stood perfectly still, savoring her first view of wild horses. Though she remained quiet, she was doing somersaults inside. In her mind she was wildly dancing and singing and clapping her hands in sheer delight.

She was really here. In the Montana wilderness, just a hundred yards away from a herd of mustangs.

She wasn't even aware that she was crying until Grace drew an arm around her waist and offered her a handkerchief.

Surprised, she dabbed at the moisture running down her cheeks.

"I understand," Grace whispered. "I've had that same reaction so many times."

Hearing her, Vanessa got past her embarrassment over being all weepy, and simply savored the moment.

She was here. The horses were here. And her heart was nearly bursting with a feeling of wild joy.

They spent the rest of the day watching the herd.

Vanessa had assumed Grace would move closer and maybe even walk among them. But all the older woman did was sit on the boulder, aiming her camera at the various mares, and often at the stallion, snapping off picture after picture.

By the time the sun had made its arc over the distant mountains, Grace beckoned Vanessa to follow, and they made their way back to camp.

Once they were out of sight of the herd, Vanessa was free to give voice to her enthusiasm.

"Oh Gracie, I can't believe I'm here, doing something I've always dreamed of doing. I admitted to Matt that I was horse crazy as a young girl. I wouldn't let up until my parents allowed me to take jumping lessons at a nearby stable. And then I grew up and life and work got in the way. But now...these wild horses..." She gave a dreamy sigh. "It's my dream come true. They're so beautiful. And those foals. Just so precious." She danced around, unable to contain herself any longer.

Then she paused as a thought struck. "Did you see the way the stallion watched us?"

"I saw."

"Was he thinking of charging us if we moved too close?"

Grace chuckled. "If we were predators, he would. But with people, whenever he feels threatened, he simply leads his herd to safety."

"So he knows the difference between people and other animals?"

Grace smiled. "Indeed. And because this herd is so isolated, he may not even feel threatened if we moved among them. But for today, I wanted to let him get used to seeing us."

"Did you see how many mares had foals?"

"Six. I counted them."

"I did, too. They're so cute. I could hardly keep from dashing into their midst and hugging them."

"I wouldn't advise it, Nessa." Grace gave a dry laugh. "Did you see the roan mare? The red one? She looks like she'll foal any day now."

"Do you think you'll get to capture it on film?"

"Oh, I hope so." After walking around their campsite, quietly studying the truck and their gear, Grace went to her camera equipment, sorting through lenses and cameras. "I hope you don't mind if I delay fixing something to eat until after I've assembled everything I'll need to take along tomorrow."

"You do that, and let me handle fixing our supper."

"You don't mind, Nessa?"

"I'd love to. After all, Yancy did all the hard work. All I have to do is choose what to heat up." Vanessa opened the metal container and began rummaging through the labeled packages of prepared food. "Do you have anything in particular you'd like to eat, or would you like to be surprised?"

"Surprise me."

Later as they sat around the fire, contentedly enjoying Yancy's thinly shaved roast beef sandwiches with thick potato wedges and creamy coleslaw, Grace looked over. "Excellent choices, Nessa."

"Thanks. Not that it matters. I don't think Yancy is capable of fixing anything except the best." She bit into her last potato wedge. "How long has he been your ranch cook?"

"I guess it's over thirty years now."

"How did you find him? Did you advertise for a cook?"

"Advertise? I'm afraid not. It didn't happen that way." Grace sat back, sipping coffee. "It was late October or early November, as I recall. My son Patrick heard a knock on the door long after dark. He opened it and we heard him let out a furious oath." She shook her head. "Frankie hurried over to see who was there. Burke was carrying a boy, who looked to be about ten or twelve, who had blood dripping from a gash on his forehead, and he was barefoot. I don't know which was more shocking—the blood or the bare feet on such a cold night. Burke said he found the boy collapsed in our barn, trying to hide under the straw. The boy could barely walk, he was so exhausted and wounded, so Burke carried him inside and set him in front of the fire, while I ran around looking for a blanket to wrap him in. Just about that time there was a pounding on the door, and Frankie opened it to a man with a rifle in his arms and fire in his eyes. He said he was Rhys Martin, looking for his no-good son Yancy. Frankie told him he had to leave the rifle outside if he wanted to come in. So he dropped the rifle, and when he spotted the boy he was across the room in a flash and hauling him up so he could pound his fist in his face. Burke and Patrick pulled them apart, and when they got the man to settle down enough to say his piece, they learned that this boy was actually eighteen, even though he was no bigger than a ten-year-old. Rhys Martin blamed his own son for all the setbacks in his life. Because of 'this scrawny kid,' as he called him, his wife had died while giving birth to him. And ever since, all manner of bad things had happened. Cows were dying. Crops were failing. He was losing his ranch."

Vanessa couldn't hide her shock. "He thought it was all his son's fault?"

Grace nodded. "His whole life, according to Rhys Martin, was ruined because of this boy. And he was going to beat some manliness into him, if it was the last thing he ever did."

Vanessa was wringing her hands, clearly caught up in what she was hearing. "What happened then?"

Grace gave a soft smile. "We all listened in silence, and then Frank asked Yancy if what his pa said was true. Yancy said it was. Nothing had ever gone right since he'd been born. And his father held him accountable for every bad thing that had ever happened. Then Frankie asked the father if he loved his boy. Rhys Martin asked how anyone could love a misfit like that. He said not only did he not love Yancy, but he wished he'd never been born." Grace's voice lowered. Softened. "For my Frankie, that was the last straw. He told Burke to call the sheriff. Rhys Martin ran out the door, knowing he'd be arrested for abuse. Frankie raced to the door to let him know that Rhys would never be allowed to come close to his boy again. And if the sheriff found him, we would all testify against him."

"Did the sheriff find Rhys Martin?"

"There was no sign of him. He left his failing ranch behind, without a trace."

"Did Yancy ever see his father again?"

Grace shook her head. "And never wanted to. He once confided in Frankie that he believes he was born on that fateful night. Living with us, taking such joy in cooking, he found the life he'd always wanted, and he was never going back."

Vanessa poured herself another cup of coffee. "My dad likes to say that everyone has a story to tell."

"I'm sure, as a district attorney, your father hears more stories than most."

Vanessa nodded, deep in thought. "You realize you saved Yancy's life."

"We did. But he has more than repaid us in his loyalty and generosity to our family."

"I can understand why. What a hellish childhood he must have had."

"And what a good man he's become."

A short time later, as the two of them cleaned up the remains of their supper and slid into their bedrolls, Vanessa thought about the sweet cook who always had a big smile and an even bigger heart.

However painful his childhood had been, he'd risen above it.

And it was no surprise to her that the Malloy family had been Yancy's guardian angels. From everything she'd seen of them, they had the most open, loving, welcoming hearts for anyone fortunate enough to enter into and be touched by their lives.

CHAPTER SEVENTEEN

Grace was up before dawn, and the sounds of her movements had Vanessa sitting up and shoving hair from her eyes.

Grace set a coffeepot over the fire before looking up. "Good morning. How did you sleep?"

"I don't think I moved all night."

"Are you sore from all that hiking?"

"A little." Vanessa rolled her shoulders. "Nothing I can't manage. I just feel...eager to get back to the herd."

Grace laughed. "Spoken like a true adventurer. Let's eat and get started."

Within minutes Vanessa was dressed and had stored her bedding in the back of the truck.

"We'll need to bring along enough food and water to get us through the day and night."

Vanessa's eyes went wide. "We're staying with the herd?"

"Possibly." Grace gave a mysterious smile. "It will all depend on our mare. She may have already given birth. If so, we'll be there and back in no time. But if I get a chance to photograph the entire delivery, we'll stay until it's over, regardless of the time it takes."

Vanessa put a hand to her heart. "Oh, Grace, I hope we get there in time."

They ate quickly, then filled their backpacks with what they would need for the day and night, choosing to leave their bedrolls at camp and take only warm parkas for the night.

They were on the trail within the hour. And by the time they reached the herd, the sun was just climbing above the peaks of the nearby mountains.

They quickly scanned the horses, holding their breath as they counted the mares and their foals.

"The same number as yesterday," Grace whispered.

"That's good. Right?"

Grace nodded and pointed. Not far away was the mare they'd spotted the previous day, so swollen it looked as though she might explode if she didn't soon give birth.

Grace began assembling her equipment.

Vanessa watched with interest as the older woman set up a tripod, chose from an array of lenses, and then fixed one to a camera that she then mounted on the tripod. She kept a second camera dangling around her neck. In a bag at her feet were several more cameras and dozens of lenses.

The two sat down beside a boulder and watched the herd in silence.

Following Grace's lead, Vanessa learned to remove her water bottle, or a packet of food, with as little sound and movement as necessary, so as to not draw attention. Though the stallion, whom Vanessa had secretly named Ghost, continued to stand watch, he had also begun moving among the mares, even turning his back on the women to graze.

"You see," Grace said in a low tone. "He's beginning to accept our presence here."

"That's good?"

"That's very good."

In the hours that followed, the two women shared food and several long, impassioned discussions about the wild horses, and what role animal groups and the government ought to play in their lives.

It was clear, from the fervor in Grace's tone, that she believed the mustangs should be left alone as much as possible, to roam free and live as they always had.

"What about the freezing cold? What about starvation when snow covers their source of food?" Vanessa pressed the issues that were uppermost in the minds of the members of her various animal associations.

"These are wild creatures. Nature equips them to survive the cold. Unlike domestic animals, they grow a thicker, coarser coat that can see them through the coldest temperatures. They've learned to adapt. Whether it's a blizzard or a raging summer storm, they figure things out."

"Are you saying you've never fed them?"

Grace gave a mysterious half smile. "Frankie and I have hauled tons of hay up here on a flatbed truck when Mother Nature turned on us and delivered a killing winter. But if we didn't help out, most of these horses would survive, just as they have all these centuries."

Vanessa pressed her. "But some would die."

The older woman leaned close. "Here's the difference between hauling some feed, and meddling. Some years back, someone concerned about the herds of wild horses decided that they ought to set up some feeding stations and put birth control in the food. It stands to reason that would be the humane method of curbing the size of the herds. Right?"

Vanessa nodded. "Sounds sensible to me."

"Consider this." Grace's tone took on that of a lecturer. "Nature dictates a time for everything. That's why, in the wild, creatures give birth in spring, when there's an abundance of food for the mothers who nurse, and a gentle climate in which to raise up the young so they're strong enough to face winter's wrath."

"Well, yes, that makes sense."

"Except to the agency who messed with nature. Within a year or two, after the herds wandered hundreds of miles from the feeding stations, the birth control wore off, and many of the animals began conceiving at the wrong time of year. I came across mares that had foaled in the dead of winter, long before their natural cycle would have dictated. With little food, the mares' milk dried up. With several feet of snow on the ground, the foals couldn't move. Since a mother couldn't leave her foal behind, often both mare and foal froze to death in a blizzard. Those poor, vulnerable animals never had a chance."

Vanessa put a hand to her mouth, her eyes wide with shock. "Didn't those in charge research all of this before they started the project?"

"Apparently the clever committee that dreamed up the plan never gave it a thought. Often, within large agencies, compassion for the very ones they're supposed to be taking care of isn't high on the list." Grace paused. "I sent some of the photos to Washington to let them see the damage that had been caused. I never got a response."

"Oh, Grace." Vanessa was clearly moved. "I'm so sorry."

The older woman touched a hand to her arm. "Actions have consequences. So often we want to do the right thing, but if we don't think things through, we pay a high price for our well-meaning decisions."

Seeing the herd moving closer, the two women fell silent. But it was clear that the things Grace had told her left Vanessa deep in thought.

Grace lifted a hand in a silent signal.

Vanessa glanced across the field to where the heavily pregnant mare was standing. At first there was nothing to set her apart from the other mares nearby, except her size. Though Vanessa would expect the mare to be agitated, or breathing heavily, all she could see was a calm, quiet horse circling a patch of grass, but not eating.

Circling. Circling.

As though seeking a soft spot to recline.

Within the hour the mare folded her forelegs, kneeling, before dropping down in the grass. She remained very still, lying on her side, though her breathing had increased considerably.

Vanessa glanced at Grace. Between the camera mounted on the tripod and the wide-angle lens on the camera around her neck, Grace was busy catching each amazing moment on film.

A short time later Vanessa realized that the foal was coming quickly now. A gush of water, a tiny hoof visible through the opaque film of fluid, and suddenly, the foal slipped free of its mother and lay in the grass, while the mare licked it clean.

"It's so tiny and helpless."

"Only for a short time." Grace kept her focus on the mare and foal. "You won't believe how quickly that little one will be on its feet and trailing after its mother."

"Oh, Grace." Vanessa clutched the older woman's arm, so caught up in the beauty of the birth she could hardly speak.

"I know." Grace's smile was radiant. "Isn't it the most amazing sight? Every time I have the good fortune to witness such a miracle, I'm humbled and grateful."

As Grace went back to snapping off photos, Vanessa's attention was riveted on the mare and her foal.

As a girl she'd loved horses. So much so, she'd used every argument she could think of to persuade her parents to allow her to ride jumpers. And despite her mother's great fear that her only child might be seriously injured partaking in such a dangerous activity, she had reluctantly given her permission. But only, she insisted, because she could see the passion that burned in her daughter for the horses.

That passion had never died, but it had faded in her teen years. She'd thought her efforts on behalf of the animal foundations had been enough to feed that passion. Now, suddenly, in this amazing moment, it was back, and stronger than ever. Now, finally, she understood why she'd forsaken criminal law to become an advocate for the protection of wild animals. And why she'd been drawn to interview Grace Anne LaRou Malloy, the foremost expert on the West's wild horses.

She needed to be here. Right here in the Montana

wilderness, watching the birth of a foal, and thrilling to the very fact that a wild stallion, feeling edgy and protective of his herd, was allowing her to be this close to them.

Because of her father, and her government association, she'd met many famous dignitaries, even world leaders. But none could even come close to this singular experience.

Her heart was beating overtime just knowing she was, right this moment, living her childhood dream.

"Oh, Grace. I'll never be able to thank you for this experience. For this day."

"I believe this is the hundredth time you've thanked me, Nessa." Grace hefted her backpack, relieved to see their campsite up ahead. It had been a long, emotional day, and now that the adrenaline was wearing off, she could feel her energy flagging. She would be grateful for the chance to relax and unwind.

Vanessa's laughter trilled on the air. "I know. I just can't stop thanking you. This has been the most amazing day of my life." Seeing the older woman's concentration, Vanessa stopped her. "Here. Give me your pack."

"I can manage. I always—"

Vanessa took it from her and draped it across one shoulder. As she started to bolt ahead, Grace put a hand to her shoulder. "Wait. I'd like to..."

Vanessa paused. "What?"

Grace's smile stayed in place. "Nothing. I just like to check out my surroundings before I go stumbling into camp."

"Did you do this the other times we returned?"

"Of course. I arranged certain things in certain ways,

knowing if they were altered, it would mean we'd had visitors."

Because she was wearing sunglasses, Vanessa couldn't see the older woman's eyes. But she could see her swivel her head slightly, taking in the lay of the land.

Vanessa felt a prickling at the back of her neck. "Do you see something?"

"It could be nothing." Laying a hand on her arm, Grace signaled her to remain behind as she paused to pick up a zipper pull that must have fallen from a parka. "Did you lose this?"

Vanessa shook her head.

"I don't believe it was here this morning." Holding it in her hand, Grace walked to the truck and tested the driver's side door.

Though it was locked, she dropped to her knees and retrieved a piece of thread from the grass. When she stood, she plucked her phone from her pocket. Seeing that it had no signal, she lifted her rifle in the air and fired a shot.

The sound of it echoed and reechoed across the hills.

Vanessa flinched at the sound of the thunder of the gunshot matching the thundering of her heart. She hurried to stand beside Grace. "What's wrong? Are we in trouble? Has somebody been here?"

Grace nodded. "I need to see if anything's missing."

While the two worked side by side checking their supplies, a horse and rider appeared over a ridge.

Vanessa stared in stunned surprise to see Matt dismount and hurry over.

"Your grandmother only fired her rifle a minute ago. How could you possibly get here so quickly?"

"I was...nearby."

He turned to his grandmother, who pointed to the truck. "I did what you told me, Matthew. I tied a thread to the door handle." She held out the piece of thread. "I found this in the grass. Torn in two. Have you seen anything out of order?"

"Not a thing." He walked a short distance away, studying the ground. "The grass isn't flattened by tires or hooves. No tracks. If anyone tried to jimmy the lock, they came here on foot."

"In the middle of the wilderness?"

He nodded. "I know it sounds crazy. But we've been guarding the perimeter since you arrived. No vehicles in or out. That doesn't mean they couldn't have come in by horseback. If there were only one or two of them, they may have managed to sneak past us."

Vanessa knew her jaw dropped. "You've been guarding us?"

Ignoring her question, Grace looked skyward. "A plane? A helicopter?"

"We'd have seen and heard them."

"Then someone went to a lot of trouble to come all this way without taking anything. When they found the doors of the truck locked, they could have broken the windows, or jimmied the locks, and helped themselves to anything they wanted."

Matt's eyes narrowed. "You had your rifle with you?"

She nodded.

"They may have come to steal it, hoping to leave you helpless. But I agree that they could have forced their way inside the truck and helped themselves to the rest of your supplies, unless..."

"Unless what?"

"My first thought is the thread could have simply snapped in the breeze." He shrugged. "Or, if someone was here, maybe they saw the thread after they tried the door, and realized they'd been detected. There was no way to tie it back together and hope you wouldn't notice. So they decided to leave it in the grass just to let you to know they know you're on to them. Even if they couldn't accomplish much, they've managed to add another layer of fear and intimidation."

Grace mulled that for a moment before nodding. "All right. So now we know that they know where we are. But they have to know we'll redouble our efforts to evade them."

"Maybe they spotted our wranglers in the area, and realized they would be caught if they didn't run immediately."

"Maybe." Grace saw the way Vanessa was staring at the two of them, and realized that an explanation was in order. She turned to the young woman and extended a hand. "I'm sorry, Nessa. It isn't right to keep secrets, but I didn't want anything to spoil your first trip to the wilderness, so I thought I'd just keep to myself the fact that our men would be looking out for us."

"I shouldn't be surprised. But now that I know, I feel terrible that my being here has caused so many people to work overtime to keep me safe."

"They're keeping both of us safe. And they don't mind." Grace turned to her grandson. "Do you?"

He kept his gaze firmly on Vanessa. "It's what family does."

Grace glanced at the cold ashes in the firepit. "As long

as you're here, Matthew, why don't you get a fire going and stay for supper?"

"Thanks. I'd love to." He winked at her. "I was hoping you'd ask."

He added a couple of logs and some kindling, and soon had a fire blazing.

Grace started toward the stream to fill the coffeepot, leaving Vanessa alone with Matt.

As soon as Grace was gone, Vanessa crossed her arms over her chest, her tone lowered with righteous accusation. "I had the right to know what this trip was costing you and your family."

"All it cost was manpower, and we have plenty of that."

"Manpower that's needed with the herds. You said yourself it takes every wrangler you have just to keep a ranch of this size working efficiently. And here I am, living out my fantasy at the expense of so many others."

Matt's voice was as calm as hers was harsh. "You're our guest, Nessa." When she opened her mouth to protest, he held up a hand. "Maybe not by your choice, but our guest all the same. And there's no way in hell my family would allow you to be in any more danger than necessary."

She lowered her arms to her sides and turned away. The only indication of her agitation was her booted foot tapping a nervous tattoo. "No more secrets, Matt. I can handle danger better than I can handle being treated like some poor helpless female."

"I can't argue with that. There's nothing helpless about you." He touched a hand to her arm. "Am I forgiven?"

She kept her face averted. "Of course. As long as you

give me your word you won't shut me out of any decisions being made about my safety."

"You have it."

"Good." She huffed out a breath before turning toward the truck.

She rummaged through the supplies in the metal container, noting Yancy's careful labeling of each packet.

Matt stepped up beside her. "Need some help?"

She held up two packets. "I'll let you decide. Turkey and stuffing, or roast beef and gravy?"

"Turkey." He held out his hand. "I'll set it on the grate."

She found a packet of mashed potatoes and walked up behind him. "You can heat these, too. And I'll find that container of salad I spotted yesterday."

They worked companionably together, assembling plates and utensils.

When at last Vanessa dropped down on a sun-warmed rock, Matt sat beside her. "So. Has your wilderness experience been all you'd hoped for?"

"Oh, Matt." She looked up at him, eyes shining with excitement. "It's been amazing. We found a herd. The stallion didn't challenge us, and today we got even closer and watched a foal being born." She shook her head, as though unable to take it all in. "Your grandmother caught it all on film. And it was..." She took in a deep breath. "I know you'll think I'm being melodramatic, but it was magical. I was afraid to move. Afraid even to breathe. I was sure at any moment our presence would spook the herd and they'd scatter. Or worse, I'd wake up and discover it was all just a dream."

He was staring at her in a way that had her going still and silent.

"What's wrong?" she asked.

"Nothing. Just wondering who you are and what you've done with that cool, unemotional workaholic lawyer named Vanessa Kettering."

She started to laugh, but she was cut off as he kissed her. She absorbed little sparks all through her overcharged system.

When he lifted his head she leaned in. "Do that again. Please."

"My pleasure, ma'am." With a wolfish smile he dragged her close and kissed her until they were both breathless. "Want more?"

She put a hand on his chest. "Anything more and I'd have to crawl inside you, which could prove embarrassing when your grandmother returns."

At the mention of Grace, she shot him a puzzled look. "Where is Grace? She was just going to the stream for water."

With the thought of danger uppermost in their minds, they were both up and running, fearing the worst.

Before they were halfway to the stream Grace came strolling toward them, hair dripping, carrying her hiking boots.

"I thought I'd give you two a few minutes alone. And then, once I got there, the cool water looked so inviting, I had to wash." She shot a girlish glance at her grandson. "If you hadn't been here, Matthew, I'd have probably walked back to camp as naked as the day I was born to slip into something clean and warm. But I was feeling charitable, and I decided that wasn't a memory a grandson of mine ought to bear for the rest of his life."

"Thanks for that." He managed a smile, though his

heart was still pounding. "But next time you decide to give us some time alone, don't wander so far away from camp."

Grace turned to Vanessa. "You see? Let a man into your adventure, or your life, and he just has to start giving orders."

CHAPTER EIGHTEEN

Nessa tells me you found a herd." Matt sat in the grass, his back resting against a rock, feet stretched out to the warmth of the fire, enjoying dinner and the pleasant company.

"We did. Not the one I've been looking for this past year, led by that magnificent white stallion." Grace glanced at Vanessa. "This one had a gray leader."

"I named him Ghost," Vanessa admitted.

"You named him?" Matt gave her a bemused look. "Next thing you know, you'll want to take him home with you and make him your pet."

She blushed like a schoolgirl. "I don't know why I admitted that to you. Now I'll probably never hear the end of it."

"You've got that right."

Watching the two of them, Grace couldn't help smiling. "I hope at least a few of the photos I took of a mare delivering her foal are good enough to put up for sale."

"Gram Grace, I've never known any of your pictures to be less than exceptional."

Grace winked at Vanessa. "He's just a little bit prejudiced."

"As he should be." Vanessa set aside her empty plate. "There aren't too many men who can brag about their famous and talented grandmothers."

"Now you sound like my Frankie." Grace sighed. "That man just purely dotes on me."

"I noticed. And I can see why." Vanessa shared a smile with Matt. "Does he ever come with you on these wilderness treks?"

"When he can spare the time. I love having him along. He does all the grunt work and allows me to concentrate on my photography."

Matt chuckled. "Is this an invitation for me to stay and shoulder Grandpop's load?"

"I was hoping you'd take the hint." Grace looked at him over the rim of her cup. "Especially now that we've had proof of a visitor."

"Then it's settled." He put his hands under his head and glanced skyward. "Looks like a perfect night for sleeping under the stars. Especially since I texted the others to let them know I was here."

Grace crossed to him and kissed his cheek. "Bless you, Matthew."

As she walked toward the truck to retrieve her bedroll, Vanessa turned to him. "Your grandfather's not the only one who feels the love. She dotes on you, too."

He merely grinned. "It's my charm."

When she tossed her pillow at his head, he caught it one-handed before dropping it. "Careful, woman," he drawled. "That's an invitation to a duel."

"Pistols at dawn? Will I be branded a troublemaker?"

"I might have something else in mind. But be warned. You'd be branded all the same."

His words, spoken lightly, sent a thrill along her spine.

Grace returned and set out her bedroll near the fire. She snuggled into its warmth and drew up her knees, wrapping her arms around them. "Nessa, tell me how a smart big-city lawyer took up the cause of wild animals. Has this always been your passion?"

Vanessa smiled. "I think so. I wasn't always aware of it, but my dad says he recognized it way back in my earliest days. He tells me I was always the champion of the underdog, including Jeepers, our third-grade mascot."

Grace smiled indulgently. "A dog?"

"A hamster."

Grace exchanged an amused look with Matt before asking, "What made Jeepers an underdog?"

"Over our midwinter break, we came back to discover that the student who had volunteered to take him home for the holiday had forgotten and left him behind in the classroom. The poor little thing was hiding under his empty food dish and shaking so badly when he saw us, our teacher thought he was having a seizure. I insisted on holding him until the tremors subsided. After class I told my teacher I was taking him home so he wouldn't have to be alone overnight."

"So a hamster changed your life." Matt winked at his grandmother.

"Jeepers may have been the start, but it was a coyote while I was in high school that sealed the deal."

"A coyote in Chicago?" Grace was laughing. "This should prove to be quite a story."

"Yes. Poor thing made the headlines. A lost, terrified coyote was spotted dodging cars along Division Street, and before an animal control officer could catch it, a woman screamed that she was afraid for her life and a police officer was forced to shoot it, even though the poor, frightened thing was running away from her, and not toward her. That's when I realized that wild animals needed an advocate."

Grace glanced at her grandson, who was staring at Vanessa with a look that was both fierce and tender.

She'd seen that look before. In her son's eyes when he'd looked at his bride at the age of seventeen. In her husband's eyes the first time Grace had seen him, riding into her camp, demanding to know who she was and why she was on his land. She'd lost her heart to him in an instant, just as he'd lost his heart to her.

She pretended to yawn behind her hand as she slid deeper into her bedroll. "I hope you two don't mind, but after the day I put in, I really need to sleep."

Matt blew her a kiss, while Vanessa called, "Good night, Gracie. Thanks again for this amazing day."

Though Grace could have stayed awake another hour or more, the sound of their muted voices, and the gurgle of the stream nearby, soon lulled her into sleep.

Matt filled two mugs with coffee and held up a bottle of whiskey. At Vanessa's nod of approval, he splashed some into each cup before passing one to her.

He sat beside her, and they leaned against his saddle while stretching their legs toward the fire.

"How do you like sleeping under the stars?"

Her smile was radiant. "I'm loving it."

"Really?" He turned to study her. "You're not missing all the comforts of home?"

"I'm not. And that surprises me. I expected to feel out of my element here. I mean, no showers, no shampoo, no change of clothes. And the bedroll isn't much of a cushion against the hard, cold ground. But—" she sighed "—instead of feeling like a homesick kid at camp, I feel like I was meant to be here."

"I'm glad. I know it can't be easy, finding yourself far from everything familiar."

"That's just it. Though I've never been here before, I feel as though somehow this place has been waiting for me to discover it." She turned to him. "I hope this doesn't sound crazy, but this whole day has been like a dream come true for me. The herd. The mare giving birth. Watching the stallion not only accepting our presence but turning away, ignoring us, as though he'd already figured out that we weren't there to do harm. It was"—she exuded barely controlled excitement and energy—"too amazing for words. And I've embarrassed myself by thanking your grandmother so many times, she's probably sick of hearing my voice."

"I can't imagine anyone who wouldn't enjoy hearing that voice." He lifted a hand to the lock of hair that had drifted across her cheek. He tucked the hair behind her ear, then kept his hand there, his fingers stroking the side of her neck. "You voice is mesmerizing. And so are you, Nessa."

He leaned close and brushed a soft kiss on her lips. She kept her eyes open, seeing herself reflected in his dark gaze.

As he started to pull back she lifted a hand to his cheek. "Could you...? Could you just hold me a little longer?"

"It would be my pleasure, ma'am." He gathered her close.

It started off as a mere touch of mouth to mouth, but it quickly turned into a sizzle of heat that had them sighing as they took it deeper, lingering over the kiss until they were struggling for breath.

Matt glanced toward his grandmother's bedroll. "We'd better think about getting some sleep."

"I should be tired." Vanessa sighed. "But the truth is, I'm so keyed up, I'm not sure I'll be able to sleep at all." As he started to move away she put a hand on his arm. "If I haven't told you, Matt, I'm so relieved to have you here."

"Even though I've intruded on your privacy?"

She bit her lip. "I know I reacted badly, and I'm sorry for that."

"I'm sorry, too. I never wanted anything to spoil your grand adventure."

"I thought it couldn't get any better than today, seeing the herd of mustangs, and the bonus of seeing a foal born. And Grace is so comfortable here in the wilderness that I trust her to know exactly what to do. But in truth, I feel safer having you here with us."

"Careful. I could be your biggest threat of all." He swept another quick kiss over her mouth before getting to his feet. He walked to the far side of the fire and tossed down his saddle before lying beside it. Wrapping a parka around himself, he winked before closing his eyes.

Vanessa smiled and turned to stare into the flames.

She'd been so surprised when Matt had turned up at their camp, just minutes after Grace fired off a shot. And she'd been stunned and horrified to think their entire family and their ranch hands had been forced to forego their own chores in order to keep her safe. Still, the more she thought about it, the more she realized that it gave her great comfort to know Matt had been around the entire time, watching out for their safety.

Watching out for their safety.

It was Matt's way. Seeing to his younger brothers, his uncle, his grandparents. Whether he'd chosen this path, or it had been chosen for him by the Fates, he was singularly qualified to take responsibility for everyone he cared about. The land. The ranch and wranglers. And now, a woman who had come unbidden into his life and couldn't leave until the threat of danger was eliminated. And though she was secretly terrified, not only for herself but for her father, she felt somehow safer knowing Matt was here. His strength, not only physical, but that inner core of steel as well, made her believe that no harm could come to her as long as Matt Malloy was beside her.

It was, she realized, one very compelling reason to love him.

Love?

She rolled to her side, watching the flames flare up, sending sparks into the darkness.

It didn't seem possible that she could have such feelings for a man she hardly knew.

She was attracted to him. She trusted him. And she was

enchanted by his family. Plus, because of him, she was living her dream. But that didn't add up to love. Did it?

Hadn't her father once joked that every young woman he knew fell in love with the idea of love at least once in her life before finding the real thing?

There had been boyfriends, dates, flings, and one rather serious relationship that had ended badly, though in truth she couldn't believe she'd ever shed a tear over such a shallow man. And though she'd had varying degrees of joy and sorrow, over-the-top happiness and moments of sheer bliss, she'd never felt like this. Out of her depth, and floundering, and doing her best to stay one step ahead of a man like Matt.

A man like Matt.

He wasn't like the boys she'd grown up with, the young lawyers she'd competed against, or the men with whom she now worked. There was a toughness to him, a rough-around-the-edges attitude that let you know he meant what he said and did what he thought right, no matter the consequences. He had a shrewd mind. A head for business. Could hold his own in a debate. A true cowboy.

He was a man's man. And yet, he treated her with almost old-fashioned courtliness. He was such a contradiction.

How would she know if what she was feeling was real or some glorified idea of the old fairy tale every child had been fed? Handsome prince discovering the princess of his dreams. Superman and Lois Lane.

But was it love?

She should call it what it was. Lust. Oh yes, now that was something she could admit to. She wanted Matt. Couldn't get him out of her mind. With every day that passed, she found herself more and more tempted by the idea of making love with him. But making love wasn't the same as loving someone completely, unselfishly.

They lived in two very different worlds. When the trial was over, and the threat removed, she would return to her life, and all of this would just be a pleasant memory.

She closed her eyes, weary of the debate she was waging with herself. This need to examine every side of an issue had always been both her blessing and her curse.

For now, for this night, she needed to turn off her logical lawyer's brain and just let it be. It was enough to know that Matt was here, just a few feet away, ready to slay any dragons that threatened.

Not that she needed any help with dragons. She'd been fighting them alone for years now, thank you very much.

But having a partner nearby, someone watching her back, was a real comfort.

It was her last conscious thought before drifting off to sleep.

CHAPTER NINETEEN

The morning was cool and damp. The mountain peaks were cloaked in mist. After a quick breakfast, they packed up the gear they would need for the day and started out across the high meadow.

Matt held his horse's reins loosely, choosing to walk with the women and lead his horse. They had tied their supplies behind the saddle, freeing their hands.

Grace's eyes were crinkled with happiness. "Matthew, I must admit, having you and Beau has lightened our load considerably." She turned to Vanessa, who was walking beside Matt. "Don't you agree, Nessa?"

"Absolutely. Those backpacks were getting heavier each day."

"That's because I kept adding more camera equipment each day, or didn't you notice?"

Vanessa chuckled. "Oh, I noticed." She glanced at Grace's rifle, which Matt had shoved into a boot of the saddle. "I didn't want to admit this, but the last time I carried your rifle, I almost knocked myself out when I turned too quickly."

"That's quite a visual. The next time you're in DC, presenting your thoughts to your wildlife commissions, that ought to keep you grounded."

Matt's dry remark had the three of them laughing.

"I'll leave that part out of it while I brag about my adventures in the Montana wilderness. And I guarantee that I will brag about it."

Matt shot her an admiring glance. "I'll just bet you will."

"You can't blame a girl for doing whatever it takes to impress the bureaucrats in Washington."

Grace nodded in approval. "Oh, I'm sure you've already impressed them, my dear. How many of their young attorneys would bother coming all this way just to see for themselves how their rules and regulations affect the very creatures they're hoping to protect?"

Vanessa's cheeks flamed. "You make me sound noble. The truth is, I'm having the time of my life. I wouldn't trade this for all the personal meetings with congressmen and -women, or those boring cocktail parties I'm forced to attend just to make the proper connections."

Grace looped her arm through Vanessa's. "I'm sure there are a lot of ambitious young lawyers who would be thrilled to have your job."

"Oh, don't get me wrong. I love my job. But these last few days are so far outside my realm of experience. I'd always hoped to have times like this, but I never really believed it was possible." She squeezed Grace's hand. "Thanks to you, I'm living my dream."

* * *

By the time they reached the herd of mustangs, the sun broke from behind the clouds. Soon after, the day quickly heated up. Each time they removed a layer of clothing, Matt stored it in his saddlebags.

Grace set up her cameras, then snapped off shots of the various mares and their precious foals, and often took aim at the majestic stallion, alone and aloof, standing on a sloping meadow, keeping watch over his herd.

Vanessa appointed herself keeper of the equipment. Whenever Grace wanted to move the tripod, or requested a change of lens, or another camera, Vanessa was there to assist. She had soon stripped down to her shorts and a tank top, and was still too warm.

For his part, Matt hauled the supplies, set up a campfire far enough from the herd that they wouldn't be spooked, and prepared a lunch that had both women sighing with pleasure when they finally took a break.

"Matthew, have you been taking lessons from Yancy?" Grace sat in the grass, polishing off the last of her skillet potatoes and roast beef.

He chuckled. "All I did was warm up whatever he sent along."

"It tastes amazing." Vanessa took a long drink from her water bottle.

"Hiking for miles in all this fresh air makes everything taste better." Matt studied the way she looked in denim shorts and a white tank, revealing that willowy body and long, shapely legs. He couldn't keep his eyes off her. It was all he could do to keep from drooling.

At the end of their meal Matt passed around chocolate

chip cookies. "I'll concede that Yancy's cookies could win any baking contest hands down."

"They could indeed." Grace savored every crumb.

A short time later she stood. "Time to get back to the horses. I want to take advantage of all the sunlight I can."

Vanessa held up her water bottle. "I'm heading to the creek to fill this. Anybody else need water?"

Grace shook her head. "I have enough. I'll see you back at the herd."

Vanessa ambled to the stream and knelt on the banks. When she stood, Matt came up behind her and dropped his hands to her waist, pulling her firmly to him.

"I've been thinking about this all morning." He spoke the words against her ear, sending shivers along her spine.

"So have I." She turned into his arms and offered her mouth.

He took it with a hunger that had them both sighing.

Vanessa wrapped her arms around his waist and slid her palms up his back. "I didn't think anything could ever distract me from wild horses, but right now I'm not even tempted to watch the herd. I just want to stay here in your arms."

"Talk about a distraction." He looked her up and down with a smile of pure pleasure. "I don't believe I've ever seen a woman look as sexy in shorts as you look in these."

"Then I'll have to remember to thank Trudy Evans for recommending them."

"I'll just thank heaven for the way you look in them." He nibbled a trail of kisses from her throat to her ear. "You feel so good here, I'd gladly stay for hours. But I'm afraid if you don't go, and soon, my grandmother might stumble across a shocking scene."

She couldn't help batting her lashes at him. "Now that's mighty tempting, cowboy." She gave him one last kiss before pushing free of his arms. "But I really do have an obligation to save Grace from shock."

He turned her into his arms. Against her temple he growled, "It's gotten so bad, I actually found myself praying for rain this morning, just so our fearless leader might be persuaded to head back to the ranch. I figured somewhere between here and there I could get you alone."

She touched a hand to his cheek. "There's always tomorrow."

"Another day?" He groaned. "Woman, you've got a very mean streak in you."

Her smile was quick and dangerous. "So I'm told."

As she started away he bent to pick up the bottle that had slid from her hands. "Don't forget this."

She glanced back, then burst into laughter. "I guess that kiss had my mind a little more muddled than I thought."

"Care to try again?"

She caught the fierce look in his eyes and shook her head. "One more and I'd never be able to leave." She took the bottle from his hands and sprinted up the hill, leaving him staring after her with a look of naked hunger.

Late in the afternoon the clouds returned, completely obliterating the sun.

Grace lowered her camera and glanced at Matt and Vanessa. "Why didn't one of you mention that storm coming in?"

"I didn't want to bother you." Matt was busy loading

her discarded equipment into his saddlebags. "That brooding sky should make for some impressive pictures."

"Until it opens up," Grace remarked drily. She snapped off a few shots of the angry sky before removing the camera from around her neck and placing it in a waterproof case.

Vanessa hurried over to help her pack up the rest of her cameras and lenses.

When they had everything stowed in their backpacks, Matt secured them behind the saddle, and the three of them turned toward their base camp, while keeping an eye on the storm clouds.

They paused at the top of a meadow and caught sight of Frank's truck parked alongside Grace's.

"Oh, Frankie's come to join us." The radiant smile on Grace's face said more than her words. She quickened her pace, and Matt was left to lead his mount more slowly, with Vanessa by his side.

He turned to Vanessa with a smug smile. "My prayers have been answered."

"You wanted another storm?"

He shrugged. "I just wanted anything that would give us an excuse to leave here and slip away by ourselves. Are you game?"

She smiled, and it was answer enough.

By the time they reached the trucks, Grace and Frank were locked in a tender embrace.

Grace stepped back a little, to touch a hand to her husband's cheek. "Is something wrong back at the ranch, or did you just miss me?"

He gave her a smile that banished all the dark clouds.

"I always miss you, Gracie Girl. And there's nothing wrong. I just wanted you here in my arms."

Then he glanced over at Matt holding his horse's reins, as a jagged sliver of lightning streaked the sky, followed by a rumble of thunder. "Storm's rolling in fast."

"I noticed." Matt crossed the distance between them to hug his grandfather.

Frank tugged on a lock of his wife's hair. "You find a herd?"

"I did. Not the big one, but this one had a mare ready to foal, and I caught it all on film."

"I'm glad, my girl. Does that mean you're ready to head home, or do you need more time up here?"

She shook her head. "I have all the pictures I need for now. And with that storm, your timing couldn't be better."

He nodded. "If we play our cards right, we ought to get back to the ranch in time for supper." He turned to Matt. "How about I drive Gracie in my truck, and you and Nessa can ride in Gracie's?"

"That'll work." Matt tied his horse behind Frank's truck. "You mind hauling Beau?"

"Not at all. But why don't you take him?" Before Matt could answer, Frank got busy stashing his wife's camera equipment in the backseat of his truck. "Let's get out of here, before we get blown away. We'll celebrate a successful trip with one of Yancy's fancy chicken dinners."

Matt's tone was deliberately bland. "You might want to eat without us."

Frank sent him an assessing look. "You're staying here?"

Matt gave a negligent shrug of his shoulders. "I

thought I'd check on that old range shack along the way. But you don't have to worry about us. If the storm gets too rough, at least we'll have shelter."

"Sure thing." Frank looked at Matt's horse. "I'll see old Beau gets an extra portion of feed tonight."

"Thanks, Grandpop."

Frank glanced beyond his grandson to the young woman standing quietly to one side. "I guess this is good-bye then. We'll see you back at the ranch, Nessa."

She merely nodded.

Grace hurried over to hug her. "I'm so glad you came with me, Nessa. I've never had a better companion."

"Thank you so much. I've fallen in love with your mustangs. You'll never know what this time in the hills has meant to me."

"I think I do." Grace gave the young woman a final hug before turning away and climbing into the passenger side of the truck.

Frank put the vehicle in gear and, with Beau trotting along behind, they started across the meadow. He watched the young couple in his rearview mirror before turning to his wife. "Did you know that was coming?"

Grace's voice was warm with laughter. "The story about needing to check on the range shack?"

He chuckled. "Then you're not buying it either?"

"Not a word of it." She laced her fingers with his. "I'm not sure they're even aware of how much their eyes reveal. But Frankie, those two are head over heels. And tumbling faster every minute."

He squeezed her hand and put a foot on the brake. "Want to go back and rain on their parade?"

"Don't even think about it." She patted his shoulder.

"Though it would be great fun to see their faces if we showed up to spoil all their plans."

He paused for a moment more before leaning over to kiss her mouth. "Okay. I'll go along with whatever you say. But only because if I turned back now, I'd ruin my carefully planned night alone with you, Gracie Girl. I have to say, that bed's been awfully empty without you."

He turned on the radio, and the two of them began humming along with Barbara Mandrell and the old country-and-western tune about sleeping single in a double bed. That had them both laughing out loud as Frank carefully navigated the rolling hills and meadows that spread out before them, leading them home.

CHAPTER TWENTY

Matt watched his grandfather's truck until it dipped below a ridge.

When he turned, Vanessa was staring at him with a puzzled look. "You need to check out a range shack?"

"Yeah." He circled the truck and opened the passenger door, helping Vanessa inside before walking to the driver's side, climbing in, and putting the vehicle in gear.

"Is it nearby?"

He seemed to be deep in thought. "What?"

"The range shack."

"Oh." The corners of his lips curved slightly. "It's a fair distance, but it was the best I could come up with on such short notice."

She removed her wide-brimmed hat and shook her hair. "You're not making any sense."

"I know. That's what you do to me."

She was grinning. "Now this is all my fault?"

"You bet. If you weren't wearing those sexy shorts and that second skin you call a tank top, I'd have probably had enough self-control to head home. But now, having been forced to spend the day looking at you, I'm barely holding it together."

"Ah." She said the word on a sigh as the truth dawned. "This is all just an excuse to get me alone."

"Now you're thinking." He shot her a dangerous smile. "Alone and naked."

"Couldn't you have come up with something a bit more believable than checking out a range shack?"

"Do you object?"

"Not at all, cowboy. Although I do object to having to drive a fair distance."

"We could always stop right here."

She glanced at the black, swirling clouds overhead. "Not on your life. I want shelter from this soon-to-hit storm, and I want it as fast as possible."

"Yes, ma'am." He floored the accelerator and the two of them were laughing like children as they flew up ridges and down gullies until, at last, they caught sight of a cabin looming in the distance.

She turned to him with a look of surprise. "Isn't this the same cabin where we first met?"

"It is."

"Well, aren't you the clever one."

"Yes, ma'am. I am. Or at least I try to be, as I said, on short notice."

He pulled up beside the cabin and helped her from the truck. Before they could take a single step his arms were around her, dragging her close in a fierce embrace. "I know we should get inside, but this can't wait."

His hungry mouth found hers and nearly devoured her.

She responded with equal hunger, her arms around his neck, holding on to him like a lifeline as a wicked wind blew up and buffeted them with such force it nearly blew them apart.

They were so caught up in the kiss, they were startled when the sky opened up and they were hit with a drenching rain.

Matt lifted his head, struggling to get his bearings. "Sorry. Looks like we didn't beat the storm after all. My key..." He fumbled in his pocket before turning toward the door, all the while keeping his arm firmly around Vanessa to shield her.

As he struggled to unlock the cabin door, she put a hand over his. "Let me help."

"Or we could just stand out here and try that kiss again."

"Not until you get me out of this rain."

Laughing, they turned the lock and stumbled inside.

"Oh yeah. This is better." He backed her against the closed door before pressing his body to hers and taking her mouth in a kiss so filled with desperate need it had her head spinning.

She kissed him back, pouring herself into it, impatient for more, until they were both struggling for breath.

"I need to..." He stripped away her tank, revealing a tiny nude silk bra that had his eyes narrowing. "Oh, lady, you do know how to get my blood hot."

"You're welcome." Her lips curved as she reached for the buttons of his shirt.

As it dropped to the floor she ran her hands up his arms, across his shoulders, and down his chest, making little humming sounds as she did. "You have the most amazing body."

"Why, thank you for noticing, ma'am. It's all yours. Do with me what you want."

She gave a tortured laugh. "That's really generous of you."

"Anything for my lady." He shucked his boots and jeans and dragged her close, pressing hot, wet kisses to the sensitive hollow between her neck and shoulder.

She arched her neck, loving the feel of his clever mouth on her flesh. But when he moved lower, down her throat, then lower still, to take one erect nipple into his mouth, all she could do was sigh and clutch blindly at his waist.

As he moved from one breast to the other, the pleasure continued building until it became so intense, she whispered, "Matt. Please. I don't think I can wait."

"Now I'm 'Matt' instead of 'cowboy.' "

"I thought that would get your attention faster."

"You have my complete attention, Nessa." He tugged away her shorts and the tiny nude bikini beneath.

For the space of a heartbeat, all he could do was stare. "God, you're incredible. I can't wait to get my hands on you."

And he did. Touching her everywhere. With teeth and tongue and fingertips he took her on a wild, dizzying roller-coaster ride that had her writhing with frantic need and trembling for more.

"Matt . . ." When she touched him as he was touching her, she could feel the raw passion blazing through him.

The moment her hands came in contact with him, he

pressed her back against the rough door and kissed her until they were both struggling for breath.

His eyes were fixed on hers. "I thought I could be civilized, and show you all kinds of clever, seductive moves, but I can't wait. I need you now, Nessa. This minute."

With her back to the rough door he lifted her off her feet.

"Yes." The single word was torn from her dry throat. She could barely speak over the feelings that had completely taken over. "I need you, too. Now." She wrapped herself around him and let her head drop back as he thrust into her.

Her body had become a mass of nerve endings. Raw. Sensitive. She could feel him in every pore. His hands, those wonderful, calloused, rough hands, moving over her. His mouth burning a trail of heat down her throat.

He began to move with agonizing, deliberate slowness, and with each thrust she was moving with him, desperate to find release.

His thundering heartbeat kept time with hers.

As his movements increased, she moved with him, climbing frantically upward, higher, then higher still.

She could feel him pulsing with that same need, and rockets began going off in her head.

Her heart racing, her breath hitching, she climbed up and up, moving with him until behind her closed lids, brilliant fireworks exploded.

At his shuddering response she opened her eyes to see herself reflected in his blue depths, and could feel her body, her mind, her heart exploding in a shattering climax.

She shattered into fiery pieces before drifting slowly to earth.

"Sorry." Matt's face was buried in the hollow of her throat.

"Umm. For what?"

He knew he could die happy now. Or maybe he had. Maybe this was heaven. "I was rough." He struggled to lift his head. He looked into Vanessa's eyes. "I really intended to get us to the bed."

"There's always next time."

His smile bloomed. "So you'll go for seconds?"

"Or thirds." She managed to move enough to bring a hand to his cheek. "As long as you promise you'll do all that again."

"Deal. In fact, I really wanted to do more. Lots more. But then I lost control."

"Did you ever."

"And it's all your fault. You and that sexy smile."

"I thought it was my sexy shorts and tank."

"Those, too." He caught her by the shoulders. "You okay?"

"A little weak in the knees. Hold on to me."

"Happy to. I'll never let you fall."

"I know. That's one of the many things I lov—" she caught herself in time and said simply "—like about you."

He lowered his head and took her mouth. "That was pretty amazing."

"Yeah." She heard the torrent of rain on the roof. "Did I imagine fireworks?"

"I thought I heard some. Saw bright lights, too."

She nodded. "Exactly. That was some trick, cowboy."

"Wait till you see what else I can do."

"You going to show me?"

"You bet." He scooped her up and carried her across the room to the bed. "This is a tight space, but then I don't think either of us will complain."

"Not on your life. Now"—she wrapped her arms around his neck—"about those things you're going to show me..."

"Did anybody ever tell you you're a glutton, lady?"

"Hey. I've been on a starvation diet."

"Me, too." He nibbled her shoulder. "And now, if you don't mind, I'd like to feast—" he moved lower, and heard her little hum of pleasure "—on you."

Vanessa stirred and felt the mattress sag seconds before she looked up to see Matt beside her, holding out a glass of red wine.

She shoved hair from her eyes and sat up. "I can't believe I dozed in the middle of the day."

"Only for a few minutes. And only because you had some great exercise." He handed her the wine and settled himself beside her in the narrow bunk. "It gave me time to haul in the supplies."

Thunder boomed overhead, shaking the cabin. "It's still storming."

"From the looks of things, it may rain all night."

"Gee." She shot him a sideways glance. "How original. A storm holding us captive in this cabin, far from civilization. Whatever will we do?"

He laughed and reached for a second glass of wine on the small night table beside the bed. "Don't you worry your head, little lady. We'll think of something. Especially since you're already naked and in my bed."

"I figure I played hard to get long enough, cowboy."

"Yes, you did. And nearly drove me around the bend, woman."

"Now I'll make it easier. I'm all yours."

He drew an arm around her. "I feel like I won the lottery."

"Yeah. I'm feeling like a winner, myself." She turned to him. "This wine is really good."

"From a friend's vineyard."

"They have vineyards in Montana?"

He smiled. "Italy. Last time I was there I toured his wife's family vineyard and they shipped me a couple of cases. I told Burke to haul some up here whenever they arrived at the ranch."

"Italy. You do get around, don't you?"

"I do." His tone lowered, deepened as he kissed the tip of her nose. "But right now, there's nowhere I'd rather be than here. With you."

"I'm glad." She set aside her wine and wrapped herself around him. "I hope you don't mind if I snuggle."

He set his glass beside hers and gathered her firmly against him. "I think, Miss Kettering..." He felt the need rising again, and wondered how in the world he'd managed to wait so long for this woman. "I think snuggling is the perfect thing to do during a Montana thunderstorm. In fact, we should have tried this that first time we were up here."

She was smiling, a lazy cat's smile. "It wouldn't have been at all professional of me to snuggle with a man I'd only just met."

"I guess not. But it would have been a hell of lot more fun than discussing government regulations regarding wildlife."

And then there were no words as they shut out the thunder, the lightning, the whole universe, and lost themselves in their newly discovered world of lovemaking.

CHAPTER TWENTY-ONE

Vanessa stirred as Matt slid from the bed. "Where are you going?"

The cabin was dark, except for the glowing embers on the grate. The sky outside the window was midnight black. Though the thunder and lightning had ceased, a steady rain beat a tattoo on the roof.

"I'm going to feed you."

"Now? In the middle of the night?"

"I don't know about you, but I'm ravenous. And after all that exercise, I need to restore my energy—" he bent and kissed her mouth "—for the next round."

"You make it sound like a prizefight."

"More like a marathon. And we're both winning the race."

She chuckled. "All right. Now that I'm a winner, and awake, I'll give you a hand with our midnight supper."

She reached for his shirt, still on the floor where they'd left it, to cover her nakedness.

Matt was barefoot and stripped to the waist, wearing only his jeans, which were unsnapped.

She followed him to the little galley kitchen. "I'm glad you thought to bring along the last of our supplies. Was that by design or accident?"

He shot her a grin. "It was no accident. The minute I knew we were leaving that mountain retreat and I was going to be driving Gram Gracie's truck, I decided to confiscate whatever was left."

"Aren't you the sly one." She opened the metal container and removed several packets. "Chicken or steak?"

"Definitely steak." At her look he added, "It goes with red wine."

"Of course." She held up another packet. "Rice or potatoes?"

"I'll let you choose the rest."

"A mystery feast then." She set aside several packets and arranged the food on a cooking tin, which she then set over the hot coals.

While their food heated, Matt tossed a salad and divided it into two bowls, which he carried to the low table set in front of the fire, along with the bottle of wine.

A short time later, with a log blazing on the fire, and their meal ready, they sat, sipping wine and enjoying sizzling steak and twice-baked potatoes loaded with chives and cheese and sour cream, as well as a salad dressed with Yancy's balsamic-vinegar-and-oil.

With a plaid afghan around her shoulders, Vanessa gave a sigh of contentment as she finished every bite. "I wouldn't trade this moment for the fanciest meal anywhere in the world."

"Have you traveled the world?"

"Some. England, Scotland, Ireland." She thought a moment. "Spain. And the Greek islands."

"Italy?"

She shook her head. "That's on my to-do list. How about you? Besides Italy, of course."

He topped off her glass. "All the places you mentioned. Plus Iceland."

"Really?" She turned to him. "Why?"

"They import everything. And one of the things they import is Malloy beef."

"That's pretty impressive."

He smiled and reached over to play with a tangle of her hair that had slipped forward. "I was hoping to impress you."

She absorbed the little tingle of pleasure at his touch. "You don't need to. I'm already impressed by everything I've seen here."

"And I'm impressed by what I'm seeing." He took the glass from her hand and set it on the table beside his before leaning close to kiss her. "I could look at you all day every day for the rest of my life and never get tired of what I'm seeing."

With a sigh she wrapped her arms around his neck. "Same goes for me, cowboy. Who would have believed a hardworking rancher could be such eye candy?"

"You're just trying to flatter me so you can have your way with me."

"Maybe." She looked up at him and batted her lashes. "Is it working?"

"You bet."

They came together in a slow, languid dance of love.

Matt set a fresh log on the fire before joining Vanessa in bed. They sat side by side, listening to the soft patter of rain, sipping fresh coffee, and talking.

"That day we took a ride across the hills, you told me your grandmother is a pilot. I haven't been able to put that out of my mind. I'm so impressed by her. How did that happen?"

"When she married Grandpop, there wasn't much civilization around these parts except for a few dirt roads. The quickest way to anywhere was to fly, and at first she relied on her Frankie to take her. But then, after she found herself alone on a ranch with two sons, and Grandpop often a hundred miles away with a herd on one of the mountains, she figured she'd better learn to take care of herself. It was just a natural progression that my dad and uncle got their pilot's licenses as soon as they were old enough. And just as natural that my brothers and I would do the same."

"Do you remember the night your parents died?"

Matt's eyes narrowed slightly. "It's seared into my memory. The family in shock. The sheriff and Archer Stone, his deputy, trying to make sense of it. And the Great One, really agitated after returning from the crash scene."

"He went there?"

"With his movie camera. He recorded everything he could. It's just second nature to him. The snow-covered highway. The mangled car. The two blanket-covered bodies by the side of the road."

Vanessa shook her head. "I don't know how he could bear to even look at something so painful and brutal. Something so close to his heart."

"He felt responsible."

Her eyes widened. "Why?"

"He'd loaned his fancy car, the one he'd brought with him from Hollywood, to my folks for a night in town. Mom and Dad were so excited. Nobody ever drove that Rolls. It was parked in the barn, and probably would still be sitting there, unused, but the Great One urged them to take it as a special treat."

"Oh, that poor old dear. No wonder he felt responsible."

"The Great One believes this was no accident. He believes it was something sinister, and that there was a second pair of tire marks in the snow that night. We've all looked at the film, and we all agree there are other marks, but the authorities insist they were made by all the people who intruded on the scene. Besides the sheriff's squad car and his deputy's, there was a rancher passing by who saw the fireball, and a couple of wranglers tending a herd who heard the crash. And then my uncle and grandfather, who drove the Great One to the site. And there's no disputing that there were way too many tire marks littering the crash site. According to the official report, it was just a terrible case of speed, a driver handling an unfamiliar vehicle during a snowstorm, and a layer of ice that made the roads dangerously slick."

"Does your great-grandfather ever talk about it?"

"Not to us. He knows how painful it is. But I've come upon him discussing it with Yancy. Both of them are obsessed with long-ago Hollywood crimes, and I think they're always trying to find a similarity between them and our family tragedy. But the minute any of us walk in, he changes the subject. Still, I doubt he'll ever let go of his belief that a crime was committed. And it may have been avoided if my father had been driving one of the ranch trucks instead of a fancy Rolls Royce."

Vanessa brushed a kiss to Matt's shoulder. "How awful that he carries that guilt."

"Yeah." Matt stepped out of bed to retrieve the coffeepot from the fire and topped off their cups before climbing beneath the blankets.

He drew an arm around her shoulders, determined to change the subject. Even after all these years, he found it too painful to think about. "It has to be tough not hearing from your father the last few days, especially with everything that's been going on. I know you two are close."

"That's the hardest part of all this. We've always talked every day. And now, with this blackout, I don't even know how he's doing. Not personally, and not with the trial."

"I'm sure he's missing you every bit as much as you miss him. But from what I've read about him, he's tough as nails."

"That's the reputation the press gave him. The Iceman. But they don't know the man I know."

"No one ever knows family except those intimately involved." He linked his fingers with hers. "Tell me about him."

It was the best thing he could have said. It was like opening a dam.

"When I was little, he was busy working every case he could. My mom and I did everything together. And then, when I was thirteen, and my mother got sick, I remember him being home for days at a time. I kept pestering him with questions, but he was really good at evading. And then one day he just sat me down to explain that my mom wasn't getting better. That all the treatments weren't helping. And then he told me that she had cancer, and I was so scared, and so angry at him for keeping that secret from me when I could have been—" she paused "—nicer to her. Kinder. I could have tuned into her needs instead of selfishly worrying about school and tests and friends." She took in a breath. "I told him I felt cheated. He understood my anger. And he promised me that he would never again keep anything from me."

"And then I did the same thing as your father. I thought I'd spare you by handling things myself."

"Exactly. I hate being afraid. But even more, I can't stand being kept in the dark. I have a right to know what's going on, so I can find a way to deal with it."

The lines of worry in her face relaxed. Her voice lowered, softened. "As for my dad, once we got past the secrets, we formed a pact. And now, he's just the best father. He really cares about everything I do. After my mother passed away, he did double duty, being both father and mother to me. He never missed a school event. He even took off work whenever there was a parent-teacher meeting or an after-school activity. He was just always there for me." She sighed. "And now I can't even imagine how hard it must be for him to pour himself into all the details of this trial while being forced to trust his daughter's safety to others."

"I'm sure he has plenty of eyes and ears. Not just the Chicago PD but any private investigators they've brought onto the case. You're the daughter of an elected official. They're all feeling responsible for your safety. They're charged with reporting to him or to his office on a daily basis. I'm betting he knows more about you and your daily activities than you do about him at this point."

She sighed. "I hope you're right, Matt. And I hope it isn't distracting him from the trial. He really needs to feel free to do his job, no matter the outcome. This man he's prosecuting is a vicious criminal disguised as an important city official."

Matt squeezed her shoulder. "You heard what he told you by phone. In a matter of days or weeks, this will be resolved once and for all."

And then, seeing the tension returning to her eyes, he drew her close for a kiss. And another.

As they came together, all the troubles of the past and present slipped away.

Later, while he watched her sleep, Matt thought about all they'd shared. Now, finally, he understood her need for complete honesty. Even though her father's intentions had been admirable, hoping to spare her the pain of her mother's illness, his secrecy was hurtful.

As for Matt, he'd revealed more personal history with her in this one night than he'd ever told another living soul. Not even his own family. He and his brothers never talked about the loss of their parents. And because of the pain he could sense in his family, he'd refrained from bringing up the subject. But with Vanessa, all that changed. She was so easy to talk to. She listened. Really listened to all he had to say. But it was deeper than that. She was smart. She was sensitive. And she really cared about him, his family, his life.

He liked the fact that she was crazy about her father. Coming from a close, loving family himself, it mattered to him. *She* mattered to him, though he didn't want to probe the why of it too deeply.

She was getting to him.

Who was he kidding?

She'd gotten to him the minute they met.

Then she was just a sharp mind in a pretty face wrapped up in a gorgeous body.

Now she was so much more.

He wasn't ready to admit just how much more. But the fact was, he wasn't looking forward to the day she would be free to leave.

Free to leave.

The thought rankled.

He didn't want her to leave.

Not now. Not ever.

And that fact was so alien to a man like him. He'd spent a lifetime caring for his entire family and had never once given a thought to his own future, other than how it would be linked to this ranch.

He'd always kept outsiders at arm's length. And now, though it was far too soon, he found himself thinking about how Nessa fit into the picture. She was no longer an outsider. She mattered to him. Perhaps more than she ought to.

And that fact scared the hell out of him.

CHAPTER TWENTY-TWO

Vanessa lay very still, listening to the sound of birds outside the cabin. After a day and night of storms punctuated by thunder and lightning, and of rain drumming the roof, it was a soothing, relaxing sound.

She looked over at Matt, who was gloriously naked, one leg resting over hers, an arm wrapped protectively around her.

She felt safe with this man. Safe in all ways. Not just safe from the outside world, but safe to be herself. No pretense. No airs.

She could tell him anything, and knew instinctively that he would listen and not judge. Except for her father, she couldn't think of another man who bore that distinction.

But why? What was it that set Matthew Malloy apart from others? He was handsome, but then, so were dozens of other men. He was smart, but she'd attended law school with plenty of smart men who had never affected her like this. He was serious and funny. Shrewd and charming. All business, until he decided to play. His playful side, such a contradiction from the man she'd first met, delighted her more than she cared to admit. In truth, she loved everything about Matthew Malloy.

Loved?

Though the word teased the edges of her mind, she didn't want to probe this too deeply. It was too soon. Her life was too complicated. She didn't want or need another complication. Wasn't it enough that she was the object of death threats? Even though she felt safely removed from them, they were there in the background, real, deadly, taunting her. And there was the absence of her father. She missed his presence in her life. Theirs was such a comfortable, loving relationship. She hated that he was dealing with not only a career-changing trial but also a dangerous foe who had threatened to stop at nothing to walk free. And he was doing it alone, as he'd been forced to deal with everything alone since the death of her mother. On the one hand she wanted to be there with him, to offer aid and comfort. On the other she knew that he was grateful to have her here, safe and protected, so that he could give his full attention to the trial.

She struggled to put aside such thoughts. There was nothing she could do to help her father, except to stay here and to stay safe. But she felt a measure of guilt that, while her father was forced to slay his dragons alone, she was here having a grand time with Matt.

Matt. His hand moved along her side and she felt the now familiar sizzle of anticipation at his touch. His hands were work worn. A working cowboy's hands. Strong. Steady.

She loved his hands. Loved having them on her.

His breath was warm as it tickled her cheek. She delighted in kissing him. His face. His body. His mouth.

She leaned in, hoping to touch her lips to his.

It was then she realized that he was awake and watching her.

She paused. "I was planning on kissing you awake."

"Be my guest."

She laughed. "It won't work now. You're already awake."

"Part of me is. But one kiss, and you'll wake the rest of me."

"Oh." Such a small word for the rush of feelings that surfaced as an image came to mind. An image of their glorious night of lovemaking.

She leaned even closer. With her eyes on his she nibbled a chaste kiss to his mouth. His arms came around her, pinning her to the length of him. And then she was lost. Lost in the wonder of the pleasure only he could give.

"I need coffee." Matt slipped from bed and stepped into his jeans.

"I saw some sort of biscuit dough in the supplies. Maybe I'll try my hand at pancakes."

He looked at her. "Pancakes?"

She flushed. "Or not. But I'll try."

"Pancakes are good." He rummaged through the metal container and lifted a package. "But even better with crisp bacon." He set out strips of bacon on the cooking tin.

Vanessa pulled on a pair of denims and a T-shirt and joined him in the kitchen area, looking through the supplies until she found the biscuit dough.

After reading the directions, she turned with a smile. "I can do this."

"Great. I didn't know you cooked." He stood watching as she mixed it with milk and poured several large circles of thin pancake batter beside the bacon.

He placed the tin over the hot coals. A short time later, when their breakfast was ready, he set a log on the grate, and they settled in front of a roaring fire to enjoy their meal.

"Perfect pancakes. Yancy had better watch his back." Matt sat back, smiling over at her. "You're just full of hidden talents, aren't you, ma'am?"

"I've barely scratched the surface."

He shot her a look. "Now you tell me. What else am I missing?"

Her voice was a soft purr. "You'll just have to wait and see."

His grin was quick and dangerous. "I'll show you mine if you show me yours."

She slapped his hand. "You're such a guy."

He shrugged. "Can't blame a guy for trying."

They shared a laugh.

He sat back and finished his coffee. "We'll have to pack up soon and head back to the ranch."

"I know." She laid her hand over his. "This time alone with you has been special."

"For me, too."

She could feel him studying her. As he'd been studying her ever since she'd first arrived here in Montana. It warmed her. It thrilled her. It frightened her. Not Matt, she realized, but the feelings he aroused in her. She'd never felt like this about any other man, and it was delicious and oddly uncomfortable, all at the same time.

"There are things I want to tell you."

"Things?"

"Feelings. They're..." He paused. "They're still pretty new, but since we're sharing secrets..."

"I don't know if you're ready to hear this, but I need to say it anyway. In all these years, I've never before known a woman who's ever made me think about love, commitment, and happily-ever-after."

Seeing her look of stunned surprise, he squeezed her hand before getting up and crossing the room to pull on his shirt, parka, and boots.

"Wait, Matt. You tell me something this important, this earth-shattering, and then you just calmly turn away?"

"I realize this came out of the blue. Sorry. I'll give you some time. If I had my way, we'd never leave. So, if we hope to get out of here"—he kept his back to her—"I'm going out to chop some wood."

Then he turned and gave her a blinding smile. "We have a rule up here. A cowboy never leaves one of the range shacks until he's replaced whatever was used while he was here. That way, the next one who has need of shelter will find it ready."

"Sounds like a good rule."

"Yeah." He returned to bend close and give her a long, slow kiss.

"Another rule?"

"That one was just for me. Never leave your woman without first kissing her." He straightened and walked outside.

Your woman.

His woman.

Warmed by his words, thrilled by them, she stared at the closed door and sat back as a slow smile spread across her lips.

Matt loved her.

And she'd said not a word. Though her heart was in her throat, and in her mind she was dancing on clouds, she'd remained still and mute.

Maybe because she was afraid to admit just how she was feeling. It was too new. Too delicious.

She couldn't recall another time when she'd done so little and had so much pleasure doing it. No alarm clocks. No fast-paced schedule to adhere to. No airports from Chicago to DC and back. No small talk with people she barely knew. No fighting to change rules set in stone by some bureaucrat years before she'd been born.

Here in this simple place, she'd found peace and contentment.

And love.

She drained her coffee and carried their dishes to the small sink.

To the steady sound of an ax splitting logs, she made up the bed, tidied up the space, and looked around with a nod of appreciation. This little cabin had been her sanctuary and her heaven. It was primitive by any standards. Just a rough bed, a fireplace for heat, and cold water. But she wouldn't trade it for the finest spa or resort.

Because of Matt.

Just the thought of him warmed her. He loved her.

Love.

She touched her hands to her hot cheeks and couldn't help grinning.

She looked up as a rumble, like thunder, seemed to echo

across the hills. Another storm blowing through? Would Matt try to drive through it, or remain here until it blew over? She hoped they could remain. It would be such fun to extend their time here.

Fun? It would be heavenly. Another day and night in Matt's arms, with no distractions. No ranch chores. No loud, teasing brothers or family members to intrude.

She blinked. In truth, she was already missing his rowdy brothers and raucous family. After a lifetime alone, she loved the crazy laughter, the wild teasing, the loving interaction of the entire Malloy clan.

One thing was certain. Despite the threat of danger hanging over her head, she'd never had a better time anywhere than she had here, with Matt and his large, loving family.

She grabbed a battered denim jacket from a hook by the door when she realized that the chopping had stilled. She would help Matt haul the logs inside and see what their plans would be going forward.

She ran to the door. Before she could reach it, it was yanked open, and a burly figure seemed to fill the entire space.

The stranger was tall, bearded, and menacing. And in his hand was a terrifying looking automatic weapon aimed directly at her.

"Matt...?" She couldn't seem to make her mouth work over the constriction in her throat.

"Your cowboy's dead."

The roar. Not thunder. Gunfire.

Matt dead?

"No! Matt—" She tried to push past the man, but he

swung the weapon in a wide arc, hitting her in the head so hard it knocked her to the floor.

Pain, hot and swift, crashed through her brain. She struggled to clear the black spots dancing in front of her eyes. She touched a hand to her head and felt the wet, sticky mass of blood oozing through the hair at her temple.

Ignoring her obvious pain, the stranger grabbed her arm, hauling her roughly to her feet and dragging her through the open doorway.

In the clearing she saw a second man standing beside Grace's truck. Through the open doorway of the vehicle she saw Matt slumped behind the wheel. The front of his parka was stained with his blood.

The man cupped his hands to shout, "Got him inside, though it was like lifting an elephant. This cowboy's all muscle."

"Quit complaining and get that truck going. We need to move now."

The second stranger started the engine before slamming the truck's door closed. Reaching inside the open window, he engaged the gear. The truck lurched forward.

The vehicle moved slowly toward a rock ledge. The same ledge Matt had once pointed out to her. At the end of it lay a sheer drop-off that fell thousands of feet to a heavily wooded canyon below.

Vanessa watched in horror as she realized what they intended.

Tears of pain and rage blinded her as the truth dawned.

The truck, with Matt inside, could rot in that primitive forest for years without ever being spotted from above.

No one would know what had happened here. She and

Matt would both be dead, and the killers would be free to return to Chicago, to report to the vicious thug who had ordered all this, without fear of reprisal.

Without Matt's body, without hers, the crime would go unpunished.

Her father would know, and the knowledge would eat at him for a lifetime. And there was nothing he could do to stop this madness. Worse, nothing she could do.

Still holding her firmly by the arm, the bearded stranger shoved her into the passenger side of an SUV, its windows tinted so that the occupants couldn't be seen. Her wrists and ankles were bound by plastic restraints. Her cell phone was taken away and pocketed by her captor before he climbed behind the wheel and waited.

Minutes later there was a terrible explosion sending flames high in the air.

The sound of it, and the heat it generated, were so overwhelming, the very earth beneath them trembled. The vehicle gave a great shudder. Vanessa realized that Matt's fate had been sealed. At the knowledge that he was lost to her, she was overcome with such grief, all she could do was sob helplessly.

While the flames turned black, whirling and dancing on the breeze, the second man settled into the backseat.

"Okay, Homer. That's done. Let's roll."

As they started away Vanessa turned for a last look. The once peaceful cabin was cloaked in a thick cloud of black, choking smoke curling up from the ravine far below.

Could anyone survive such an explosion? The thought had her going as still as death.

"Oh Matt," she whispered, though she wasn't even aware that she was doing so. She tried to envision him rising up from the smoke and ashes. "Please. Please." Was it a prayer or a plea? Whatever it was, she couldn't put the rest of her thoughts into words. It was all too painful. Too deep. Too real. Too...impossible.

Unable to wipe at her eyes, she blinked several times, and fell into a deep, dark well of utter despair.

CHAPTER TWENTY-THREE

The SUV kept to the high meadow, moving steadily through a wooded area that shielded them from view of anyone who might pass that way. Since it appeared to be the same vehicle that Vanessa and Matt had come upon the day of their ride, its occupants had apparently learned their lesson. On a ranch of this size, they might encounter employees or family members anywhere, so they kept to secluded places where they were less likely to be seen.

Occasionally Vanessa caught glimpses of herds in the higher elevations, and the thought of wranglers just out of reach had her throat clogged with unshed tears. While the crew went about the business of running a ranch, they were unaware that killers were hiding among them.

"Where are you taking me?"

"To Disneyland," the driver said with a sneer.

The man in the rear seat laughed at his partner's joke.

"My father will hunt you down and find you if it takes him the rest of his life."

"If Mr. D. has his way, that ought to be real soon. When we're done with you, we have orders to get rid of him next. But not until he's done as he's told."

Another burst of laughter from the backseat, and the two men exchanged knowing smiles in the mirror.

The driver's tone was smug. "We figure, once your daddy gets our little video, he'll have to walk away from his day job to search for his little girl."

Video.

They weren't going to kill her yet. They needed her alive if they were planning on sending her father a video.

She knew how this sort of thing worked. A tearful kidnapping victim. Something that would prove the date, so that they could point to the fact that, at least for now, she was still alive. And probably a time limit, which, if not met, would end with the threat of her execution.

"My father would never leave in the middle of a trial."

"Oh, I'm betting he can't refuse to take the bait we offer."

Vanessa fell silent, her heart pounding. How far along was the trial? Had the prosecution concluded its testimony yet? Was that why these men had acted now? Had DePietro concluded that he was going down in defeat?

Mr. D. Of course. Running scared and taking desperate measures.

Beware desperate men, her father often said. When backed to the wall, they become more vicious than feral animals.

As the SUV passed through a thick wall of trees and came up over a rise, the land that was spread out below them appeared as wild and desolate as a moonscape. Here there were no herds. No wranglers. No buildings. Only wilderness for as far as the eye could see.

Vanessa's heart froze. The perfect spot to make their video and send it to her father, as instructed.

As the vehicle slowed to a halt, Vanessa steeled herself. She needed, more than ever, to look calm and composed. She would rather die here and now than give them what they wanted. She would not break down and weep like a frightened victim while they recorded every tear, every quivering moan or sob. She was determined to swallow her terror and show her father a defiant, uncompromising woman who would make the district attorney of Cook County proud.

The driver unlocked the car doors, and the man in the backseat stepped out and cut her ankle restraints before hauling her out roughly by the arm.

"Where do you want her?"

The driver pointed to a large, flat rock. "There."

She was pressed down, arms behind her back, facing a cell phone camera. While the driver recorded, the other man held a Chicago newspaper up to the camera, showing the masthead, the date, and the headline, which read: DePietro Jury to Begin Deliberations.

The driver snarled, "Tell Daddy you've been a bad girl and got yourself caught by the big, bad wolves."

Vanessa kept her silence and lifted her chin defiantly.

His big hand slashed out, slapping her so hard her head snapped to one side, and she saw stars. She was infuriated when tears pooled in her eyes and she bit down hard on the cry that almost burst from her lips.

He swore. "This may be your last chance to say anything

to your daddy. You wouldn't want to leave this world without telling him how much you love him. Right?"

She clenched her jaw.

His voice grew shrill with agitation. "Suit yourself. As for you, Mr. Big Shot DA, take a good look at your smart-ass daughter. She may be a good actress, pretending she's too good to cry, but the blood you see is just a sample of what you'll see in the next video if you don't do exactly as you're told."

Vanessa had forgotten the blood. The sight of it would horrify her father.

The stranger had already turned away, electronically sending the video that would shake her father's world to its very foundation.

The second man yanked her to her feet and hauled her back to the car. Once inside, he affixed fresh restraints around her ankles before slamming her door and climbing into the back.

Minutes later they were once more on their way, keeping always to the wooded areas, away from civilization.

Burke, standing with his wranglers as a herd of nervous cattle milled about, saw the plume of black smoke and whipped out his phone.

"Something's wrong. Get the crew up here now."

He rang off and drove his truck toward the range shack.

By the time he got there, Luke was just parking his Harley, and Reed and Colin were stepping away from their all-terrain vehicles. The three were racing toward the ridge, where the smoke was so thick it burned their eyes.

Because they couldn't see through the black cloud to

the bottom, they began the treacherous descent into the gorge.

Burke hurried toward the cabin, where the door was standing open. An ominous sign. Inside, he stared around, noting the half-burned log in the fireplace, proof that its occupants had been gone only a short time. As for the rest of the cabin, it was spotless. As though Matt and Vanessa had been preparing to leave.

Outside, half a dozen logs were neatly stacked, with one log uncut, the ax lying on the ground nearby.

Burke knelt and touched a hand to the dark moisture in the grass.

Blood. Quite a lot of it.

With a heavy heart he turned away and followed Luke, Reed, and Colin down the circuitous route to the bottom of the gorge.

Darkness came early in the hills. Once the sun had set behind the mountain peaks, the land became cloaked in shadows.

The driver seemed sure of himself as he guided the car across shallow streams and around rocky outcroppings before coming to a halt inside a cave.

Of course, Vanessa thought. These two men had planned this carefully. If anybody happened to be searching by air, this hiding place would never be spotted.

The driver opened the door and stretched his arms over his head, leaving Vanessa to his partner.

As before, her ankle restraints were cut away before she was hauled from the car and shoved roughly to the cold ground inside the cave. Once there her ankles were restrained tightly, and a rope was tied from her feet to her neck, making movement of any kind painful. Making escape impossible.

The driver retrieved a backpack from the rear of the vehicle and set it inside the cave before announcing, "Honey, I'm home."

Again the two men shared a laugh at his little joke. They were, Vanessa noted, in high spirits since sending the video.

She watched as the driver zipped open the backpack and began removing bottled water and wrapped food.

She asked, "How long will we be here?"

The driver answered for both. "We're here until we're told to leave."

Her throat burned with fury. "I know it was that monster, Diomedes DePietro, who sent you."

The driver's head turned, his eyes hot with anger. "Shut your mouth. You're not fit to speak his name."

"You make him sound like some sort of holy man."

"Compared to your old man, he's a saint." The driver sat down, his back against a boulder, and began devouring a sandwich.

The other man followed suit.

When they'd each eaten several sandwiches, the driver produced a bottle of whiskey. He took a long pull before passing it to his partner, who did the same.

After several minutes he drank again before looking over at her, more relaxed now. "After my father died and my mother was sick, Mr. D. saw to it that she got the finest medical care in the world."

Vanessa wanted him to talk, to keep her from thinking about Matt. And about what was going to happen to her when this ended. "How did your father die?"

"In a shoot-out with a cop who'd caught him during a stakeout, passing money to a Chicago alderman."

Vanessa thought back to the many charges against DePietro. Bribes, money laundering, supplying drugs and prostitutes to politicians in exchange for favors. But none as critical as the murder of a witness set to testify against him.

"Your father died for DePietro?"

"Any one of us would have done the same."

"How does a man like that earn your loyalty?"

He took another long pull of whiskey before passing it to his partner. He crossed his arms over his chest and stretched out his legs, trying to get comfortable on the cold, hard ground. "You tell her, Jasper."

The taller of the two men, whose hawk-like face bore a jagged scar from his eyebrow to his chin, nodded. "Mr. D. rewards loyalty. The pay's good, but the benefits are even better."

"Benefits?"

He and his partner chuckled.

"What sort of benefits?"

"If we're in trouble with the law, he provides us with lawyers. If we do time, he takes care of our families until we get out."

"And why shouldn't he? He's the reason you're in trouble with the law. It's the least he can do for the people he hires to do his dirty work. Wouldn't it be better if he found you honest work to do, instead of sitting back and allowing men like you to get caught up in criminal activities?"

The driver's tone grew sulky. "Shut up and get some sleep. You're going to need it for the morning, Daddy's Girl."

She felt a shiver of apprehension, wondering what could be worse than what she'd already gone through.

As the two men drifted into sleep, she lay awake and troubled.

Each time she closed her eyes, she could see Matt slumped behind the wheel of the truck, blood smearing the front of his parka, and then the terrible sound of an explosion as a plume of black smoke rose up, covering the area with its acrid smell.

She fought tears of pain and rage at the helplessness of the situation.

She was trying to put up a brave front for the sake of her father. But inside she was waging a losing battle, knowing that Matt had paid the ultimate price because of her.

Because of her, the man she loved was dead.

The man she loved.

Now there was no need to dissect those strange, troubling feelings she'd been trying to deny. It was love, plain and simple. And now, he was lost to her forever, and oh, the pain of that knowledge was almost more than she could bear.

All this heartache and loss, brought to the very doorstep of the Malloy Ranch. All these good, sweet people, who didn't even know her father or his opponent in the trial, were now forced to risk their lives for having welcomed her into the circle of their safe retreat, believing the trial would end quickly and they would be relieved of any responsibility.

Frank and Grace had lost a beloved son and daughter-in-law all those years ago, and had helped raise three grandsons. And now, they would be faced with the horrible news of yet another loss.

Matt was a pillar of strength to them. Their firstborn grandson. The strong, steady one among them who, after the loss of his parents, had appointed himself leader of his siblings. He'd worked and studied to become the shrewd business leader of their vast enterprise.

Picturing the grief the entire Malloy family would suffer when they learned of their loss had Vanessa's heart breaking into millions of pieces. And knowing she couldn't be with them, to grieve, to comfort and to take comfort from them, just added to her misery.

While the two killers snored, deep in sleep, she gave in to the feelings of despair and wept bitter, scalding tears.

CHAPTER TWENTY-FOUR

Elliott Kettering sat in his office, surrounded by Chief McBride and his men, forced to watch the video yet again. They'd played it dozens of times now, each man in the special crimes unit looking carefully for anything that would tell them where DePietro's men were holding Vanessa.

While they dissected it frame by frame, Elliott shoved away from his desk to pace. Though he'd remained silent for the most part, a voice in his head was swearing, screaming obscenities at the vicious killer who thought he was above the law.

And for now, he was. That's what had Elliott almost mad with fear. At a thug's command, his precious only child could be brutalized, tortured, murdered. All the power of the Chicago PD, all the wealth of knowledge at the district attorney's service, were helpless to keep Vanessa safe.

A phone call to the Malloy Ranch had only added to Elliott's frustration. The family insisted that Vanessa was with the oldest son, Matthew, in some secluded cabin, and being guarded by a team of wranglers. But when pressed, they had admitted that they had neither seen nor spoken to Vanessa nor Matthew since the previous day. And the wranglers couldn't be reached to confirm their safety.

He should have ordered her to a safe house as soon as this threat had surfaced. And now he was paying the price for his tenderhearted gesture in permitting her to stay at a remote ranch in Montana. To Elliott, it was like sending her to the dark side of the moon. He didn't know these people, or their ranch hands, or their intentions. Despite assurances from his investigators, for all he knew, they could be on the payroll of Diomedes DePietro.

"You know the spot?" Chief McBride's words penetrated Elliott's dark thoughts.

He turned and stood behind the chief, who was seated at Elliott's desk, using a speaker phone.

Sheriff Eugene Graystoke's gravel voice on the other end was loud in the silence of the office. "After viewing the video, Frank Malloy tells me he knows it well. It's on the North Ridge, in a high meadow that isn't used for the herds. Too many dangerous ravines in that area."

"What does he hear from Matt?"

"No word yet. But Burke Cowley, his foreman, should be checking in soon. There's limited cell phone service in the area, and we often don't hear from the wranglers for days at a time."

Elliott's voice cut like a whip. "I don't give a damn about cell service. Get somebody up to that cabin and find the son of a bitch who allowed these bastards to kidnap and video my daughter, bloodied and helpless."

The sheriff's tone was incredulous. "Have you positively identified her as your daughter?"

"You think I don't know my own daughter, you—?"

Captain McBride lifted the receiver, effectively cutting him off. "Sheriff, my entire team has seen the video. It's Vanessa Kettering. Now I know the Malloy Ranch is big, but you need to get somebody up to that cabin right away."

"We're on it."

"Good. I expect to hear from you within the hour."

He disconnected while the sheriff was still responding, and turned to the DA. "I know how you feel, Elliott."

"Do you?" Kettering's face was as dark as thunder.

"Your job is to keep this under wraps until the jury reaches a verdict. Our job is to find your daughter. And we *will* find her, Elliott."

"Don't insult me with platitudes." Angry, frustrated, helpless, Elliott Kettering turned away, too agitated to sit, too furious to meet the eyes of the men scattered around his office. He wanted to put a fist through the wall. He wanted to lash out at someone, anyone. He wanted...

...to hold his daughter in his arms. Just to hold her, and know that she was safe from all harm. Instead, he was forced to pretend to the world outside this room that everything was fine, and that his only concern was awaiting the jury's verdict. A verdict that he prayed would put away for a lifetime the spineless, heartless thug who had ordered this vicious crime against his Vanessa.

His baby girl. His sweet, beautiful Vanessa.

The words played like a litany through his tortured, troubled mind.

Burke thrashed through the brush, cursing his age and arthritis, desperate to get to the bottom of the ravine. The dampened handkerchief tied around his nose and mouth did little to protect him from the smoke that burned his eyes and had him coughing with every intake of breath.

Ahead of him, scrambling over rocks and fallen tree branches, was Luke, who had tossed aside his Harley like a toy on the rock ledge above before jumping into the search. Reed was swearing at the brambles that tore at his flesh with every step, and Colin, always the stoic, silent uncle who kept his thoughts and words to himself, moved doggedly forward.

None of them knew what to expect. All they knew was that something had caused an explosion and a fire, and Matt and Vanessa were missing from their cabin, along with Grace's truck.

It wasn't possible for Matt to lose his way and drive off that rock shelf into such forbidding terrain. He knew this land better than anyone. There wasn't a careless bone in his body.

Burke heard Luke's shout, and followed Reed toward the sound of it. The two arrived at the bottom of the ravine to a scene of such devastation, they were speechless.

"It's a truck," Luke shouted. "I can't tell if it's Gram Gracie's. Too much damage."

He peered through the smoke and flames before shaking his head. "I don't see anyone. Maybe they..."

At a moan, Burke turned. A body, bloody and wreathed in smoke, lay in a snowbank beneath a cluster of evergreens. Because of the dense underbrush, the rain had yet to melt the snow.

"Here!" Burke shouted. "Over here! It's Matt!"

Luke and Reed gathered around while Burke and Colin knelt beside Matt, checking for a pulse.

The old cowboy looked up. "He's alive." To Matt he muttered, "You're one lucky guy. If it weren't for this snowbank, the fall from that burning truck would have clean killed you, son."

He looked over at the others. "Let's get him out of these wet things."

They quickly removed Matt's still-smoldering parka, all the while checking for wounds.

"So much blood." Reed, accustomed to treating animal injuries, probed Matt's chest and shoulder until he located the source of the blood. Leaning close he whispered, "Can you hear me, Matt?"

His brother's eyes flickered, then opened. "...hear you."

"You're bleeding from the shoulder. Did it happen during the accident? Broken glass, maybe? Or did something stab you?"

"...shot."

"You're saying you took a bullet? Who would shoot you?"

"Thugs. Got Vanessa."

The four men looked at one another in stunned surprise.

Luke's voice was suddenly filled with anger. "She's been kidnapped?"

Matt nodded. "All my fault. Get me up."

Colin put a hand on his chest. "You shouldn't be moved until we're sure nothing's broken."

"Get me the hell up. Now."

His two brothers put their arms around his shoulders and gingerly lifted him to a sitting position. Moments later they helped him to stand, but kept their arms around him to steady him.

Matt's voice was raspy from the smoke. "They got a head start. We need to find her. Now."

Burke shook his head. "It's a long climb up, Matt. You'll never make it."

Through gritted teeth Matt said, "I don't care what it takes. Just get me up there."

"I'll take care of this." While the others watched, Colin sprinted up the ravine and out of sight.

Minutes later he shouted to watch for a rope, which was soon seen snaking down.

"Wrap it around your waist, Matt," he ordered. "I'll use Burke's horse to slowly pull you up."

With Luke on one side, and Reed on the other, and Burke close behind to catch him if he fell, Matt made his way slowly, torturously, up the steep climb until he was on level ground.

For long moments he lay on the ground, breathing labored, eyes closed, as he fought his way through waves of pain. Then, forcing himself to his knees, he looked at the others.

"I counted two men. The SUV with the tinted windows. Sheriff Graystoke has a partial license number, unless they've stolen new plates. They have an automatic weapon, and they have Vanessa. Now get me to the ranch so I can report what I know. Then we're heading out to find her."

Burke glanced from Luke to Reed. "As soon as you get

your brother to the ranch, call for a medevac. He needs to be flown to a hospital."

"Not until I get Vanessa away from those thugs. This is all my fault, Burke. If I hadn't asked you to have your wranglers back off and give me some time alone with her, this never would have happened. I gave those monsters the perfect opportunity to do their dirty work. Now I have to make it right." He turned to Luke. "Your Harley is faster than Reed's ATV."

Colin lay a hand on his nephew's arm. "Luke's may be faster, but Reed's is safer."

"Safe doesn't count right now. You heard me. I have no one to blame but myself." Matt turned to Luke. "Let's go."

With Luke driving, and Matt holding tightly behind him, they left in a roar of engines.

Burke gave a shake of his head. "I know he's hurting. I know he needs a doctor. But with the load of guilt he's carrying, I'd say Matt won't even be able to think about anything until he finds Vanessa, or dies trying. And God help him if anything bad happens to her. I doubt he'd ever recover."

Reed and his uncle nodded their agreement.

They all knew Matt well enough to realize the truth of the old man's words.

CHAPTER TWENTY-FIVE

Oh, Matthew." Grace hugged her grandson fiercely the minute Luke's motorcycle arrived at the back door of the ranch.

Within minutes the rest of the family pulled up in their various vehicles and gathered around. It was clear that all were stunned by the look of him. Between the blood that smeared his clothing, and the smoke and soot from the explosion, he looked more dead than alive. But the fire burning in his eyes left no doubt that he was very much alive and ready to go to war with his attackers.

He brushed off all their questions. "How much do you know?"

It was Frank who answered. "Eugene Graystoke sent us a video uploaded to Vanessa's father by her kidnappers. We feared they had killed you to get to her."

"They think they did. What's this about a video? I want

to see it." Matt strode inside, and the others trailed behind.

Frank put an arm around his wife and bent to whisper, "Courage, Gracie Girl."

Her eyes reflected the pain she felt. "Did you see the blood? Frankie, he needs a doctor."

"You saw the look on his face. He's still standing. That will have to do for now."

Colin, who had remained behind, nodded to his parents. "I've never seen him like this before. And it isn't just his injuries. Our Matt is carrying a heavy load of guilt."

"What does he have to be guilty of?" Grace demanded.

"He asked Burke to keep the wranglers away from the range shack so he and Vanessa could have some privacy."

"I see." Now that she knew, the old woman saw much more. Her grandson had found that one special woman, who had driven him to throw caution to the wind in order to be alone with her. And now he was riddled with guilt for having risked her safety.

Grace sighed and allowed herself to be led indoors.

In the kitchen they gathered around the table and watched Matt's reaction as he viewed the video. At the first sighting of Vanessa, he flinched as though struck by a whip before his eyes narrowed in fierce concentration.

He waited until the short video was over before muttering, "They hurt her. She's bleeding." His hands clenched at his sides in impotent fury. "They hurt her."

Nobody said a word.

He sucked in a breath. "I need to call her father."

Nelson started to say, "I don't think that's a good—"

Grace shot her father a look, and his words of disapproval died.

They watched and listened as Matt called Elliott Kettering at the number Captain McBride had promised would be a direct line to both Kettering and the Chicago PD.

The phone was answered on the first ring.

"Mr. Kettering, Matt Malloy."

Elliott's voice was both angry and weary. "Tell me what happened. And tell me how they managed to take my daughter without taking you."

As briefly as he could Matt described being shot and put into a truck, which was sent crashing into a deep ravine, where it exploded into flame, before he was rescued.

While he spoke, his family looked stunned and horrified to hear him speak so calmly about all that he'd gone through.

"I'm grateful you survived. And now?" Elliott asked.

"I'm back at the ranch and was just shown the video Nessa's kidnappers sent."

Elliott's voice mirrored his fury. "They dared to hurt my daughter."

"Yes, sir. I saw the blood. I want you to know that I hold myself personally responsible."

"I don't see how you can make such a claim when you were shot and nearly burned to death."

"All because of my own carelessness. None of that matters now. But your daughter's safety does. And I give you my word that I'll get her back to you or die trying."

"There's no need. Our state police are working with your authorities there. Let the professionals do their job."

"You don't understand." Matt's voice was pure ice. "Nessa's safety is on me. I allowed this to happen. I won't rest until I find her."

He disconnected then, leaving Elliott Kettering no time to voice any further argument.

He turned to his family. "Play the video again. I want to be certain of the location."

While Yancy complied, Frank said softly, "They'll be long gone from there by now, son."

"I know that." Matt studied the video again before saying, "But I'll start there. They may have left something, some tracks or even something at the scene that I can follow."

Grace looked alarmed. "First, Matthew, you have to see a doctor."

"Not now. There's no time." He turned away. "I need a rifle."

Luke raced from the room and returned with an armload of weapons and ammunition from a locked cabinet in the office.

As he passed them around, Matt said, "I'm taking a truck. Grandpop, I'd like you and Gram Gracie to go up in the plane. Maybe you'll spot something from the air. And Great One, you and Yancy man the phones here, in case the authorities report something. You can relay the information to all of us."

Luke closed a hand over his brother's arm. "I'm going with you."

"No." Matt shook off his hand. "Take your Harley." He turned to Reed. "Your ATV can go places other vehicles can't. Colin, Burke, you and the wranglers take trucks and fan out."

His uncle Colin paused. "Sheriff Graystoke may have something to say about this."

"He and his men will do what they're trained to do. But

I'm not waiting around for anyone. This is on me, and I'm going to do what feels right."

Grace pressed an emergency medical kit into his hand. He shot her a look.

"There's something for pain and an antibiotic to hold back any infection from that bullet."

"Thanks." His tone was dismissive. "I'll take the antibiotic, but I'm not going to risk getting muddled with pain meds."

As Matt walked away, old Burke paused to say to the others, "I know he's been wounded, and he's going on pure adrenaline. I know you're all worried about him. I am, too. But even so, I'd rather have Matt, injured and angry, than just about any damned army in the world. So if those kidnappers are still anywhere in Montana, my money's on Matt finding them."

Frank squeezed his wife's arm before starting for the door. "You heard the man, Gracie Girl. Let's trust his word and follow our leader."

Sheriff Eugene Graystoke and Deputy Archer Stone arrived at the Malloy Ranch with a swarm of police vehicles. A team of state police sharpshooters had been brought in by helicopter.

The sheriff entered the ranch house and found only Yancy and Nelson in the kitchen. He looked around with a puzzled expression. "I was expecting everybody to be here by now. Where are they?"

"Here and gone." Nelson pointed to the sky. "Frank and Grace are airborne. The rest have scattered, searching for the bad guys."

The sheriff's eyes narrowed with anger. "This isn't

some cops-and-robbers movie, Nelson. This is real life, and an innocent young woman's safety hangs in the balance. Captain McBride wants this played by the book."

"I guess we didn't get that memo." The old man shot the lawman a wry grin.

Archer's voice was low with sarcasm. "How did Matt let this kidnapping happen? I thought he'd appointed himself Miss Kettering's personal bodyguard, and the rest of you his backup army."

As quickly as possible Nelson described what Matt had endured at the hands of the kidnappers.

The sheriff blanched. "How in hell is Matt still standing?"

"He's a Malloy," the old man said simply.

With a muttered oath the sheriff and his deputy turned their backs and strode outside to join their men.

After a lengthy meeting to outline their strategy, they separated and went in various directions, the sheriff still muttering about how he hoped to hell the Malloy family didn't get in his way. Just to make certain, he pulled out his phone and called Matt.

"Yeah, Sheriff." Matt's tone was abrupt.

"I'm at your ranch, where the Great One informed me that you and your family are already out searching for Miss Kettering."

"That's right."

"Just so you know, her safety is our main concern. I don't want any would-be heroes barging in and causing her any more harm than has already been done to her."

At the ominous silence on the line, the sheriff cleared his throat. "Look. I heard what they did to you. I know that this isn't something you asked for, Matt. But now that it's happened, I want you to remain in contact with me and my men every step of the way. The State Police have men trained for this very thing. There are more of them than there are of you and your family. But if you happen to find where they've taken her, I want your word that you'll step back and allow us to do our job."

At the continued silence, his voice took on a low note of authority. "Do I have your word, Matt?"

"I've already given my word to her father. I'll see her returned safely to him, or die trying."

"My men and I are here to prevent anyone's death. Yours and Miss Kettering's. So see that you rein in that famous temper, and ask the rest of your family to do the same. You got that?"

In reply, the phone went dead.

Sheriff Eugene Graystoke uttered every rich, ripe swear word he knew as he made his way to his squad car.

Captain Daniel McBride stood before a giant map of the town of Glacier Ridge, Montana, and the thousands of acres of land that made up the Malloy Ranch.

It was one thing to imagine a sprawling ranch, and quite another to see thousands of acres mapped out in three dimensions, with every hill, mountain, ravine, and lake dotting the landscape. The sheer size of the place was mind-boggling. What was even more amazing to a man born and bred on the south side of Chicago was the isolation of the place. He figured there were more cattle per square mile than humans. Thousands of acres of uninhabited land where a couple of thugs could hide without ever encountering another human being.

And in the middle of all that was Elliott Kettering's

daughter. A helpless young woman at the mercy of men hired by a man who, if convicted by a jury, had nothing to lose by ordering another murder. And all that stood in the way of that death sentence was a small-town sheriff and a handful of Montana State Police.

Captain McBride pulled out his cell phone. If he couldn't be there to handle things, he could at least direct the operation and give them the benefit of his years of experience with Chicago thugs.

As soon as he heard Sheriff Eugene Graystoke's voice he took charge, barking orders. "I want all roads leading into and out of the Malloy Ranch to be sealed at once."

The sheriff's tone was gruff. "These men don't need roads. They're so deep in the wilderness, they could drive for days without seeing another human being."

"Then you need aircraft and an army of sharpshooters."

"Already got 'em. They've targeted the area where the video was shot."

"How about trackers?"

"One of the best is already on it."

"One?" McBride's tone was incredulous. "Shouldn't you have dozens?"

"This one knows the land better than anyone. It's Matt Malloy."

"The stupid cowboy who allowed her to be captured? I don't want that clown anywhere near this investigation."

The sheriff's eyes narrowed. It was one thing to have his feathers ruffled when the Malloy family stepped on his toes. It was another entirely to hear a city cop demean the family that had offered shelter to a stranger. "You might want to check that attitude, Captain. We may be small town, but we know how to fight for what's right. Matthew Malloy is one tough cowboy. In a fight, I'd rather have him on my side than a dozen of your finest."

Captain McBride stared at the phone in his hand before letting loose with a string of curses. And though he would never say it out loud, he didn't give Elliott Kettering or his daughter much hope for a happy ending to this mess.

CHAPTER TWENTY-SIX

While Frank piloted the Cessna, Grace sat beside him, her binoculars trained on the land below.

She pointed. "There's Matt's truck."

They circled the area, and could see their grandson kneeling in the grass.

Grace dialed his cell phone number and turned on the speaker so both she and Frank could hear.

"Yeah." Matt's voice showed signs of frustration. Or perhaps pain. It was clear that he hadn't bothered to look at the caller ID. "This is Matt."

"We're above you, darlin'."

"Sorry, Gram Gracie." He looked up and saluted. "Any sign of them?"

"Nothing so far." Grace paused a moment. "Are there any tracks you can follow?"

"Enough to know they're heading west. Straight into the wilderness."

"That could work to our advantage," Frank said. "We know this land. They don't."

"But they've been here long enough to study a map of it." Matt sighed. "If so, they've figured out that just over these hills is a cattle trail that leads to an old, abandoned road that will eventually connect with the interstate. Once on that, it's clear sailing."

"So we need to patrol this area until they decide to make a run for it?"

At his grandmother's question, he hesitated before saying, "Once that happens, it will be too late for Nessa. If this thug directing the operation is found guilty, I don't believe they have any intention of taking her with them."

There was total silence as his grim words sank in.

Grace put a hand to her mouth to cover the little gasp that escaped. "Oh, dear heaven." She looked over at her husband, who gave a slight nod of his head.

Matt's voice sounded a long way off, as though thinking aloud. "These men are hiding somewhere until they get the word from their boss."

Frank cleared his throat. "Then we'll keep searching until we find out where those rats are hiding."

"That's the plan." Matt paused before adding, "How are you at praying, Gram Gracie?"

"I've had a lot of practice over the years."

"Good. I think we could all use some now."

As dusk stole over the land, Vanessa listened to the drone of a plane's engines. Earlier, it had been directly overhead, as though circling, and her heart had nearly burst out of her chest at the thought that someone was searching for her. But now it could be heard growing more and more distant. As the sound faded, and the night grew quiet, all she heard was the snoring of the two men. After they'd polished off several sandwiches and an entire bottle of whiskey, she wasn't surprised that they'd offered her nothing. Why bother to feed someone they considered as good as dead? They'd made it clear to her that their loyalty to DePietro was absolute. Whatever he ordered, they would do without question.

Did her life or death depend on the jury's verdict? Or had this vicious criminal known all along that once she was taken, there would be but one ending?

She shivered as she faced the very real possibility that her fate had already been decided. These two couldn't let her live to identify them. And if, as her father believed, the case against DePietro ended in a guilty verdict, her death would be a criminal's final show of power against the lone man who had stood up to him and his empire.

It was clear that these two were simply awaiting the final word from their leader.

Matt glanced skyward, where the far-off drone of the Cessna told him that his grandparents were heading back to the ranch to refuel and wait until morning to resume their search.

He ought to do the same, but the slim chance that the kidnappers might risk a fire had him still driving slowly across the barren hillside, hoping against hope for any sign of them.

He'd hoped the view from the air would reveal a glint of vehicle somewhere in this vast area. Apparently the kidnappers had given this a lot of thought. There were so many heavily wooded areas, as well as rock ledges and caves, where they could take refuge.

He parked at the top of a hill and stepped out of the truck, staring around at the darkened outline of rocks, trees, and distant mountain peaks. Somewhere in this vast wilderness, Vanessa was cold and frightened. And hurt. The very thought of the blood he'd seen in the video had fury bubbling to the surface. It was that fury, that knowledge that she was hurt, that kept him going.

He'd long ago stopped feeling his shoulder, where a bullet was lodged, radiating an all-consuming pain from the top of his head, down his spine to his toes. His body was now simply numb. But he couldn't stop the thoughts that drove him nearly insane. Vanessa in the clutches of madmen. Men awaiting orders to kill her. Men who didn't care about the pain they inflicted. Men who may have been given license to do whatever they wanted with her before disposing of her body.

His hands clenched into fists at his sides and he closed his eyes against the thoughts and images torturing him. Because of his carelessness, he was reduced to this—chasing after shadows while the woman he loved was suffering.

The woman he loved.

Why hadn't he said more when he'd had the chance? He'd begun to declare his love, and then, seeing Vanessa's wide-eyed reaction, he'd backed off and left the cabin to chop wood and work off some of his restlessness. He'd believed it was too soon to shock her with so many personal feelings. And now he would live with that regret for a lifetime.

He'd known. Maybe not at first. It had been perfectly

normal to confuse lust with love. Vanessa Kettering was gorgeous, smart, funny. What man in his right mind wouldn't be attracted? But long before he'd given in to his passion, he'd known it was so much more. And still he'd worked overtime to keep those feelings low-key.

It was that damnable Malloy pride. Look at his uncle. Colin was forty, and still determined to remain a bachelor. He loved to boast that the woman wasn't born who could tie him down. That same mantra had been adopted by all of them. But they'd all known it was a joke, used to cover up any deep feelings they had. They were all very good at repressing feelings. Of loss. Of pain. But love? Frank and Grace were perfect examples of the way love ought to be. And hadn't his own parents been wildly in love?

It was what he wanted. What they all wanted.

Maybe that was why he'd wanted to soft-pedal his declaration of love. It was the most important emotion in the world, and it could be snatched away in an instant.

What he wouldn't give to be able to declare his undying love to his beautiful Nessa this very minute.

Sweet Nessa. How she must be suffering.

He'd asked his grandmother to pray.

It would take a miracle to find where those monsters were hiding her in this vast tract of wilderness.

Vanessa had put in the worst night of her life. Afraid. Alone. And plagued with horrible images of Matt, dead at the bottom of a ravine.

She needed to get free. But she couldn't imagine a scenario that would persuade these two to release her for even a few minutes. When she'd begged for a bathroom break before dark, the beefy, coarse one, Homer—whom she'd mentally nicknamed Bulk—had told her to soil herself, except he hadn't used such proper terms. And once again the two men had enjoyed his little joke, laughing themselves silly.

So what would persuade them to untie her?

Throughout this endless night, she'd played with a dozen different ideas. Feigning sickness. Pretending to be unconscious. Nothing seemed compelling enough to work to her advantage. They didn't care about her state of health. They had no reason to revive her if she fainted. She was already dead to them.

Dead.

It was so hard to concentrate when her mind always circled back to Matt. The thought of him, lying dead at the bottom of a ravine, his sweet, loving family grieving their loss, brought tears spilling down her face.

Had the wranglers in the distant hills seen the pall of smoke? Had someone come to investigate? Had they made the descent into the fiery hell that had enveloped his body? Would they even be able to identify the truck or the burned body?

Matt, her strong, fierce cowboy, his life cut short because of her. He didn't deserve this. All he'd done was offer his ranch as a sanctuary until the threat of danger was gone. And now she would never see him again. Would never hear that deep, sexy voice. Would never feel those strong arms holding her as gently as though she were some delicate, fragile flower. Would never again know the fierce wonder of his love.

The tears flowed until her throat was raw. She lay on the cold, hard ground of the cave and allowed herself to give in to a feeling of complete, absolute despair that settled over her like a dark cloud.

Hawkface, as Vanessa thought of Jasper, the tall, muscled man who always rode in the backseat, woke from a drunken sleep and got to his feet, swaying wildly.

His movements woke Homer, the driver, who aimed a fist into his middle, dropping him to his knees. "What're you doing?"

"Going out for a pizza." Jasper wheezed out a pained breath before getting to his feet. "Whadda ya think I'm doing? I'm going out to pee."

"Watch out for rattlers."

That made Jasper stop in his tracks. "Do snakes come out before daylight?"

"Who the hell knows? Just saying, there could be wolves or bears or all kinds of wild things in this place."

"It gives me the creeps. This whole wilderness thing creeps me out." Jasper stopped just short of the cave entrance. "Maybe I'll just take a whiz in here."

The driver swore. "Take it outside. I don't want to have to smell it in here."

When Jasper hesitated, Vanessa's mind went into overdrive. "Homer has my phone. If you turn it on, it'll give you enough light to see what's close by."

He reached out a hand to the driver. "Give it to me. I'm not taking any chances on stepping on a rattler."

A scant minute later he turned on the phone before stepping away from the cave.

Watching, Vanessa sucked in a quick breath. Would her little trick work? She strained to peer in the predawn darkness, but could see little more than a thin, tiny circle of light, no bigger than the flare of a match.

Minutes later the hawkfaced man returned and handed over her phone to the driver. "I saw something move in the bushes and it had me so spooked I pissed on my shoes. But at least there weren't any bears or wolves."

"Good. Now shut up and let me get back to sleep."

Vanessa lay in the dark and wondered if anyone in Chicago had time to note that brief instant her phone had been engaged. Had it been on long enough to alert them of her location? Not likely. But it had been worth the effort, if only to lift her spirits.

Now her mind was even more alert than ever. She knew she ought to grab some sleep while these two slept, but it was impossible. Her thoughts kept circling back to Matt. The sudden shocking sound of a gunshot, and then the sight of him, bloody and unconscious, behind the wheel of the truck as it went over the ravine.

My fault, she thought fiercely. *All my fault.*

If she hadn't whined and complained about going to a safe house, he and his family would have never become involved in any of this. And right now he would be home with that big, rowdy family, ready to face another glorious day in his Montana paradise.

Instead, because of her, he would never again work or play or laugh.

Or love.

The pain was sharp and swift.

Like his parents, he was in the prime of life, and far too young to die. Unlike his parents, he left no children to carry on his legacy.

Because she'd lost her mother at such a tender age, she

knew only too well that death claimed the young as well as the old.

There was no denying the fact that death was a harsh reality in her life. One that had left her and her father deeply affected.

Her father.

He would be inconsolable. Whatever the outcome of this trial, he would lose. And would pay the price for as long as he continued to live.

She refused to let that happen. She struggled with the restraints at her wrists and ankles until her flesh was raw and bloody. Though she knew it was an impossible task, she had to try. There would be no superhero flying in to save her. She would have to save herself.

CHAPTER TWENTY-SEVEN

Luke parked his Harley on a flat plateau and walked to the edge, to stare at the surrounding hillsides below. All around him the land lay in darkness.

He slipped his cell phone from his pocket and touched the number that connected him with the others.

"I'm on Glacier Plateau. All's quiet here."

Reed's voice answered immediately. "Eagle's Ridge here. Nothing moving."

Their uncle's words were hushed. "Burke and I are at North Ridge, and we haven't seen anything out of the ordinary. Matt? You there?"

Matt's voice was low, though whether in pain or anger, the others couldn't tell. "I'm at the mouth of Glacier Creek. Plenty of caves and cliffs around here big enough to hide a vehicle or people, but no trace of any, so far. It's still too dark to see what's out here."

"You should head to town, Matt." Colin chose his

words carefully, knowing his nephew didn't want to hear what he had to say. "Check into the clinic and have that bullet removed before the wound becomes infected."

Burke added, "Colin's right, son. The doctor could pump you full of painkillers and antibiotics before you pick up the trail again in a couple of hours."

"I can't leave. No time." Matt's words were clipped. "I have to—"

At the sudden silence, the others held off the questions they were burning to ask.

For what seemed an eternity, they waited.

Finally Matt's voice came back over the line. "I think I saw something."

"What?" Luke demanded.

"I'm not sure. It looked like a small flicker of light in the darkness. Just a quick little flash, and then gone. If I would have blinked, I'd have missed it."

"A cigarette?" It was Reed's voice.

"Maybe. Maybe a lighter or match." He breathed in the cold air. "So far I don't smell smoke, but it's too soon for the odor of cigarette smoke to drift this far."

"What direction did the light come from, son?" Burke's voice had gone soft as a whisper.

"North of here. Maybe a thousand yards. A quarter of a mile or so. I know it's a long shot, but I have to check it out. Since it didn't seem natural, it had to be man-made. I'll go on foot. If it's our kidnappers, they'd hear my truck's engine."

The sheriff, plugged into their line, swore. "Matt, you need to wait—"

Before anyone could say more, the line went dead.

* * *

Matt tucked away his cell phone and snatched up his rifle before starting out in the direction he'd seen the light.

Had it been a light? He was already beginning to question himself. His eyes and his mind could be playing tricks on him, because he wanted it so desperately. If DePietro's thugs were nearby, they would naturally take every precaution to slip away undetected. Still, as eager as they would be to get back to their own comfort zone in the city, the thought that they were alone in this vast tract of wilderness may have caused them to become careless. He sincerely hoped so. He could feel his strength flagging with every hour that passed. In order to overpower two armed men, he would need both the element of surprise and an almost superhuman strength to take them both down without causing harm to Vanessa.

Dear God. Vanessa.

Just the thought of her at the mercy of those animals had his heart rate speeding up.

Fear was an alien feeling for Matt. In his entire life, he'd always been fearless. But now there was a knot of it in the pit of his stomach. Not for himself. His life didn't matter at this point. The fear was that he wouldn't find Nessa in time. A terrible dread that he would fail her when she needed him most.

As soon as Matt disconnected, the others held a hasty phone conference, deciding on the best course of action.

Luke voiced his concern. "If Matt's right, we need to be there as backup. I'm worried about how long he can hang on before he collapses."

"Exactly." Reed said what the others were thinking.

"There are two armed thugs, and only one wounded man standing between them and their goal to harm Vanessa."

"If they haven't already killed her and disposed of the body," Colin muttered.

"They might need her alive for now," Luke reminded them. "I'm thinking that if DePietro is found guilty, his ultimate revenge against the DA will be another video showing her pleading for her life before being killed."

"And what if Matt's wrong?" Old Burke's voice had them paying attention. "Right now we're spread out across some miles, and there's a good chance that one of us might spot them trying to get away, if not now, then as soon as it grows light." He paused before adding, "If we miscalculate, boys, we could all be backing up Matt on a false alarm, while the bad guys make a clean get-away."

Eugene Graystoke's gruff voice cut in. "Burke's exactly right, boys. You need to stay where you are. I've just heard from the Chicago PD. Miss Kettering's phone was engaged for a minute. They're tracking the location now."

Luke was the first to respond. "I hear what you're saying, Sheriff. But I trust Matt's instincts. I'm not waiting for word from Chicago. I'm heading that way now."

Reed could be heard climbing aboard his ATV. "I agree with Luke. I'm on it."

Colin slapped Burke on the arm. "I agree with everything you said. But my gut tells me to go with Matt."

The old man gave a grim smile. "All right then. We're all in. We win, or we lose everything."

They climbed into the ranch truck and turned toward the hills at the mouth of Glacier Creek.

* * *

Before dawn the phone rang in the kitchen of the ranch house. Nelson, who had fallen asleep in his favorite chair, barely stirred. But Yancy, who had paced the floor between cups of coffee, snatched up the phone before it had a chance to ring again.

"Yes?" His single word sounded like a growl in the silence of the room. He listened, then replaced the receiver.

Nelson lifted his head. "Who called?"

Frank and Grace, already dressed after a few hours of restless sleep, hurried into the kitchen in time to hear Yancy say, "Captain McBride in Chicago. There was a report of Nessa's cell phone being engaged, but only for a minute. They waited for her to speak, but it went silent again."

Grace shared a look with her husband. "Is this good news or bad?"

Frank shrugged. "It could mean she tried to make a call and couldn't finish before her abductors stopped her. Or it could be nothing more than someone stepping or sitting on her phone for a moment before they realized what they'd done and moved it."

Grace touched a hand to Frank's shoulder. "I'm going to hope it means that Nessa was reaching out to let her father and all of us know that she's still alive."

"Hold on to that thought, Gracie Girl." Frank turned to Yancy. "Load us up with some food and coffee, Yancy. By the time we finish eating, it will be light enough for us to get back in the air."

Streaks of dawn light painted the hills with pink and mauve ribbons. The air was still, and scented with the earthy fragrance of tiny shoots spearing up through the spring soil.

Matt moved cautiously through clusters of trees, around boulders, his eye on the spot where he thought he'd seen that tiny spark of light. Had he simply imagined it, wanting so desperately to see something, anything, that might give him hope?

It was too late to second-guess himself. Now that he was committed, he would move forward and check out the area.

As he rounded a huge outcropping of rock, he stopped dead in his tracks.

He spotted a cave that was almost completely hidden by a wild tangle of brush. If he'd been driving, he would have gone past it without even seeing it.

Yet here it was. Big enough, from what he could judge, to park a vehicle inside. Tall enough for a man to stand in. Secluded enough for stashing a body that might never be found.

He paused to listen. A sound. Low, rumbling, rhythmic. At first he struggled to identify the kind of machine that would make such a sound. But then, as he pressed closer to the opening of the cave, it dawned on him.

Snoring.

He moved tentatively, one small step at a time, squinting to peer into the darkness of the cave.

It was easy to spot the hulking shadows of the two men, chests rising and falling with each nasal sound.

It took an agony of seconds before he spotted a smaller figure some distance from them.

It had to be Vanessa.

It took all Matt's discipline to keep from rushing to her side. He ached to free her. To save her from her tormentors.

He ached to hold her. Just to hold her.

Instead he circled around the outside of the rock formation, careful to make no sound, until he was on the side of the entrance nearest Vanessa. With his ear pressed to the rock he heard the slight shuffling that told him she was alive.

Alive.

He looked around the entrance and saw her working on her restraints. Blood streamed from her wrists and ankles, where the plastic had cut through her flesh. The rope tied from her feet and wrapped around her neck had her neatly hog-tied, and probably blind with pain, yet here she was, still fighting.

He dug out his knife and stepped inside the entrance, intent on freeing her.

Her head came up and her eyes went wide before flooding with silent tears.

He knelt in front of her, pressing a finger to her lips to keep her from crying out.

In the hazy light of the cave he cut through her restraints and gathered her close.

In that same instant he felt the muzzle of a gun pressed to the back of his head, freezing his hand in midmotion, as a voice broke through the silence.

"Move a muscle, cowboy, and you're dead."

CHAPTER TWENTY-EIGHT

Y ou're alive." The words were wrenched from Vanessa's heart as she reached for him.

There was no time to respond. To reassure her.

Matt turned, keeping himself between the beefy gunman and Vanessa.

In one smooth motion his hand swept out, knocking the gun from the man's hand. Matt was on him in the blink of an eye, wrestling him to the floor of the cave and pounding his fist into the man's face.

He caught the burly man by the front of his jacket and hauled him to his feet, before shoving his head as hard as he could against a boulder. With a moan of pain the man slumped to the ground and lay there, his breathing labored, his broken nose streaming blood.

Matt spun around, determined to get Vanessa away from here, but when he turned, the second, taller man had a choke hold on her, and was pressing a knife to her throat.

"On your knees, cowboy."

Matt dropped to his knees and lifted his hands in a signal of surrender.

Vanessa tried to cry out, but the blade of the knife, sharp as a razor as it pierced her skin, made it impossible.

The man holding the knife to her throat shouted, "Get up, Homer. Hurry. I need your help."

With a scream of fury the hefty kidnapper lumbered to his feet and knocked Matt to the floor of the cave, before kicking him viciously. Then he grabbed up Matt's rifle and used it to batter him about the head until Matt was unconscious.

When his rage was spent, Homer looked at his partner. "I thought we killed this cowboy back at that cabin."

"Maybe he's like a cat, with nine lives."

Jasper chuckled at his own joke, but Homer's eyes were fastened on Matt with a look of pure hatred. "I don't care how many lives he has, he's about to lose all of them."

He swung the rifle one more time against Matt's head with all his strength, determined to beat him to death, but the sound of a text on his cell phone distracted him, and he dropped the rifle.

After reading the text he shot a look at his partner. "The verdict is in. Guilty."

Jasper tightened the knife against Vanessa's throat. "So. Now do we get to kill her?"

Homer nodded. "But first, we send one more video, guaranteed to make her daddy understand the price he has to pay for what he did to Mr. D."

Ignoring Matt's unconscious body, the two men dragged Vanessa roughly out of the cave.

She blinked furiously against the stab of morning light, her eyes gritty from all the tears she'd shed while she was forced to watch helplessly as Matt was being beaten.

Matt. She'd thought him already dead. But now, seeing him alive, and then being forced to watch that horrible attack, she absorbed a heart-wrenching sense of despair.

He'd come back from a gunshot and a fiery explosion, only to endure even more pain at the hands of these madmen. After that last attack, he'd stopped fighting. Had even stopped moving.

As the two thugs began choosing the spot for their final video, she resigned herself to her looming fate. Though it was small comfort, at least, she thought, she would die alongside the man she loved.

While Frank Malloy did a careful preflight check of the Cessna, Grace loaded their supplies. Rifles, ammunition, high-powered binoculars. A duffel was stuffed with medical supplies and blankets.

To fill her restless, sleepless hours she had come to a decision. Though she knew the odds of finding the proverbial needle in a haystack, she would remain optimistic and make plans to take both her grandson and Vanessa to the clinic in Glacier Ridge as soon as they were located. She would hold to that thought throughout their ordeal, no matter how long it took.

When her husband climbed up and settled himself in the pilot's seat, she fought back tears.

Seeing her struggle, he closed a hand over hers. "A lot of chatter on our frequency overnight. It seems an hour or so ago Matthew saw something that could have been a light near the mouth of Glacier Creek. The others are headed that way. We'll join them."

He squeezed her hand before taking the controls. "All right, Gracie Girl. From the looks of that sky, the Lord is about to give us a bright, clear day. Let's put it to good use."

She nodded, not trusting her voice. The lump in her throat threatened to choke her.

They rolled along the asphalt strip behind the barn before lifting into the air. As they climbed, Grace felt the familiar lurch in her stomach that she always experienced when the plane became airborne. Though she'd been flying for more than fifty years, it was still a bit of a mystery to her that a craft the weight of a truck could soar like a bird.

As they left the barns and outbuildings behind, she picked up her binoculars and trained them on the ground below.

Luke parked his motorcycle beside Matt's empty truck. Tossing aside his helmet he grabbed up his rifle and started walking north.

He looked up, enjoying the way the dawn crept across the sky, switching on pale lights here and there in the darkness. Everything here in the hills looked and smelled clean and fresh.

He knew it was possible for bad things to happen even on deceptively peaceful days, but his heart kept denying what his mind calmly accepted.

From somewhere behind him a truck door opened and closed, and he sensed that Colin and Burke were just arriving on the scene. The low hum of Reed's ATV went suddenly silent, signaling that he'd joined them.

Luke didn't slow his pace, knowing they'd catch up eventually. He was grateful for the alone time. Since he had no idea what he would find up ahead, he needed to formulate a plan.

The problem was, he couldn't think beyond the fact that Matt had been here ahead of anybody, and the area was as silent as a tomb. Not a good omen. There should have been gunshots. Shouts. A scuffle. Anything.

There was nothing. No sound. No birds overhead. Not even the buzz of insects. A very bad omen.

He paused in a cluster of trees, watching and listening, and decided he would wait here for the others. They would make a much more imposing threat to a couple of Chicago thugs if they marched in like the Marines.

"I want the morning light behind me." Homer turned this way and that while holding his cell phone, trying for the clearest shot. He pointed to a flat stretch of earth. "Take her over there."

Jasper grabbed Vanessa's arm and dragged her roughly across the clearing. "Here?"

Homer took aim and motioned. "That's good. Now I want her kneeling, with her hands in front of her, so I can film the blood."

"Why not tie her up again? That'll look better in the video."

After a moment's thought, Homer nodded. "Good idea."

He waited while Jasper threw Vanessa down in the dirt, securing her wrists and ankles before tying the rope around her neck and feet, causing her to cry out in pain.

"That's good. I want that scream. Step out of the picture and we'll have her do that again."

When Jasper stepped away, Vanessa worked furiously to blink back her tears. She thrust out her chin in a haughty pose, refusing to show pain or fear, despite the fact that the plastic restraints cut her already raw wrists to the bone.

"You want me to knock her around until she cries again?" Jasper seemed almost eager to inflict some pain.

"Never mind." Homer took a video of Vanessa, showing a close-up of her bound wrists and ankles, and lingering on the blood streaming from her raw flesh. "Now cut her loose and we'll get her on her feet."

Vanessa bit down hard on the cry that threatened to escape when Jasper cut through all the restraints and yanked her to her feet.

She staggered, unable to get her balance, and Homer chuckled while recording it. "That's it, honey. Look like a drunk for Daddy."

Immediately aware of how this would look on the video, she struggled to remain as still as possible, knowing that these brief scenes would be the last images her father would have left to carry in his memory for a lifetime.

"Do another choke hold and put your knife to her throat. If you have to, cut her. I want a close-up of her face showing real pain and fear."

Jasper was only too happy to do as he was told.

Matt was entombed in a deep, dark hole. He couldn't see through the darkness. Couldn't concentrate on why he was here. Couldn't rise above the pain that enveloped him in a web of agony.

He knew there was something he had to do. Some evil

he had to overcome. But his mind and body refused to do his bidding.

He heard a cry. A woman's cry.

Nessa.

That single name pierced the fog, and he struggled to sit up.

He tried to see past the darkness, but it was punctuated with painful stabs of light that had him blinking rapidly.

He saw twin figures. Two huge shadows. Then two more, tall and muscular and menacing. And then two women, both of them Vanessa Kettering.

Nessa.

He could vaguely recall the beating he'd taken at the hands of the towering thug. Too many blows to his head, and now he was seeing double. But none of that mattered. What did matter was the fact that Nessa was still alive.

And right now, this minute, all the kidnappers' attention was focused on her.

If he hoped to rescue her, it had to be now.

On hands and knees he crawled slowly, painfully, toward his rifle, which was lying in the dirt a few feet away.

Using it as a crutch, he got to his feet and struggled to remain upright. Any slip now, and those two would be on him before he could fire off a shot.

At the entrance to the cave he heard the beefy thug say, "Mr. D. ordered us to film her dead body. And he wants it all to make the evening news. That'll show Mr. Big Shot DA just who has the real power in his town. If Mr. D. has to do time, he'll be greeted by the other prisoners like a freaking rock star."

Laughing, Jasper said, "Why don't we film her would-be hero lying next to her, covered in blood? That ought to grab some headlines."

"Good idea. Go get the body."

As the tall man started toward the entrance to the cave, he stopped dead in his tracks at the sight of Matt covered in blood and holding a rifle aimed at Jasper's chest.

"Take a look at this cowboy, trying to be a hero when he can barely stand up. Look at him, swaying like a drunken—"

Before he could finish, a single shot rang out, echoing and reechoing across the hills.

CHAPTER TWENTY-NINE

Luke was just greeting Reed, Colin, and Burke, when they looked up at the sound of a plane's engines. Seeing the Cessna in the distance, Luke dialed his grandfather's number and put the call on speaker as the others gathered around to listen.

Grace answered. "Yes, Luke? Any news?"

"Matt thought he saw a flash of light, so we've come here to back him up, in case he's found the kidnappers. We're all here now, at the mouth of the Glacier."

"We're almost right above you. In fact, we can see your vehicles." She glanced at her husband before adding, "Captain McBride reported that Nessa's phone was engaged for a minute before going dark. Could that be what Matt saw?"

"We'll find out soon enough. We figure Matt's somewhere ahead of us, though to be honest, I haven't heard or seen any sign of life."

His grandfather's voice came on the phone. "I'm going to give your news to Sheriff Graystoke. He can send in backup while alerting the Chicago authorities."

"The sheriff knows. We talked to him earlier."

"Good." The old man's voice was rough with impatience. "I'm going to land wherever I can find a clear spot. Keep us in the loop, son."

"Will do, Grandpop."

The group looked grim as Luke replaced his cell phone.

"It's too quiet," Burke muttered.

"I'm thinking the same thing." Colin motioned to the others. "Let's keep to the trees as much as—"

The report of rifle fire had them stopping dead in their tracks before they started out at a run.

Matt watched as the scene before him unfolded.

For the space of several seconds Jasper stood perfectly still as the bullet ripped through his chest. Then, as if in slow motion, blood spurted from the wound, and he staggered before falling face-first in the dirt.

Even before he dropped, Matt was moving forward, taking aim at the big man towering over Vanessa.

He blinked several times. When his vision cleared, he realized that the thug was holding a gun aimed directly at him.

"No." With a shout, Vanessa kicked out with her foot, knocking the gunman off stride, and the shot went wide, spewing dirt several feet from Matt.

Before Homer could take aim for a second attempt, Vanessa grabbed up the rope that had been tied around her neck and whipped it at his eyes.

He cried out, half blind with pain as he reached out a hand to stop her.

Matt took that moment of distraction to charge the thug, taking him down and throwing several punches that had his already-broken nose streaming a fountain of blood.

The gun dropped from Homer's hand. Before he could snatch it back, Vanessa kicked it and sent it flying out of his reach.

Enraged, the thug pummeled Matt with several vicious blows that had his ears ringing and his vision blurring.

Unable to see, Matt struggled to protect himself while returning punches.

Once Homer realized that he had the upper hand, he moved in for the kill, pounding Matt's head against the ground, fists sending blow after blow to Matt's face and chest.

Vanessa could see the fight turning as Matt's strength began to drain away completely. She couldn't imagine how he was still moving. His wounds were too severe, his body too drained to continue. Yet she watched him fight on valiantly, presumably going on nothing but pure courage.

She picked up the gun and wondered what good it would do her. She'd never fired one and was terrified that she would hit Matt instead of the thug.

Desperate, she fired into the air, and at the sound of it Homer brought his head up sharply. As he knelt over Matt, he saw the way Vanessa's hand was shaking.

"Firing a gun is the easy part, Daddy's Little Girl. Firing it at someone you intend to kill is something altogether different. Especially if you hit the wrong target."

His evil smile spread across his lips and turned into a leer. "Now you give me that gun, and I'll show you how it's done."

When she merely stared at him, face pale, lips quivering, Homer laughed. "I get it. You thought I'd just put up my hands and surrender, didn't you? But you don't have the guts to actually shoot."

As he lifted a fist to Matt's face, Luke's voice broke the stillness. "Ask us if *we* have the guts to shoot."

Homer turned to see the entire Malloy family, even Frank and Grace, who had landed their plane nearby, forming a ring around the area, and all of them holding weapons aimed directly at him.

He had no sooner raised his hands when Luke grabbed him by the front of his parka and hauled him to his feet. Then, before anybody could stop him, Luke drove a fist into the gunman's middle and dropped him to his knees, where he wheezed out a breath.

Luke was about to throw another punch when the sheriff's voice sounded from nearby.

"I'll take that piece of garbage..." He glanced at Vanessa before adding, "I'll handle the prisoner from here, Luke."

Several police officers stepped forward to handcuff the prisoner and lead him away. And then the scene became one of complete chaos.

A team of state police sharpshooters, weapons still in place, surrounded the area. Another group of officials moved about. One checked Jasper's vitals and declared him dead, another bagged evidence, while others roped off areas of the ground darkened with blood to collect samples.

Vanessa raced to Matt's side and dropped to her knees. Feeling for a pulse she shouted, "He's alive."

Her tears, held back for so long, now began streaming down her face, as she gave vent to all the raw emotions churning inside. Her composure, so tightly controlled, now slipped away completely. "He needs help. Now. Please. Somebody help him. You can't let him die."

With the Malloy family standing anxiously by, a team of medics hurried over. When they attempted to move Vanessa, she clung to Matt's arm, her tears falling harder and faster.

"Please don't die, Matt. Please stay. You fought so bravely. You endured so much. Please..."

"You need medical attention, Miss." A stocky medic wrapped his arms around her waist, and, with the help of a second man, attempted to place her on a gurney.

"No!" She fought off both of them and raced back to kneel beside Matt. "He's the one who needs help. Please. You can't let him..."

Her tears fell harder and faster as she saw just how badly wounded he was.

Frank dropped to his knees beside Vanessa. "Hush now, Nessa girl. Everyone's doing the best they can."

The stocky medic hovered nearby, while the other took Matt's vitals and hooked up an intravenous tube to administer something for pain.

Grace looked at the man, who shook his head gravely. "I have orders from Chicago authorities to get Miss Kettering to the nearest hospital as soon as possible."

"All we have in Glacier Ridge is a clinic," Frank explained.

"Then we'll head there first." The medic reached for Vanessa's hand, but she shrank back.

"I won't go without Matt."

"He'll be on the next copter, ma'am. I promise you."

"But what if he...?" She couldn't speak about her greatest fear. That he might not survive his terrible injuries. The words, once spoken, would be too final. "Please let me stay."

"They can't do that, Nessa." Frank studied the somber faces of the two medics. "They have their orders."

Vanessa watched as a member of the medical team assessed her wounds. When she saw the way he shook his head, she dug in her heels. "I'm not going without Matt." She turned, searching until she saw Grace kneeling nearby, fighting tears.

"Grace." She stretched out her bloody hands and the old woman hurried over to embrace her. "Make somebody understand that I'm not leaving Matt. If not for him, I wouldn't be here. He sacrificed so much for me."

"I know." Grace stroked her hair.

"He's my hero. Please tell them..." Nessa's voice broke. "Please, Grace, tell them I need to stay with Matt. Oh, I love him so."

The old woman sent a warning look to the medics, who nodded their agreement. "You'll fly to the clinic with Matthew. It's what you need. What you both need."

"Thank you. Oh, thank you."

Grace pressed a kiss to her tear-streaked cheek as the team lifted the gurney bearing Matt's unconscious form. "Go with them. And hold on to the thought that it's all in heaven's hands now."

Minutes later the Malloy family watched solemnly as

a medical helicopter lifted into the air with a flurry of blades that flattened the grass and had the trees bending in a furious dance.

While several police units remained to photograph the crime scene and scour the area for evidence, a convoy of planes and vehicles began making its way from the Montana wilderness, all of them bound for the distant town of Glacier Ridge.

The scene at the tiny clinic in town was even more chaotic than the crime scene. A team of medics kept getting in the way of the lone, aged doctor, Leonard Cross, who had single-handedly run the Glacier Clinic for more than fifty years. Dr. Cross delivered babies, set broken bones, treated infections, and helped his patients through terminal diseases, and all with the same optimistic good cheer. But today, that cheer was being sorely tested.

He'd just brought his niece, Anita, here from Boston's finest hospital, in the hope of persuading her to join his clinic. For the past few years he'd been thinking of a way of cutting back to take some time for himself without leaving the citizens of Glacier Ridge without a doctor.

Since Anita had arrived several days earlier, her uncle had been extolling the virtues of small-town medicine, boasting that she would find plenty of time to pursue her dream of practicing family medicine while also writing novels set in the Old West.

As he dashed from one examining room to the next, he muttered to her, "Sorry. This wasn't exactly what I had in mind for your first days on the job. This isn't the good impression I was hoping for."

She shot him a sweet smile. "Uncle Leonard, no matter what life throws at me here, it can't possibly compare to my hectic hospital days in the trauma unit in Boston."

"That's good to hear." He led the way into the room where the entire Malloy family had gathered around the examining table.

Seeing them he skidded to a halt. "Is this Matthew?" The old doctor couldn't tell with all the blood and dirt that masked the patient's face.

Colin assigned himself speaker for the family. "My nephew Matt's been shot, Doc."

"I can see that." Dr. Cross watched as his assistant, Agnes, cut away Matt's bloody parka and shirt to expose his chest.

"And he survived a fiery truck crash." Colin stared at his nephew lying so still on the table, and forced himself to swallow.

Anita Cross, noting his pallor, put a hand on his arm. "Sir, if you faint at the sight of blood, you may want to leave the room."

He shook off her hand before giving her a look of pure outrage. "I've never fainted in my life."

"There's always a first time."

His eyes narrowed on her. "Look Miss..."

"Doctor. I'm Dr. Anita Cross."

"My niece," the old doctor said as he began to probe Matt's chest.

"Dr. Cross, I'm not leaving this room until I know my nephew will live."

Colin's harsh tone would have been enough to frighten most people, but seeing the fierce look in his eyes had Dr. Anita Cross nodding. "I understand completely. If you could step back a pace, we'll share everything we can with you." She turned to include the others. "With all of you. But this could be difficult, even painful, to watch. It might be better if you wait in the lobby."

In answer, they crossed their arms over their chests and planted their feet.

It was answer enough for her.

When the young doctor turned to her uncle, she saw him vainly attempting to remove a young woman who was clinging to Matt as though to a lifeline.

Her voice lowered to a command. "Young lady, you have to give us room to do our job."

As Vanessa looked up, her movements were slow and measured, as though she'd turned into a robot. Her face had gone ghostly white, and her hands were trembling.

Dr. Anita Cross took a firm hold of Vanessa's arm. "This woman is in shock and needs a bed immediately."

Before she could press an emergency button, Colin stepped up and swept Vanessa into his arms. "Where do you want her, Doc?"

The doctor turned to Agnes. "Show them to examining room two, and I'll be there as soon as possible."

As Vanessa was carried from the room, the others went deathly silent as the two doctors bent to examine Matt.

Dr. Anita spoke in low tones to her uncle. "Looks like he's been through a war. How is his heart?"

"Strong. But then, I'm not surprised. Some men might be taken down by a bullet, or a fiery crash." Dr. Leonard Cross muttered, "Though he's been through both, I'm thinking it will take more than that to do in a Malloy."

He stepped away and turned to the family, while his niece left the room to examine her next patient.

"I know you want to stay close. But I have to take Matt into surgery right now. We'll get that bullet out, set any broken bones we find, and deal with his burns and other wounds. Since it'll take the better part of the day, I suggest you return to the ranch, and I'll phone you when surgery is over."

Frank said, "We're not leaving, Doc." He turned to the others. "While you go to the waiting room, Gracie and I will head on over to the other room and check on Vanessa. She'll want to know that Matthew is going into surgery."

The family made their way from Matt's room, and Frank and Grace walked down the hall.

Posted outside the door to Vanessa's room stood two uniformed officers from the Chicago PD.

One of the men held up a hand. "Sorry. No one is allowed inside without permission."

Frank shot them a look of authority. "We are Frank and Grace Malloy. Vanessa stayed at our ranch during the trial."

The officers held a whispered conversation before one of them pulled out his cell phone and spoke into it. Listening intently, he stepped aside and held the door for the elderly couple.

As they paused just inside the door, a tall, handsome man in a rumpled white shirt, his tie undone, his mussed hair gray at the temples, looked up from the side of the bed with a look of pure anguish.

"Mr. and Mrs. Malloy, I'm Elliott Kettering." He offered his hand.

"Frank and Grace," Frank said as he accepted the handshake.

"I was on a plane from Chicago as soon as the verdict

was returned. Captain McBride kept me aware of what was happening during the flight. How is your grandson?"

"Doc is taking him into surgery now." Grace studied the young figure in the bed. "And your daughter?"

"I've never seen her like this. She was highly agitated and making little sense, insisting that she wouldn't accept any medical help until she knows what happened to her hero. That's what she kept babbling about. Her hero. Her Superman. And saying she was in love with him and willing to give up her own life if it meant he could survive." He ran a hand through his hair in frustration. "Obviously she's too badly traumatized to know what she's saying. I demanded that the doctor give her something for pain. Dr. Anita said the wounds to her wrists and ankles are deep and need to be treated for possible infection. Apparently the plastic restraints those thugs used cut clear to the bone."

Grace caught the young woman's hand, noting the heavy dressings at her wrists, and the bag of intravenous fluid hanging from a pole beside the bed. "I'm glad she's no longer awake and suffering."

"I'm glad, too. I had a wildcat on my hands until she was sedated. This terrible ordeal has really scarred her..." His tone softened. "My daughter needs the best possible care, so I've made a decision. Since the doctor said it would be a matter of weeks before she can completely forego pain medication, I'm taking her back to Chicago immediately." His tone turned businesslike. "I'm grateful for all they did here at the clinic. I hope you understand. After all we've been through, I don't want her out of my sight for a minute longer than necessary. Vanessa's all I have."

Grace managed a halting smile. "I understand completely."

Frank moved in to lay a big hand on Vanessa's arm. "I know you can't hear me, darlin', but I hope you'll let your father pamper you. He's earned that right. And so have you."

Grace kissed her cheek. When she straightened, she turned to Elliott Kettering. "When Matt's surgery is over, we'll call you."

"Of course. I appreciate that. And I want you to know that you have my heartfelt gratitude for everything your family did for my daughter. You'll never know what agony I went through these past weeks."

"No more than we did." Frank cleared his throat. "We're grateful for the outcome. There were some moments…" His voice trailed off.

After more handshakes, while Frank and Grace watched, Elliott Kettering was flanked by the police officers as he followed the gurney toward a waiting ambulance that pulled away from the clinic the minute they were settled inside.

It was their last glimpse of the young woman who had come to mean so much to all of them.

A young woman who had changed and been changed by their grandson forever.

CHAPTER THIRTY

Matt lay a moment, eyes closed, listening to the now-familiar beeps and pings of monitoring equipment and the sudden squeeze of an automated blood-pressure cuff. He would rather face stampeding cattle than another day in this sterile room at the clinic.

He'd been here nearly a week now. Seven long days of being numbed with pain medication, shutting down his mind. He'd been poked and prodded, and forced to listen to plans for physical therapy in the coming months.

Seven long days of waking to find his family keeping vigil, taking turns being with him day and night. When he'd asked them to go home, they'd agreed to cut back on their visits, and then promptly doubled up their time with him.

The one face he'd longed to see was missing.

He'd called and left dozens of messages on her phone.

At first her father had answered, saying she couldn't be disturbed. After a while, the calls had simply gone unanswered.

It had to be by design.

As soon as the family noted his agitation, Dr. Cross had ordered all phones removed from Matt's room, including his cell phone.

As the days stretched on, and his questions to his family were met with silence, he gave up asking.

Every time he closed his eyes, he could see her as she'd looked that last time, before he'd lost consciousness. Her wrists and ankles raw and bloody, the fierce look in her eyes as she'd knocked aside Homer's gun and then whipped him with her ropes, desperately fighting to keep him from ending Matt's life. She'd been fighting for both of them.

What an amazing woman.

And yet, because of his carelessness, she'd nearly lost her life in the Montana wilderness. It wasn't something he could ever forgive himself for, nor forget. He'd let her down. Badly.

No wonder her father had whisked her away to Chicago. To have his own doctors care for her. To keep her safe and to ensure that she could resume the life she was meant to live.

Time spent back in her own environment had surely given her a chance to clear her mind and make her realize all she'd been missing.

A woman like that didn't belong here, on thousands of uninhabited acres, chasing herds of mustangs, sleeping in rough cabins or, worse, under the stars. She might have rhapsodized about the wonder of it all, but that was sim-

ply because she was, for a brief time, living her childhood
fairy tale. Now it was time for a reality check. She was
an urban career woman, chasing what everyone wanted—
success on her own terms.

Over time, when her wounds were completely healed,
and she was back at work doing what she loved, the time
spent on his ranch would fade into the background. He
and his family would become a pleasant memory.

A feeling of desolation swept over him, dragging him
down.

Colin and the pretty young doctor walked into his
room talking quietly about something. When they realized he was awake, they hurried to his bedside.

"Hey, Matt." Colin started to punch his arm, then
checked himself and squeezed his hand instead. "How're
you feeling?"

"Fine." He hated being coddled. Hated being the object
of so much concern.

He turned to the doctor. "When can I leave?"

She smiled at him. "Your uncle and I were just talking
about it. I think, if you promise not to do too much, you
can go home today."

Matt brows shot up. "You mean it?"

She nodded.

He turned to Colin. "Get my clothes."

"Right. Quick, before she changes her mind."

Colin and the doctor both chuckled before she left the
room, giving Matt enough privacy to dress. With his uncle's help he managed to get into his jeans, but when he
lifted his arm to slip on his shirt, the shaft of pain in his
shoulder had him swearing.

By the time he was completely dressed, he was sweating and hating the fact that he felt as weak as a newborn calf.

Agnes arrived with a wheelchair, and he gave her no argument, grateful he didn't have to walk.

At the door to the clinic, Dr. Anita was waiting with a list of medications and physical-therapy sessions already scheduled.

"One thing before you go, Matt." Her tone went from sweet and sunny to one of authority. "From everything I've learned about you, you'll go home and expect to resume your ranch activities tomorrow. Please don't push your body. It was seriously damaged, and it's healing. But in order to avoid any setbacks, let it dictate when you're ready to do all the physical activities you once did."

"Sure thing." He would say whatever it took to get out of here.

She glanced over his head to where Colin stood watching and listening. "I hope you'll convey to your family what I said. When you see Matt pushing himself, remind him that he still has a lot of healing to do."

"I will." He stuck out his hand. "And thanks, Doc. For everything."

Burke stepped out of the ranch truck and hurried around to help Matt up to the passenger seat. Colin stayed back to say something more to the young doctor before climbing into the rear seat.

As they started toward home, Matt was unusually quiet, holding himself tensely.

Burke glanced over. "That niece of old Doc Cross's is one damned fine-looking woman. Quite an improvement over her uncle."

"I didn't notice." Matt gazed hungrily at the scenery outside the window, grateful to be free of the clinic.

Burke chuckled and gave his elbow a nudge. "I guess your injuries were worse than we thought if you never even noticed a beautiful woman. Now if this had been your uncle, he'd have probably insisted on staying another week, just to have an excuse to look at pretty little Dr. Anita Cross every day."

When Matt didn't even smile, Burke exchanged a look with Colin in the rearview mirror. They both knew it wasn't only Matt's physical injuries that were causing him such pain. The damage to his heart was another matter altogether.

It looked like that injury still had a heap of healing to do.

Despite the doctor's warning, Matt eased back into ranch life, mucking stalls, tending to the millions of chores required to keep a ranch of this size operating smoothly.

But when the chores were done, his family watched helplessly as he rode off alone to the range shack to brood. The same shack where Vanessa had been abducted. The same shack where they'd once loved.

There, alone in his beloved wilderness, he chopped wood until his shoulder throbbed. He sat in front of a roaring fire, remembering what his grandmother had conveyed to him when Elliott Kettering had taken his daughter home. That Nessa wanted him to know how grateful she was that he'd come to her rescue. And that she loved him.

He didn't want her gratitude. And she'd obviously had time to realize he wasn't worthy of her love.

Not one phone call. Not a word. Not that he blamed her.

Everything bad that had happened to her had been his fault. Hadn't he ordered Burke to keep the wranglers at a distance because he selfishly wanted time alone with Nessa?

Time alone. It had been everything he'd ever dreamed it would be. And then it had all gone wrong. And he'd had no one to blame but himself.

And now, judging by the silence from Chicago, Nessa blamed him, too.

Each time he returned from the hills, his family watched for any sign that he was ready to let go of the sadness they could read in his eyes. But it was always there. Like a bruise that told of a deep wound. The only problem was, a bruise around a broken heart was much harder to heal.

Burke stepped inside the barn and paused, allowing his eyes to adjust to the dim light. It was barely dawn, and already Matt was mucking stalls.

The foreman leaned against the stall door and watched for a moment before breaking the silence. "I'm worried about you, son."

"I'm not overdoing anything." Matt deposited a load of dung and straw into the honey wagon and bent to his work.

"It's not the chores that worry me. It's you."

Matt paused to lean on the handle of the pitchfork. "What's that supposed to mean?"

"You know exactly what I'm talking about. You tackling ranch chores before dawn. You riding up alone to the range shack as often as you can get away."

"That's nothing new. I've always taken my alone time there."

"In the past, that alone time renewed your spirit, son. Now it has the opposite effect. You come back sad and quiet."

"There's not much to laugh about these days."

"Things around here are the same as they've always been. Nothing's changed. Not the ranch chores or the family business. Not even the small-town gossip. The only thing that's changed is you."

As Matt opened his mouth to speak, Burke held up a hand. "And don't try to deny it."

Matt looked away before nodding. "Yeah. I know what you're saying, Burke. But I don't know what to do about it."

"You can call her."

"I tried that. She never answers. That tells me she doesn't want to hear from me. Besides, what can I say to her except that I'm sorry?"

"You've got to stop carrying that load of guilt. It's weighing you down, son, and all of us along with you."

"I can't let it go. Don't you think I try to stop playing that scenario over every day in my mind? I was the one who asked you to keep the wranglers away from the cabin so Nessa and I could have some time alone. It was foolish and selfish, and Nessa nearly paid with her life."

"Son, I think there's something you need to know. Everybody here knew what you and that pretty little lady were feeling long before the two of you did. So when you asked me to give you some space, I said I would, but that doesn't mean I called off the wranglers."

Matt's head came up. "You didn't?"

The old man grinned. "I knew what the two of you were planning on doing, and it didn't involve leaving that cabin. So I left the wranglers in place, right where they'd always been, guarding the lady."

"Then how...?"

"What none of us had counted on was having those Chicago thugs discover that old abandoned cattle trail, which they used to sneak up on the cabin, and which they'd probably hoped to use as their getaway, once they realized it was deep in wilderness. While we were watching for them, they were already in place, watching us. They spotted the guards, and to draw them away, they slit the throats of a dozen or so head of cattle. They knew once their dirty deed was discovered, the wranglers would ride out in search of the perpetrators. And that's exactly what happened. Even though we were nearby, our attention was on the herd, and not on the two of you in that cabin, as it should have been. Even when they shot you, the sound was drowned out by the lowing of cattle. If they hadn't shoved you and your truck over the ravine and caused that explosion, we wouldn't have known about their attack until hours later."

The shock Matt was feeling was evident in his eyes. "You're not just saying this to ease my guilt?"

"It wasn't your fault, son. You and Nessa did what any couple in love would do." Burke clapped a hand on his shoulder. "If you want to blame it on something, blame it on fate or timing or just plain bad luck."

Without another word the old cowboy ambled out of the barn, leaving Matt alone to mull all that he'd learned.

As he continued mucking stalls, Matt felt a measure of relief as some of the guilt began to slip away. But though these facts eased his guilt, nothing would change the fact that Vanessa didn't want to speak to him.

He swore under his breath.

He hoped the worst of her wounds had healed.

He hoped she'd been able to put behind her all the fear and pain she'd been forced to endure.

He hoped, desperately, that now that she was back to her old life in Chicago, she would think of him from time to time, and remember the love they'd shared.

CHAPTER THIRTY-ONE

After a long weekend up in the hills, Matt could feel old Beau straining to make a run for the barn. Instead he held the horse to a slow walk. His gelding might have been eager to return to the comfort of home, but Matt's heart was still at the range shack. There was no longer anything to come home to.

He'd seen the way his family tiptoed around him. He was weary of being the object of so much sympathy. He wanted things back where they'd once been. A happy, carefree family, a successful ranch business, a sense that he was making a difference.

But he had no idea how to make it happen. Ever since Nessa's abduction, he'd been feeling the way he had when he was twelve, learning of his parents' death on that snow-covered road. Broken somehow, and wondering how to put the pieces of his life back together.

Once in the barn he took his time rubbing down his

mount, then filling the troughs with feed and water, before making his way to the back door of the house.

The day had grown uncomfortably warm, and Matt, his shirt plastered to his back, was glad for the coolness of the mudroom.

As he began washing at the big sink, he could hear voices raised in laughter somewhere in the house.

He stepped into the kitchen, where the wonderful aromas of bread baking and meat roasting had his mouth watering, though Yancy was nowhere to be seen. Instead of heading toward the voices, he made his way upstairs to shower.

Half an hour later, dressed in fresh jeans and a clean denim shirt, he helped himself to a longneck from a tray on the kitchen counter and followed the sound of laughter to the great room.

In the doorway, with the bottle halfway to his mouth, he stopped and simply stared.

It was a scene he'd been a part of all his life. His family, loudly trying to talk over one another, as they shared the events of their day.

Luke, with his hair in a ponytail and a rough beard from his week with the herd, was telling them about a mustang stallion he'd spotted in a highland meadow.

Reed, also bearded, hair past his shoulders, was tipping up a longneck and suggesting that their grandmother ought to investigate, since it sounded like the white stallion she'd been trailing for over a year.

Nelson, seated in a chair next to Frank, was telling him about his latest foray into town. Someone had actually asked for his autograph, and the old man had been flattered and delighted to comply.

Though they were all talking and laughing, Matt didn't hear a thing, except an odd buzzing in his brain.

Standing in the midst of them was a vision.

She was wearing something prim and businesslike. A silk jacket and trim skirt. Her hair was soft and loose and spilling down to her shoulders.

Vanessa.

He knew he was imagining her. She looked as she had that first time he'd met her. A young professional, looking a little too intense, but doing her best to be bright and cheerful while getting her interview concluded so she could return home.

He blinked, but the image didn't dissolve. Instead she turned and stared directly at him, and he felt the quick sizzle of recognition clear across the room.

"It took you long enough, sonny boy." Frank moved aside to reveal a tall man wearing a suit and tie. "Look who's come all the way from Chicago to see us."

"There was no car outside."

Reed chuckled. "I got a call to pick up some passengers from a private jet in town." He waved a hand. "And look who I found."

"Elliott Kettering," the man said, extending his hand.

"Mr. Kettering." Matt moved woodenly across the room to offer a handshake.

"Call me Elliott. I want to thank you for all you did for my daughter. Not to mention what you did for her terrified father. It's beyond measure."

"I did what I could."

"According to my daughter, you were superhuman. After surviving both a bullet and a fiery crash, instead of sending for a doctor, as any sane man would, you just kept pushing through your pain until you found where those animals were holding Vanessa. Then, she told me, you endured even more beatings."

"Vanessa was the one who saved the day. If not for her quick thinking, I'd be dead now."

Elliott cleared his throat. "I'm here because Nessa threatened murder and mayhem until I agreed to bring her here. I tried my best to put her in a bubble and keep her away from the big, bad world, but once she realized what I was up to, she was having none of it. She let me know, in very clear language, what she thought of my tactics." He paused before adding, "I believe she has some things she wants to say."

Matt looked over at Vanessa, standing so still and quiet. He had to swallow twice. "You look good. You're healed."

"And so are you, I see." She started across the room and halted in front of him. "I'm told you tried calling me. Several hundred times."

He was aware that the others had gone completely silent. "I understand why you ignored me."

She arched a brow. "You do?"

"You needed to make a clean break. You needed time to get back to your life. The real one, not the one you were forced to live here."

"Is that what you think? That all of this was forced on me, and I was just going along, making the best of things?"

"No need to deny it. I was a witness when you learned about the threat to your safety."

She clenched her hands at her sides. "That's how it all started. And yes, I admit that I had a few bad moments." She dragged in a breath. "But then, everything changed."

"I'm sorry." Matt set aside his beer to give himself a moment to look away. The pain of seeing her, and not being able to touch her, was almost more than he could bear. But if he touched her, he'd never be able to stop. He would simply devour her. He would have to fill himself with her until he was sated. And so he stood, ramrod straight, forcing himself to breathe in and out.

"Sorry for what, Matt?"

"The pain you suffered. The fear. The danger. I thought I could keep it from you. But it was my carelessness that allowed it to touch you. To hurt you."

"You make it sound as though you're the one who kidnapped me and forced me to be with you."

"I . . ."

She put a hand on his and he was rooted to the spot, though he thought about stepping back, away from the heat. Away from the current of pure electricity that sizzled through his veins. But he needed the heat more than he'd realized, and so he stayed, feeling the touch of her all the way to his shattered heart.

"I was with you because that was where I wanted to be." She looked into his eyes. "Where I needed to be. And everything that followed can't be allowed to erase what we have, Matt."

He chose his words carefully, aware they had an audience. "I know that when two people get caught up in . . . forces they can't control, they sometimes forget for a while that they come from very different worlds. Seeing you up in the hills, sharing that once-in-a-lifetime experience with Grace and a herd of wild horses, I forgot that you were only here for a little while, and that sooner or later you would need to return to the very satisfying life you've made for yourself in the city."

"I see." She nodded. "So when I didn't return your calls, you decided, in your infinite wisdom, that like my father, you know what's best for me."

His eyes narrowed slightly. "What's that supposed to mean?"

Elliott gave an exasperated sigh. "There was a time, right after I got Vanessa back home, that I said exactly what you just said, Matt. I figured in a few days she would put the danger, and all this foolishness about spending the rest of her life on a ranch in Montana, out of her mind, so she could get back to being my success- ful, well-adjusted daughter. And when she insisted that she loved you, I decided that she was confusing gratitude with love."

Matt's gaze was fixed on Vanessa. "You loved me? You've talked about spending the rest of your life on a ranch?"

"Isn't that what you led me to believe? Or was every- thing we shared up in that cabin a lie?"

His tone lowered. Softened. "It was real. At least for me. But what about you? What about your career?"

"I represent wildlife organizations. You can't get more wildlife than here."

"You represent them in Washington, DC."

She lifted her chin a fraction. "Matthew Malloy, I know you understand the function of airplanes. I believe you use them to fly all over the world. When I'm needed in DC, I'll go. And then I'll fly back *home*." She empha- sized the word.

"Home? Here? You'd do that? You'd give up your life in the city—?"

She stopped him with a finger to his lips. "Stop talking about what I'd give up. Why don't you ask what I want in return?"

He caught her wrist and shook his head. "You've seen my life. What you'll get is hard, never-ending work. Long, frigid winters and hot, sticky summers. And more work than anyone should ever have to do."

"What I'll get in return is this big, loud, fun family." She looked at the faces, some smiling, some somber, staring back at her. "I'd have brothers. Grandparents. A great-grandfather." She grinned at Burke and Yancy. "My very own bodyguard and cook." She turned to him, and this time she touched a hand to his chest. Over his heart. "And best of all, I'd have my very own cowboy. A cowboy, I should add, who makes my heart go crazy every time he looks at me. Who fills my life with so much sizzle."

Matt had gone as still as a statue, afraid to speak, or breathe, or even blink.

Luke broke the silence. "You'd better grab the girl fast, bro, or Reed and I are going to draw straws to see which one of us gets to take your place."

The laughter that followed managed to penetrate the fog that seemed to have clouded Matt's brain. In an imitation of their grandfather he drawled, "Find your own girl, sonny boy."

He turned to Vanessa. "Is that why you're here? To declare your feelings?"

"Can't you see? I'm wearing them on my sleeve." Her voice grew soft. "Cowboy, in case you've forgotten, I learned my lesson when I was just a teen. I'm not going to be discouraged by a few setbacks. Whether you reject me or not, whether my father fights me every step of the way, I came to dance. I'm not leaving without it."

Hearing the hoots and catcalls from his rowdy brothers, he shoved open the door. "Would you mind if we took this to another room?"

Turning their backs on their audience, they walked stiffly, side by side, into the kitchen, trying not to touch.

Once they were safely inside the empty room Matt dragged her into the circle of his arms and poured himself into a kiss like a starving man. She returned his kisses with wild abandon, her arms around his neck, her body straining toward his.

They were so close they were nearly crawling inside each other's skin.

When they finally came up for air, hearts racing, breathing ragged, Nessa batted her lashes at him. "Now that's what I'm talking about. It was worth flying halfway across the country for just that."

"That's still not enough." Matt caught her hands in his. "There's still one thing missing."

Matt dropped to his knees. "I want you to know I'd crawl over hot coals for you." He stared into her eyes. "Nessa, I'm not a man who likes to beg, but please marry me. I give you my word, whenever my crazy family or the isolation of Montana gets too much for you, I'll take you away to any place in the world, as long as you promise to never leave me again."

She framed his face with her hands. "Oh Matt. This is the easiest promise I've ever made."

"Is that a yes?" He got to his feet and pressed his lips to the top of her head, breathing her in.

"Yes. Yes. Yes." As she stood on tiptoe and crushed her mouth over his, the door burst open and the entire family toppled against one another as they fell inside.

"Sorry." It was Nelson, trying to regain his dignity after being caught leaning on the door. He moved aside to make room for all the bodies spilling into the room. "We wanted to be sure we didn't miss a thing."

Matt was grinning. "You notice the rest of them didn't even bother to apologize. You're all shameless."

"Even you, Dad?"

At Nessa's words, her father managed a sheepish grin. "The Malloy family is a bad influence on me."

"They seem to have that effect on both of us." Vanessa held Matt's hand before turning to all of them. "Now it's my turn to apologize. I know I've behaved shamelessly. I should be sorry about it, but I was afraid that if I didn't bully my father into bringing me here to apologize for hiding Matt's phone calls from me, Matt would just slip further and further away."

Luke burst into laughter. "I'm just glad somebody knew how to get him out of that dark place he's been in." He turned to Matt. "Good to see you smile again, sonny boy."

Gracie hurried over to gather Vanessa into her arms for a warm embrace. "At last I get to welcome another woman into this family." She held the young woman a little away before saying, "I hope this doesn't sound too bold, but we'd be honored if you and Matthew would have your wedding here on our ranch."

Vanessa looked suddenly shy. "Nothing would make me happier."

"Here?" Elliott looked confused. "What about all our friends in Chicago?"

Vanessa crossed to him and touched a hand to his cheek. "I could say it's punishment for keeping Matt's calls a secret. But the truth is, Dad, that as much as I love you and our life together in Chicago, I've learned to love this place, too. It's become a second home to me.

"Besides, I'd really love to show off my new lifestyle to my friends. I know I can persuade my BFF Lauren to be my maid of honor on a real, honest-to-goodness Montana ranch." She looked pleadingly at her father. "Am I asking too much?"

Elliott gave a gentle shake of his head. "All I want is your happiness, Nessa."

Yancy was already rubbing his hands together. "I'd love to put together the finest banquet anyone's ever tasted."

Grace was elated. "This is more than I could ever hope for."

Frank joined her to whisper, "I'm so glad you're here, Nessa Girl."

While Luke and Reed pumped Matt's hand and hugged his bride-to-be, Burke waited until Nessa and the others gathered around her father before putting a gnarled hand on Matt's shoulder. "It does my heart good to see you two together. It's where you both belong."

"Thanks, Burke. Did you have anything to do with this?"

The old man shrugged and then grinned. "This was all on her. That little lady's got spunk, son. That one will never let you down."

Matt nodded. "You should have seen how she fought

her attackers, Burke. She was really something." He added softly, "It's not something I'll ever forget."

"Sounds like she had to fight her father, too." The foreman handed him his beer before touching the rim of his bottle to Matt's. "Every time I look at you and Nessa I see another young couple who were so crazy in love that nothing could ever come between them. Like your folks, I think the two of you are going to have one hell of a love story, son."

Matt beamed as he looked at his bride-to-be, surrounded by his family and wearing the most radiant smile as she blew him a kiss. "My love story is right there. In Nessa's heart. In Nessa's hands. And thanks to my bride-to-be, our story can have a happy ending."

EPILOGUE

Montana spring had been as brief as a wink. Cold nights and cool mornings gave way to sunshine and heat as summer followed close on its heels. The meadows, a glorious green, were blanketed with colorful wildflowers. The hillsides were dark with sleek cattle, feeding on the lush grass that grew in the highlands.

The Malloy Ranch had seen its share of parties and celebrations through the years, but the wedding of Matthew Malloy to Vanessa Kettering promised to be the biggest ever.

Almost everyone in the town of Glacier Ridge had received an invitation, and folks made it a point to arrive early so they wouldn't miss a thing.

The wranglers, sporting their best shirts and string ties, their boots polished to a high shine, were directing traffic, while two others stood on either side of the rarely used front door to show folks to the great room, where the ceremony would take place.

Because of the overflowing crowd, some chose to remain outside. There they were free to watch and listen through the open double doors as they nibbled appetizers and drank longnecks arranged on tables on the front porch, which stretched along the width of the big house.

Elliott Kettering proudly stood beside the Malloy family as they greeted the members of his staff, who had made the flight to Montana. By their smiles and looks of amazement, they were more than a little dazzled by the size of the Malloy Ranch and by the handsome, loving family she was joining.

Yancy and the wranglers, who were assisting him in the food preparation, had arranged chairs, draped in white and tied with big white bows, in a semicircle around the fireplace in the great room. Tall vases of white roses and hydrangea, with ivy trailing from each, stood majestically in front of the fireplace screen; they also flanked the banquet tables set up for the guests under a giant white tent in the front yard.

As the room began filling up, and others in the crowd ambled outside to enjoy the sunshine, Nelson whispered to Frank, who beckoned his son and grandsons, as well as Burke and Elliot, to follow.

They made their way along a gravel path to the plot of land situated on a windswept hill. Opening the wrought iron gate, they gathered around a single headstone bearing a heart, and the names PATRICK MALLOY and BERNADETTE DOYLE MALLOY. Seeing the dates of their births and deaths, Elliott lifted a brow in question.

"Some would say they died too young." Frank took in

a quiet breath. "But I've always believed their love was so great, it will continue to burn hot enough for eternity."

Luke produced a bottle of Irish whiskey and filled several tumblers, then passed them around.

"To Patrick and Bernie," Frank said softly. "For I know they're smiling down on all of us this fine day."

As one, they lifted their glasses and drank.

"To my beautiful Madeline." Nelson's voice was husky with emotion. "How she would have enjoyed this."

They drank again.

Elliott cleared his throat. "I'd like us to drink to Nessa's mother, who is right here with us, too. To Danielle O'Conner Kettering."

Solemnly they drank.

Luke and Reed shared a grin before Luke said, "To Nessa, the only one who could have ever bullied my big brother into getting hitched."

As they chuckled and drank, Matt handed his glass to Burke before turning away.

"Hey," Reed called to his retreating back. "Where are you going?"

"To face my bully," he called over his shoulder.

His words produced a roar of laughter from the others.

"I have a powerful need to see her." He quickened his pace. "Right this minute."

When he was gone, Luke said, "Matt might try, but Gram Gracie is never going to allow him to see the bride before the wedding."

Burke chuckled. "My money's on Matt. When he sets his mind to something, the whole world had better get out of his way."

* * *

Vanessa stood in the middle of the upstairs guest room, with her best friend Lauren trying to affix a veil on the bride-to-be's flowing hair.

Lauren studied Nessa's reflection in the mirror. "Maybe a couple of pins?"

"Why do I have to wear a veil?"

"It's traditional." Lauren draped it this way and that, trying for the best effect.

At a soft tap on the door, Lauren hurried over to admit Gracie, who paused in the doorway, her hand to her mouth.

"Oh, Nessa. You're a vision."

Vanessa looked suddenly shy. "It was my mother's wedding gown. I thought by wearing it, I'd feel her here with me."

"It's perfect." Grace held up a jewelry roll. "I wore this when I married my Frankie. If you don't think it's too much, I'd love for you to have it."

"You mean borrow it."

"I mean have it. In my privileged youth, my parents lavished me with jewelry, but since my life here, I have no use for such things. Since you and Matthew are planning your honeymoon in Italy, you'll enjoy wearing it."

She unrolled the satin to reveal three strands of platinum studded with diamonds woven into a stunningly simple necklace. Both Nessa and her friend gasped at the beauty of it.

Gracie fastened the necklace before stepping back to study the effect. "What do you think?"

Nessa touched a hand to it before turning from the mirror with a smile. "I think it's perfect."

"And so are you." Gracie caught her hand. "You've made Matthew so happy. If I didn't already love you, that would be reason enough. All of us are so thrilled to have you in our family."

The two women embraced just as the door opened. They both looked up as Matt stepped inside.

"Oh, Matthew, you musn't see your bride before the wedding."

Before Gracie could block his view, Vanessa stopped her with a hand to her arm.

"What's wrong, cowboy? Having second thoughts?"

For a moment he was unable to speak. He stood perfectly still, staring at her with a look of blinding love. Then, finding his voice, he gave a shake of his head. "I just needed to see you. Alone."

Lauren gave a soft laugh and turned to Gracie. "Come on. I'm so glad you still have two eligible grandsons left. Not to mention that bachelor son of yours. Can I have my pick?"

"Be my guest. The more women in my family, the happier I'll be."

The two women left on a trill of laughter.

When the door closed, Matt stepped closer. "I was afraid I'd dreamed all this. Afraid when I got here, the room would be empty."

"You're not getting rid of me that easily, cowboy. You promised me forever, and I'm holding you to it."

She stepped into his arms, and he pressed his lips to her temple, breathing her in.

She looked up with an impish grin. "Why does Gram Gracie think we're heading off to Italy?"

"Because ever since Vittorio and Maria arrived, they've

been insisting that we use their villa. Maybe this winter we can slip away for a visit." He feathered her mouth with his. "But tonight we'll head up to the cabin. Away from everyone and everything."

"Our very own simple shack in the woods."

He chuckled. "Not exactly simple. I had Burke haul up a case of Maria's wine, and Yancy threw in enough prime beef and lobster to feed an army of wranglers."

She smiled. "I hope they're both sworn to secrecy."

"They know better than to say a word to anyone. The last thing we want is the whole family barging in on our honeymoon."

Her eyes sparkled with mischief. "That might not be so bad."

"Don't even think it." His arms tightened around her. "After all the time you spent in Chicago getting ready for this, I've built up a powerful hunger for alone time with my best girl. There'll be plenty of time with the family. Just promise me that if you ever feel crowded, you'll let me know and we'll go anywhere you want."

Against his lips she whispered, "The only place I ever want to be is with you." She slipped an arm through his and started toward the door. "Now let's go make some memories, cowboy."

Memories.

As they started down the stairs toward the house overflowing with family and friends, Matt thought about how far they'd come. They'd survived the worst that life could throw at them. Had cheated death. Had begun as strangers and were now lovers, about to speak vows that would seal that love for all time.

He smiled at the memory of his mother and father, so wildly in love. As he caught sight of Frank and Gracie, hand in hand, looking so happy, his smile grew.

They already had enough memories to last a lifetime.

And they'd only just begun.

YANCY'S FANCY CHICKEN

- 3 or 4 chickens, quartered, bones in, skin on
- ¼ cup olive oil
- ¼ cup red wine vinegar
- several cloves garlic
- 4 tbsp dried oregano
- several bay leaves
- ¼ cup brown sugar
- ½ cup white wine
- 4 tbsp finely chopped parsley
- half dozen pitted green olives
- 1 cup capers

In large plastic bag, marinate chicken pieces several hours or overnight in remaining ingredients.

Arrange chicken in a single layer in large baking pans, pouring marinade over all. Bake for 1 hour at 350 degrees F. Occasionally spoon marinade over chicken to baste.

When thoroughly cooked, remove chicken pieces to a serving platter, and pour capers and juice over all for a tart delight.

Serve with rice or small garden potatoes. Add a fresh green salad and dinner rolls.

Wild wrangler Luke Malloy loves the solitary life of a rancher. But when he's thrown off his horse and meets the most beautiful woman he's ever seen, Luke finds himself flirting with forever...

Please see the next page
for a preview of

Luke.

PROLOGUE

Glacier Ridge, Montana—Thirteen Years Ago

Carter Prevost, owner-manager of the Glacier Ridge fairgrounds, stopped his pacing when rancher Frank Malloy and his ranch foreman, Burke Cowley, walked into his office.

Though Frank was owner of one of the state's biggest ranches, having amassed several thousand acres and growing in his lifetime, he was still just a neighbor and friend to the folks in Glacier Ridge. A man still struggling to pay the bills required to maintain such an operation.

"Okay, Carter. Now why the frantic phone call, and why couldn't you just tell me what you wanted over the phone?"

"It's about Luke."

The old man let out a slow breath. "It's always about my middle grandson. What did he do this time?"

"Luke signed up to compete in the motorcycle challenge during rodeo weekend."

"He did what?" Frank removed his wide-brimmed hat and slapped it against his leg, sending up a cloud of dust. "He's only fifteen, Carter."

"Don't you think I know that?" The thickset man ran a hand through the rusty hair that was now more gray than red. "But he paid the entrance fee and signed all the forms. Since there's no age limit, I didn't want to be the one to face Luke's temper, so I figured I'd call you and let you deal with it."

"Oh, I'll deal with it, all right." Frank swore and turned away. "No grandson of mine is going to risk his life jumping his Harley over a line of trucks."

"Everybody knows Luke's capable of a trick like that. If jumping vehicles was all there was to it, I wouldn't be so worried."

At Carter's words, Frank turned back. "What's that supposed to mean?"

"Jumping a line of trucks is just the preliminary. This year we're building a ramp higher than anything ever tried before. At the end of that ramp, the biker will see nothing but air. We've issued a challenge to all the professional bikers who want to enter the final. They'll have to land in one piece—and to prove they're still able to function, they'll be expected to circle the stadium. If more than one succeeds, the finalists will have to do it again, until only one is left standing. The first prize is ten thousand dollars."

"If it were a million dollars it wouldn't be enough." Frank Malloy turned to the door and stalked toward his truck.

Burke Cowley followed more slowly.

As they started toward the ranch, Burke held his silence while Frank gave vent to every rich, ripe curse he knew.

"Damned hot-headed kid will be the death of me."

Burke cleared his throat. "I know Luke's a handful."

"A handful?" Frank was fuming. "There's a devil inside that boy. I think he sits up nights dreaming of ways to challenge his grandmother and me. I swear, he's the most ornery, fearless boy I've ever known."

"He is that." Burke smiled. "But he has a way of getting under the skin. Despite all the trouble he causes, you know we can't help but love him. He has the greatest heart in the world. And as Miss Gracie likes to say, he has an old soul. Like his daddy, God rest him, Luke's a sucker for a sad story."

The mention of Frank's son, Patrick, who had been killed along with his wife, Bernadette, on a snowy stretch of Montana road, had Frank Malloy sucking in a painful breath. Their death had left a void that would never be filled. Not for the Malloy family, and especially not for Pat and Bernie's three sons, Matt, Luke, and Reed, who were left to figure out a world rocked by the sudden, shocking loss of their parents.

Burke stared straight ahead, his tone thoughtful. "Luke's the kind who will always stand and fight beside anybody who's down and out. That boy would give you the shirt off his back."

"I know what I'm about to give him." Frank's eyes narrowed with flinty determination. "God knows, I don't like coming down too hard on the boy, after all he and his brothers have suffered. But this time he's gone too far. If I have to, I'll lock him in his room until rodeo days are over."

"Pretty hard to keep a fifteen-year-old locked away."

Frank's head swiveled. "Are you on his side?"

Burke shrugged. "The boy's wild and reckless. But he's not stupid. If you forbid it, he'll find a way around you. But if he knows he has your blessing, he might look at this challenge with a clear eye. He might even be willing to back down if he sees that it's too dangerous."

"And if he breaks his fool neck?"

Burke squinted into the sunlight. "It's his neck. Like you said, there's a devil inside him. Maybe in time he'll learn to tame it. Or maybe, whenever he feels it taking over, he'll just ride that devil into the eye of the storm and see where it takes him. Either way, he's the sort who's willing to play the hand dealt him."

After a few more miles, Frank muttered, "I guess we'll see."

"You're going to give him your blessing?"

Frank shrugged. "Like you said. It's going to be impossible to keep him locked away during rodeo week."

A week later, when Luke proudly handed his grandfather a check for ten thousand dollars, the old man's eyes narrowed. "What this about, sonny boy? It's your money. You're the one who risked his neck for it."

Luke shrugged. "I heard you telling Gram Gracie the bills were piling up, and you were going to have to hold off on buying that bull you've been itching to import from Calgary."

"Are you telling me you risked your neck for a damned bull?"

"It's my neck, Grandpop. And honestly, it wasn't much of a risk."

"You weren't scared?"

The boy grinned. "Yeah. But it was really cool. I felt like I was flying."

"Here." Frank held out the check. "You earned this, boy. I won't take it."

"You know you need that bull." Smiling, Luke ambled away, leaving Frank staring after him.

It was then that he recalled Burke's words.

Despite all the worries and sleepless nights spent on his middle grandson, there was no denying that Luke Malloy had the biggest heart in the world. That breathtaking daredevil...that defiant rebel...had the heart of a champion. And the soul of a hero.

CHAPTER ONE

Glacier Ridge, Montana—Present Day

Luke Malloy sat easily in the saddle as his roan gelding, Turnip, moved leisurely up a hill. Luke had spent the last three weeks in the hills that surrounded his family ranch, tending the herds, sleeping under the stars. It was something he never tired of. Though some of the wranglers complained about the solitary lifestyle, it was the very thing that fed Luke's soul. He sometimes thought he could build a home up here, far enough from his family to listen to the whistle of the wind in the trees, yet near enough to visit when he craved their company.

The time spent alone was a soothing balm to his soul, though he had to admit that after weeks of solitude, he wouldn't mind a night in town. A night of good whiskey, loud country music, and lusty women in the smoky atmosphere of Clay Olmstead's Pig Sty. That wasn't the name on the sign above the saloon. But Clay had been a pig farmer before opening his saloon in Glacier Ridge, and everyone there referred to it as Clay's Pig Sty. Just the thought of it had Luke grinning.

Luke's body was lean and muscled from hard, physical ranch work. He was heavily bearded, and his long hair was tied in a ponytail beneath his wide-brimmed hat. He was hot, sweaty, and thinking about a swim in the welcoming waters of Glacier Creek.

As he and his mount crested a ridge, all thought disappeared at the sight of a herd of mustangs feasting on the rich vegetation of a meadow spread out below him, between two steep mountain peaks. Their leader, the elusive white mustang his grandmother had been trailing in vain for the past two years, stood a little apart from the herd, keeping an eye out for intruders. With five of the mares nursing foals, the herd was especially vulnerable to predators.

Urging his mount forward, Luke kept to the cover of the trees, hoping to get close enough for a clear photograph. With Gram Gracie's birthday approaching, he couldn't think of anything that would please her more than a framed picture of the mustang stallion she'd named Blizzard when she'd first spotted the animal years ago during one of Montana's worst winters.

Luke lifted the expensive camera hanging around his neck, a gift from his grandmother, who was widely acclaimed for her photographs of the herds of mustangs that roamed their ranchland. He focused the viewfinder and started clicking off shots, all the while urging his mount into a run. The mustang stallion's head came up sharply, scenting danger. But instead of facing Luke, the mustang turned and reared, just as a shot rang out, missing the animal by mere inches. At the sound of the gunshot, the herd scattered.

Luke's mount, caught in the midst of it, reacted instinctively, rearing up before bucking furiously, tossing its rider from the saddle.

In a single instant Luke felt himself flying through the air. His last conscious thought as he landed on his head and saw the most amazing display of fireworks going off in his brain was that once again Blizzard had managed to slip away without a trace. Damned if he hadn't just missed his best chance ever for Gram Gracie's precious birthday gift.

Ingrid Larsen came up over a rise and heard the gunshot, followed by the herd of mustangs dissolving like ghosts into the surrounding forest. One minute they were grazing, the next there was only flattened bear grass left to suggest they'd been there at all.

As she looked around she was surprised to see one horse remaining. As she drew near she could see the reins dangling. Not a mustang. A saddle horse. But where was its rider?

When she got close enough to see the wide eyes and hear the labored breathing, she dismounted and approached the animal cautiously.

"Here, now. Steady." She took hold of the reins and spoke soothingly as she ran a hand over its muzzle.

Within minutes the big red gelding began to settle down.

"I know you didn't come all this way alone. So let's find out where your owner is."

Leading the horse, she peered over the edge of a steep

cliff and caught her breath when she saw the still form of a cowboy on a narrow shelf of rock below.

"Hello." She cupped her hands to her mouth. "Are you okay?"

There was no response. The body didn't move.

With a sigh of resignation, she whistled her own horse over and removed the lariat. Tying it securely to the saddle horn, she stepped over the ravine and began inching her way to the rocks below.

Once there she touched a hand to the man's throat. Finding a pulse, she breathed a sigh of relief. Not dead.

She lifted a canteen from her pocket and held it to the man's lips. He moaned and choked before instinctively swallowing. After a few sips, he pushed her hand away and opened his eyes.

"Think you can sit up?" With her hands around him, she eased him to a sitting position.

He swayed slightly, before fixing her with a look of fury. "What the hell...shooting at...herd? You damn near killed me."

"Save your energy, cowboy." She didn't bother saying more. Seeing the blood oozing from his head, she realized he was much more injured than he realized. From the spasms shuddering through him, she could tell he was going into shock. "I'm going to try to get you out of here. I'll need your help."

She looped the lariat under his arms, around his chest, and gave a hard, quick tug on the rope.

The rope went taut, signaling that her horse had taken a step back from the edge, jerking the barely conscious man to his feet. Satisfied, Ingrid wrapped her arms around his limp body and gave a whistle.

Both figures were lifted from the narrow rock shelf and eased, inch by painful inch, up the ravine until they were on solid ground. At once Ingrid scrambled to remove the rope. That done, she wrapped her blanket around the still form of the man and began lashing tree branches together, covering them with the blanket she found tied behind his saddle. Within the hour she'd managed to roll the heavily muscled body onto the makeshift travois, which she'd secured behind her horse. From the amount of blood he'd lost, and the swelling to the back of his head, there was a good chance this cowboy was suffering some very serious injuries.

Catching up his mount's reins, she pulled herself onto her horse's back and began the slow journey toward the ranch in the distance.

Black clouds scudded across the sky. Thunder rumbled, and lightning sparked jagged flashes overhead. The wind picked up, sending trees dipping and swaying. Minutes later the sky opened up, and a summer storm was lashing the hills. By the time Ingrid's mount crested the last peak and caught the scent of home, they were drenched.

It took all of her strength to hold her horse to a walk, when the instinct to run to shelter was so strong.

When they reached the barn, an old man was standing in the doorway and watching her.

"What you got there, girl?" he asked.

"Not what, Mick. Who." She slid gratefully from her mount and looked down at the still figure. "Some cowboy shot at a herd of mustangs and got himself tossed from his horse. Landed halfway down the mountain on a pile of rock. He's out cold."

"Injuries?"

She nodded. "Pretty bad head wound. Lost a lot of blood. Wasn't making any sense."

"Going to call for a medevac?"

"In this storm?" She bent down and felt the pulse. "I guess, at least for tonight, we'll just get him inside, keep him quiet, and hope for the best."

The old man unsaddled the stranger's horse and settled it into a stall with fresh feed and water. Then he moved along beside her as she led her horse to the back door. The two of them struggled under the weight of the man as they removed him from the makeshift travois and half-dragged, half-carried him up the back steps and into the house.

"This cowboy's all muscle." Mick pulled a handker-chief from his back pocket and wiped his face, damp from the workout. "We'll never get him upstairs to a bed."

"You're right." Breathing heavily, Ingrid shed her parka before once more taking hold of her burden. "Let's get him to the parlor."

They dragged him past the kitchen and managed to roll him onto a lumpy sofa in the big room.

Mick glanced around the cold, dark parlor. "I'll get Strawberry back to the barn and bring in an armload of logs. You'll want to get this guy out of those wet clothes and wrap him in dry blankets."

She shot him a sharp look. "I'm no good at playing nurse. I'll take care of my own horse, thank you. And I can handle the logs. You can get him out of his clothes."

The old cowboy was already halfway across the room. With a chuckle, he called over his shoulder, "Your stranger, your problem."

His laughter grew as the sound of her curses followed him out the door.

Left alone, Ingrid gathered whatever supplies she could. Several thick bath towels. A basin of warm water and soap. Then she set to work washing the blood from the back of his head. That done, she folded a dry towel and placed it under his head before moving on to his clothes. Her attempt at unbuttoning his flannel shirt, which was completely soaked, was a huge effort. That done, she turned to his boots, but because they were so wet, she could barely budge them. It took long minutes of pulling and tugging, while muttering curses through gritted teeth, before she got them off. Then, with much tugging, she finally managed to get him out of the last of his clothes.

By the time old Mick returned with an armload of firewood, the stranger was wrapped in a blanket, and his clothes lay in a heap on the floor.

Once the fire was blazing, Mick walked to the sofa to stand beside Ingrid. "I brought his saddlebags inside." He hooked a thumb toward the doorway. "Tossed 'em over a chair in the kitchen. They might give you a clue to just what kind of cowboy you dragged in from the storm."

"Good idea." She huffed out a breath. "I just hope the idiot who was shooting at mustangs isn't also an ax murderer."

"I doubt he'd carry that kind of information in his saddlebags."

She turned away and headed toward the kitchen. "You never know."

"He wasn't your shooter."

She paused. Turned. "And you know that because . . . ?"

"His rifle was still in its boot. If he was trying to take down a mustang, the rifle would have been in his hands." Mick poked and prodded the flames, adding another log to the fire before ambling back to the other room, where Ingrid had spread out the contents of the saddlebags across the kitchen table.

"Find anything interesting?"

She looked up. "Where'd you get this?" She held up the camera.

"It was hooked to the saddle horn."

"German. Expensive. Not what I'd expect from an itinerant cowboy."

The old man shrugged. "Maybe he's a professional photographer."

She opened a worn leather wallet and began sorting through the cards stored inside. She picked up one. "Lucas Malloy. Twenty-eight. Height six feet two inches. Weight 185 pounds. Hair black. Eyes blue. Doesn't need glasses." She looked over. "Ring a bell?"

Mick shook his head. "The only Malloy I knew was Frank. Owns one of the biggest spreads in Montana. Frank Malloy's my age. Got a famous wife. A photographer."

"Maybe a son?" She pointed to the camera. "That makes more sense."

"What makes sense is he's probably a grandson. Unless she made medical history."

They grinned at each other.

"Okay. He's a long way from home. With a head injury, you never know what could happen. If I could find his cell phone, I'd notify his family."

"It could be back there on the mountain."

She nodded. "And trampled by a herd of mustangs."

"I'm sure you can find a number for the Malloy Ranch." Mick filled two mugs with steaming coffee. Handing one to her, he said, "Lily and Nadine have been asleep for hours. You going up to your room, or are you planning on keeping an eye on your guest?"

"He's not my guest, Mick." She picked up her mug and headed toward the parlor. "But since I was the one who brought him here, I guess it's my job to see him through the night."

"You got that right, girl." With a grin the old man shuffled off to his room next to the kitchen. "If you need me..."

"Yeah." She didn't wait for him to finish.

It took her several minutes to move an overstuffed chair beside the sofa. She draped an afghan over her lap and cradled the mug in both hands as she watched the steady rise and fall of the stranger's chest.

Her head nodded, and she felt the hot sting of coffee on her skin before setting aside the mug and snuggling deeper into the warmth of the cover.

After the day she'd put in, she was asleep before she could form a single thought.

Fall in Love with Forever Romance

RETURN OF THE BAD BOY
By Jessica Lemmon

Fans of Gena Showalter, Olivia Miles, and Jaci Burton will love Jessica Lemmon's hot alpha heroes with dark pasts and hearts of gold. Rock god Asher Knight is forced to put down roots when he finds out he has a three-year-old son. But is his newfound stability enough to convince Gloria Shields to finally surrender her heart to this bad boy?

THE WAGER
By Rachel Van Dyken

Seattle millionaire Jake Titus has always made Char Lynn crazy. He's too rich, too handsome, and too arrogant. But now Jake's stopped acting like a jerk and turned on the charm, and Char knows she's in trouble. The *New York Times* bestseller from Rachel Van Dyken is now in mass market.

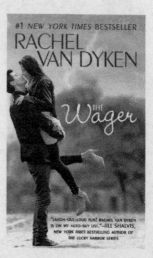

Fall in Love with Forever Romance

THE WEDDING PACT
By Katee Robert

New York Times and *USA Today* bestselling author Katee Robert continues her smoking-hot series about the O'Malleys—wealthy, powerful, and full of scandalous family secrets. In THE WEDDING PACT, Carrigan O'Malley has a parade of potential suitors, but the only man she wants is the head of a rival ruling family. To be with Carrigan, James Halloran will have to fight not only his enemies—but his own blood.

HER KIND OF MAN
By Elle Wright

I'll never let you go… Allina always dreamed of hearing those words. But when her fiancé utters them—it's a threat. Forget walking down the aisle; it's time to run. Back to Michigan. Back to Kent. Kent will do whatever it takes to make Allina feel safe, beautiful, and desirable. But as the two grow closer, and their passion pushes deeper, it's clear that something bigger than a botched wedding still lingers between them…

Fall in Love with Forever Romance

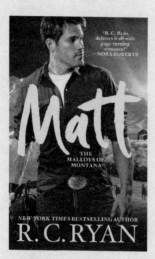

MATT
By R. C. Ryan

In the *New York Times* bestselling tradition of Linda Lael Miller and Diana Palmer comes the first in a beautiful new series by R. C. Ryan. When lawyer Vanessa Kettering and rancher Matt Malloy are forced to weather a terrible storm together, they're drawn to each other despite their differences. Can they survive the storm without losing their hearts?

HOW I MARRIED
A MARQUESS
By Anna Harrington

When an old family friend comes to retired spy Thomas Matteson about a rash of mysterious robberies near Blackwood Hall, he jumps at the chance to be back in the field. What will he do when the suspect turns out to be the most beautiful—and beguiling—woman he's ever seen? Fans of Elizabeth Hoyt will love this sexy historical romance.

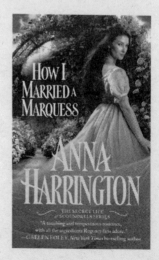